SECOND BEST

But when she knew he had gone she covered her face with her hands, and for a moment her courage failed her. She thought:
'He doesn't want me at all. He wishes he had not married me now that Gina is free. When we get back to town he'll see her. Oh, *God*, what can I do?'
The answer to that was—'Nothing.' For the first time since she had married Barry she realised to the fullest extent what she had risked when she had married a man in whose affections she had only second place. And she was afraid ... desperately afraid for her own happiness, as well as for his.

**Also by the same author,
and available in Coronet Books:**

Put Back The Clock
And All Because
To Love Is To Live
The Cyprus Love Affair
Forbidden
House Of The Seventh Cross
The Boundary Line
Laurence, My Love
Gay Defeat
Do Not Go My Love
All For You
I Should Have Known
The Unlit Fire
Shatter The Sky
The Strong Heart
Stranger Than Fiction (Autobiography)
Once Is Enough
The Other Side Of Love
This Spring Of Love
We Two Together
The Story of Veronica
Wait For Tomorrow
Love And Desire And Hate
A Love Like Ours
Mad Is The Heart
Sweet Cassandra
To Love Again
The Crash
Arrow In The Heart
A Promise Is Forever
The Secret Hour
Nightingale's Song
It Wasn't Love
Fever Of Love
Climb To The Stars
Slave Woman
Lightning Strikes Twice
Loving And Giving
Moment Of Love
Restless Heart
The Untrodden Snow
Betrayal (previously, Were I Thy Bride)

Second Best

Denise Robins

CORONET BOOKS
Hodder and Stoughton

Copyright 1931 Denise Robins

First published in Great Britain by
Hodder and Stoughton Limited 1931

Coronet edition 1966
Second impression 1966
Third impression 1969
Fourth impression 1976

---

*The characters and situations in this book are
entirely imaginary and bear no relation to any real
person or actual happening*

This book is sold subject to the condition that
it shall not, by way of trade or otherwise, be
lent, re-sold, hired out or otherwise circulated
without the publisher's prior consent in any
form of binding or cover other than that in
which this is published and without a similar
condition including this condition being
imposed on the subsequent purchaser.

Printed and bound in Great Britain for
Coronet Books, Hodder and Stoughton, London
by Cox & Wyman Ltd, London, Reading
and Fakenham

ISBN 0 340 20654 3

BOOK I

CHAPTER I

EVERYTHING was as it should be at a fashionable wedding. A big church in the West End. The long striped awning; the strip of red carpet leading up to the door of the edifice. Rows of well-washed, well-polished cars lined up in the street, and the usual crowd. That striped awning, that crimson carpet waiting for the dainty footsteps of the bride are magnets calculated to draw an amazing number of people to any church door. Few of them even know the names of either bride or groom. In all probability none of them will ever look upon the couple or their attendants again in this life. But it is a wedding. That is enough. The atmosphere is charged with excitement and curiosity.

This was a very fashionable wedding. There had been paragraphs in the leading papers for the last fortnight about the bride and her future husband. She was one of the most popular figures in young Society at the moment. Virginia Brame, only daughter of the late Sir William Brame of Wanderton Towers, Bucks, and of Lady Brame of 10, Greyes Street, Belgrave Square. She was marrying Sir Ian Kingleigh, Bart., also a popular figure in Society because he had a great deal of money and although he was not very young he was still handsome and had retired from the Diplomatic Service with a distinguished record.

The mass of humanity lined up outside the church craned their necks and stared expectantly at the church door. It was not too warm this morning. A real April day. Fitful sunshine, showers of rain, and a cool wind. But the weather behaved well and staged the affair charmingly. Just as the bridal pair appeared in the open, the sun broke through the clouds and poured what would seem a benediction upon them. Women in the crowd cheered hysterically.

The Press fought for precedence. Cameras clicked as the bride came down the steps and walked with light footsteps under the awning towards the big Rolls limousine which had pulled up at the entrance. One hand rested on the arm of the man who had been made her husband a few minutes ago; the other held a beautiful bouquet of Spanish irises—palest yellow with delicate fronds of green trailing fern. She was a golden bride. Gold *lamé* dress shimmering to the tips of golden shoes. Gold train held by a little golden page-boy. Golden, gauzy veil through which one could see smooth dark waves of hair. A cluster of orange-blossom over both ears. Virginia Brame, now Lady Kingleigh, was more than ordinarily beautiful. Hers was a face which had been photographed and published in Society papers continually since she " came out ". An oval, " madonna " face, large chestnut-brown eyes fringed with thick, black lashes, and a creamy skin. Virginia was always pale. Even now, in the midst of all this excitement, she was without colour save for her mouth, which was, as always, touched with lipstick of a bright, pillar-box red. The curved lips, so vivid a hue in the pale face, trembled very slightly as she reached the car.

Sir Ian Kingleigh took Virginia's hand and squeezed it hard. His silk hat was set a little rakishly to one side of an iron-grey head. He was much more nervous than his bride, in spite of his six foot two and squared shoulders.

"Hurry up into the car, darling. Let's try and miss the damned confetti."

But they didn't miss it. A shower from both sides deluged the bride and bridegroom. " Good luck, dear! " shouted an old woman in a shawl, and sprinkled Virginia with rice.

The faintest colour came into her cheeks now. She looked a little disdainful. She stepped into the Rolls, shaking the confetti from her veil. Her husband took his place beside her. The door slammed after them. The big car moved almost noiselessly away from the church. The sun, having done its duty, retired behind a bank of cloud and the morning was sad and cold and grey again.

Ian Kingleigh, who had been much more interested in his career as a diplomat than in women, until he reached the age of forty-five and met Virginia Brame, looked at the exquisite figure beside him with something approaching awe in his eyes. He had never thought to marry. Incidentally, he had always felt some contempt for middle-aged men who marry very young women. But who knows what one is going to do until one is faced with this problem or that? When Ian Kingleigh fell in love with Virginia, he fell badly.

It did not seem to matter in the least that she was nearly twenty years younger than himself.

The only thing that did matter was making her care for him and having her for his wife. This morning saw the achievement of ambition. Fulfilment of the most ardent longing he had ever experienced. Virginia had married him. She was his wife. His, until death parted them.

"Well, my dearest . . ." he said. "I'm glad that's over."

Virginia smiled at him. Hers was a very slow, seductive kind of smile which parted her lips and narrowed her brown eyes until they were laughing slits. The sort of smile calculated to go to any man's head. Kingleigh crushed her fingers in a grip that hurt.

"Virginia," he said. "My dear, I love you very much. I'll do everything that I can to make you happy."

"I know you will, Ian," she said.

She touched his cheek with two white fingers which had nails like glittering rubies. He kissed the palm of that hand which was redolent of the scent which she used and with which he was now so delightfully familiar.

"Frightful effort, a wedding—isn't it?" he said, and laughed in a shy way—the typical Englishman, embarrassed by intense emotion.

Virginia looked through the windows of the car at the moody April sky. They were nearing Belgrave Square and the little Georgian house wherein she had lived for the last ten years alone with her mother. A house never empty of friends and acquaintances. She and her mother were noted for their hospitality. They had always entertained freely, gone everywhere, and "done" everything.

But the girl who was now Lady Kingleigh stared out of the window of her husband's Rolls and thought, not of the charming house or her popularity amongst her friends, but of the bills—the horrible pile of bills which had been accumulating rapidly day after day for the last few months—a sea of debts in which she and her mother had been swimming. Both of them by nature extravagant, heading for the rocks of bankruptcy and unable to fight against the tide. Sir William, with his restraining influence as husband and father, was dead. Unfortunately, he had not tied up what money he left. Now most of it was gone. The house in Greyes Street was heavily mortgaged; cash had been borrowed and raised and scraped up from all sources. The ocean of debts had swelled to an alarming size. A crash had been in sight. Financial and social ruin stared mother and daughter in the face.

And then—Ian Kingleigh fell in love with Virginia. Marriage to Ian meant not only a title; a lovely country house in Sussex; a villa in Rome and a flat in Town; but the money necessary to keep up such acquisitions.

A month ago, when Virginia's engagement to Sir Ian was publicly announced, the stormy sea of debts remained, but had calmed down considerably. Lady Brame and her daughter found themselves able to sail gracefully into harbour. Creditors were content to wait. They knew bills would be settled once Miss Brame became Lady Kingleigh. The relief on both sides was considerable.

Now there was no need to worry. The golden bride in the Rolls Royce possessed a distinguished husband and an income of £10,000 a year which was her marriage settlement. Generous, but not too much for Virginia, who could spend money like water.

What a good thing that Ian had come along just at the crucial moment. And how lucky that he was such a dear; she might have been a victim to an old, horrible man. Ian wasn't young, yet fifty-five was not old and he was still good looking. A little stodgy, perhaps a little boring. But she liked him. Respected him. He would be heart-broken if he thought she had married him to save the financial situation. But why need he ever know? And she was giving him something in return. Herself. Her lovely, carefully tended body; her wit; her charm. She had all three. He couldn't complain.

"My wife. D'you love me?" said Kingleigh huskily, against her ear.

"Of course," said Virginia.

And then she shivered a little.

"You're cold, my darling," he said. "Your lovely dress isn't very warm. Put on your coat."

She shivered, not with cold, but with nerves. Her nerves were in an awful state. She knew it. She hadn't been eating or sleeping well. The last three weeks had been a hectic rush—over to Paris and back—from shop to shop—from modiste to milliner. Buying her trousseau. All in such a hurry because Ian was so much in love. He hated long engagements and wanted an immediate marriage. Her mother had encouraged it—terrified of finding herself flung once more on to that harassing, ghastly sea of liabilities which she could not meet.

"I'm tired out," Virginia told herself. "I shall feel better now. We shall be on our way to Italy tomorrow. I can forget all the worry."

But there was one thing which she could not forget— she knew it was futile to delude herself. She saw herself sitting in front of the fire in her bedroom last night, tearing up old photographs and letters. There had been one photograph and one bundle of letters which she had been slow to destroy. She had felt that it meant the destruction of something fine and real and decent in herself. She was a particularly cool, level-headed girl, who despised emotions and trod on her own ruthlessly. She rarely shed a tear over anything or anybody. But last night she had cried. Cried over those letters before she put them in the fire; over that photograph which was the enlarged snapshot of a young man with a gay, charming face, sitting on the steps of a bungalow out East. It was signed: " Yours, Barry."

The letters had all been signed " Barry," and one or two special ones just " *Your lover.*"

He was the only man for whom she had ever really cared. Last summer when he was back on leave from Ceylon he had asked her to become engaged to him. She had said she couldn't make up her mind. He had no money. At least, from hers and her mother's point of view, no money. Not enough. But she gave him hope. He was extraordinarily attractive and he roused something in her which no other man had ever roused. Real passion—if not real love. Love of the selfless, sacrificial order, Virginia did not know. She was, perhaps, incapable of it. In her fashion she had loved Barry Elderton.

She sent him back with hope—and for the last twelve months she had written to him often and he had written to her every mail. He was faithful and he had never loved any woman except Virginia. For four years he had loved her. She had been eighteen and just out of school when they first met at Wanderton Towers in Buckinghamshire.

He fell in love with the eighteen-year-old Virginia from the hour that they played tennis together as partners on the first day of their meeting. It was a devotion from which he had never swerved during the four years that followed.

Virginia had known all the way along that Barry was the one and only man for her. That knowledge was confirmed every time he came back from the East and she saw him. She met so many men during those four years that he was in Ceylon. Men who fell in love with her. Men whom she could like and admire. But there was never anybody quite like Barry; Barry who was such a vital, enthusiastic young man with an immense amount of energy and personality. Barry, so good to look at with his athletic body, hard and disciplined; his brown eager face. He was tireless and nobody ever got tired of him. He was amusing; a little dry and satirical without being too much of a cynic. And what Virginia had liked most about him was his reserve. He always had that power of reticence which kept his ardours, both bodily and mental, in check. Never on any occasion had Virginia known Barry to let his feelings run away with him. And as she herself, up to a point, was built like that, she appreciated that part of his make-up. He was deeply and steadfastly in love with her, but he did not bore her with his love. He kept it in restraint. It was only once, on the last day of his last holiday, he laid aside the usual gay banter and chaff, and told her that he wanted her to be his wife.

The companionable days at Wanderton were over then. Virginia had grown up considerably, and the lovely, spoiled girl was still lovely and still being spoiled, but up in Town, sharing responsibilities and financial difficulties with her mother. Barry knew about them. He had worried over her. He could not marry her until he had a better position. He was hoping to become manager of the tea estate up in Nurwaraylia at the end of the year. He asked her to join him in Ceylon as his wife when that position was secured.

Virginia had wanted to marry Barry. He could have held her affections always, and she knew it. But the question of money remained an insoluble difficulty. She was not born to be the wife of a struggling tea-planter, and she knew it. He must have known it in his heart. But he was in love and he wanted her, so he had tried not to think too much about the money. He was not altogether without prospects. It was an accepted fact that Barry would inherit his uncle's money, and that, by now, was no mean sum.

Virginia knew perfectly well, however, that it is a poor game to wait for a dead man's shoes. John Elderton was sixty-four, but a perfectly healthy old man. It might be another ten years before Barry came into the money. She had hesitated to give him a definite answer. And he had said :

" You're still very young, sweetheart, so don't worry about an engagement if you'd rather not, until I come home again."

He had taken her in his arms as a lover for the first time. When she surrendered to his kiss she had almost let her emotions run away with her and told him to take her then and there, and marry her. His lips and arms had been extraordinarily thrilling and satisfying to her. But the practical side of her nature won in the end and she sent him back to Ceylon without a definite promise. But Barry took it firmly for granted that she did care for him and that they would fix things up when he came back from Nurwaraylia as manager of the Jungwood Estate.

All these things, these memories of Barry, came back to Virginia vividly as she sat in the Rolls beside the man she had married this April morning. Came to torment and reproach her. She had been a coward. She knew it. She had been afraid of poverty—not only for herself, but for her fond and foolish mother, whom she sincerely loved. She had taken the easiest way out and " married money ". But there was a horrible little ache in her heart for Barry. She would never see him again. Would she be able to bear it ? She had been so treacherous to all those lovely hours and days they had spent together. And so much of a coward, indeed, that she had even shirked writing the plain truth to him. Somebody else—anybody else—must tell him that she had married Ian Kingleigh. She couldn't, or rather, wouldn't. She avoided the painful things in life. It would be so painful to write and tell Barry that after his four years of adoring her and hoping to marry her she had failed him and gone beyond his reach. It would hurt her. She didn't wish to be hurt any more than was necessary. So, when she had started the affair with Ian and let it develop, she had just stopped writing to Barry. That was all. She received several letters from him telling her that she was a lazy little brute not to write to him ; chaffing her, scolding her. But never once had he seemed to doubt that things were all right. He was confident of her. Such confidence, such loyalty on his part, frightened Virginia. Heaped coals of fire on her head. She allowed Ian to hustle her into an immediate marriage because she was half afraid of throwing away the big chance he was offering, and of cabling to Barry to come home and take her back to Ceylon.

There had come one letter from Barry—a month ago—less confident—a little anxious. But she had left it unanswered, like the rest. And after that, silence. No more letters from Ceylon. She wondered if the news had leaked out and if he had just dropped her like a stone. It made her miserable. She had behaved badly. She ought never to have given Barry so much encouragement. But she had been so fond of him, in her fashion. And if it hadn't been for the money—she would have married him.

She didn't like the idea of losing him altogether. They had been friends so long. There had been quite unforgettable moments during his last leave. She would miss him sorely. His devotion. His friendship. His gay, amusing personality.

What a horrible thing money was. The need of it. The lack of it!

Virginia stared out of the window of the Rolls a little blindly. She saw, not the Georgian house in Greyes Street outside which a crowd waited to see the bride, but the brown laughing face of Barry. And she supposed when, if ever, she saw him again—he would not smile at her. He would have nothing but contempt for her. Unless his love carried him even through his disappointment. Unless he understood how difficult things had been for her.

"I'd better stop thinking about Barry," she told herself. "It's Ian I ought to be thinking about."

"Here we are, darling," said the grave voice of the man at her side.

With a feeling almost of pride, Virginia pulled herself together and spoke to her husband.

"I could do with a cocktail, couldn't you, Ian?"

She spoke flippantly. She felt the need to be flippant—to drown that feeling of panic in her heart.

He helped her out of the car. She was glad a sudden gust of wind blew the golden veil across her eyes, because they were full of tears.

CHAPTER II

WHILE the bride changed into her travelling dress, the guests poured to and from the drawing-room and dining-room. Everybody seemed to be holding a glass of champagne and a *foie-gras* sandwich or a piece of the immense glittering wedding cake which Virginia had cut just before she vanished. Everybody seemed to be screaming in order to make their voices heard.

Sir Ian stood in the centre of a circle of admiring bridesmaids—tall, willowy golden girls with big picture hats and bouquets of yellow Spanish irises. Lady Brame fluttered from one group of guests to another, performing her duties as hostess in her inimitable fashion. A *petite* woman, Millicent Brame, with a carefully preserved figure and face; pink cheeks and snow-white hair which gave her a fragile, porcelain appearance, and eyes that were still fine—that same warm chestnut-brown which she had bequeathed to Virginia.

She was always a gay, chatty, vivacious little woman. Nobody—not even Millicent Brame's intimate friends—ever knew the weight of the financial burden which she had carried on her shoulders since her husband's death. Dear Milly was extravagant—everybody knew that—and absurdly generous. Her friends saw to that. But that she was floundering in a sea of debt—who should guess it, from her happy, chirrupy voice and incessant tinkle of laughter?

Like an exquisite porcelain figure in a long, high-waisted dress of blue silk taffeta with a big blue hat on her waved white hair, Lady Brame flitted from friend to friend, putting in her charming word.

Always sweet and grateful and charming to everybody. Little Lady Brame was a great favourite and there wasn't a woman of her age in the room who did not envy her. So fortunate of Milly to have married her daughter to such a delightful, distinguished man. It was far from easy these days for match-making mothers to find husbands, really nice, with means for their daughters.

The long mahogany table in the dining-room groaned

under a load of wedding presents. Only half of them were on show. Lady Brame said to everyone:

" So many beautiful gifts—and our little home isn't large enough to hold them—so I've just put out the smallest, loveliest things...."

Crowds gathered round the table and fought in an amiable, well-bred fashion to see the presents. Glittering crystal glass; delicate, coloured china; silver, old and new, books, antiques; a variety of things.

Lady Brame finally slipped away from her guests and tripped upstairs to her daughter's bedroom. She wanted to make sure the darling girl was all right. In Virginia's big bedroom there was a good deal of chattering going on. One of the bridesmaids—Virginia's great friend, Eleanor Canfax—was helping Lady Brame's maid to finish the packing. Another bridesmaid sat on the edge of the bed, holding a suit of golden brown velvet with a great cross-fox collar. The bride's going-away suit. Indescribable confusion everywhere. Trunks, suit-cases, still open. Cardboard boxes, tissue paper, paper and string all over the floor. The lovely golden wedding dress and veil were stretched over the pillows. The golden bouquet had been thrust in the wash-basin into water.

" Hello, my dears," said Lady Brame, beaming at the bridesmaids. " Where's my little girl?"

" She was here a moment ago, having her hair done," said Eleanor Canfax. " I think she's in the bathroom collecting a sponge, Lady Brame. Shall I call her?"

" No, dear, I'll find her," said Lady Brame, and tripped from the room again.

Virginia was not to be found in the bathroom. Lady Brame had a brain-wave and went along to her own bedroom. Perhaps Virginia had left something in there.

" You here, darling?" she asked, pushing open the door.

Virginia was there. She was still in her house-coat. She sat on the edge of her mother's bed, holding a sponge-bag in her hand. She was staring at the carpet, and on her face was set an indescribable expression of misery which wiped all the proud beauty from it. Lady Brame gave her a look of horror and rushed up to her with a sharp rustle of taffeta dress.

" Oh, Gina, my *darling*, what *is* it?"

Virginia raised her head.

"Oh, hello, Mother," she said. Her voice was dead, miserable, like her face.

"Darling, what *is* it?"

"Nothing. I came in here for a moment's quiet. It's like a bear-garden downstairs and there isn't much peace in my room with Eleanor and Kitty and Edith all talking nineteen to the dozen."

"But aren't you *well*, dearest?"

"Absolutely. I'm just going to get into my suit."

Lady Brame stared at her anxiously, sat down beside her and encircled her with an arm.

"Gina, aren't you happy? I can't bear to think you aren't happy. I mean—you wanted to marry Ian—didn't you?"

Virginia's red-brown eyes held a hunted look for an instant. She was on the verge of breaking down, and she knew it. She mustn't break down. She patted Lady Brame's hand, then stood up. She swung the sponge-bag round and whistled a tune to it.

"Come on, Mother. I'm better now. My head was aching."

Lady Brame, not quite reassured, followed the beautiful figure with troubled gaze.

"Gina, you looked so miserable. I can't bear . . ."

"I'm not miserable. But if you want the truth, I'm a bit worried about Barry. I've behaved rather foully to him, haven't I?"

Lady Brame's heart sank. She might have known it was the thought of Barry which had sunk Virginia. But she was determined not to let her make a tragedy out of it.

"Darling girl, don't be foolish. You *couldn't* have married Barry. The dear boy hadn't any money."

"No," said Virginia in a bitter voice. "Money is damnably necessary, isn't it?"

"You *know* it is, darling," said Lady Brame.

Virginia smiled— not a very happy smile.

"I'm very lucky, and Ian's a dear."

"You do like him, don't you, Gina?"

"Immensely. I'm sure we shall get on very well."

Lady Brame walked beside her daughter to her own bedroom. She squeezed her hand.

"Better not brood about Barry, dearest."

"Much better not," said Virginia with a grim smile. "Don't worry any more about me."

She started to whistle again; entered her room whistling. She took off her house-coat and stood up straight and beautiful in an ivory satin slip.

"Hurry up, Edith—my dress."

"Coming, miss," said the maid.

"What a seductive slip that is, Gina," said Eleanor Canfax, who was a tall, blonde girl with fine eyes and a bad-tempered mouth. She was a sister of Rupert Canfax the portrait-painter, and, with her brother, led one of the most ultra-modern artistic sets in town. She had been Virginia's closest friend since they had met three years ago, when Canfax had painted Virginia's portrait.

Virginia liked Eleanor because she was witty and amusing and go-ahead and always had something to say.

"My slip isn't half as seductive as my black chiffon nightie, my dear Eleanor," said Virginia. She held up long, slim arms while her maid stripped off the satin sheath and put a silky yellow one in its place.

"Poor old Ian," said Kitty McKyler, a pretty Irish girl distantly related to the Brames. "Even a clever ex-diplomat won't have a chance against a black chiffon nightie."

Lady Brame clicked her tongue and tripped from the room, shaking her head.

"Really—you girls today—most indelicate."

Eleanor Canfax laughed. Kitty giggled. The face of Edith, the maid, remained sober, but she stored up the remarks for the servants' hall. Ian Kingleigh's wife laughed and, picking up a lipstick, ran it over her lips with a swift, restless movement. Her nerves were jumping. And she didn't particularly want to think about seducing Ian. He didn't need it, poor dear. He was terribly in love. Of course it was nice to be adored. He'd give her whatever she wanted; obey her least wish. But the trouble was she was not in love with him. There was scarcely a thrill for her in the thought of her marriage. But if it had been Barry . . .

To the devil with the thought of Barry. It was spoiling everything. Virginia took the chic little hat which Edith handed her and crushed it down on the sleek dark waves of her hair.

"Give me that diamond bar I wore on my veil," she said curtly. "I'll stick it through the brim."

Virginia pinned the diamond bar in her hat and then sprayed herself with Jean Patou's "*Amour-amour*" from a tall crystal bottle.

Her thoughts were similar to Eleanor's now.

"Money means a devil of a lot . . . and I'm not the girl to give up a luxurious life for a struggle out East as a planter's wife in a damned uncomfortable bungalow."

She was escorted downstairs by her two chief bridesmaids. Lovely, perfectly dressed in the gold-brown velvet suit with the collar framing her exquisite face.

Kingleigh met her at the foot of the stairs. His heart beat quicker at the sight of her loveliness.

"My darling," he whispered when she was close to him.

She screwed up her red-brown eyes in that warm, alluring smile of hers, and buried the torment in her heart which was for Barry and a "damned uncomfortable bungalow" in Ceylon.

CHAPTER III

IN a less congested corner of the reception-room, a girl sat alone, scribbling busily on a block of paper. She was a rather short, slimly-built girl, soberly attired in a dark suit with a black helmet-shaped hat on her head. She was not as smart as most of the women in that festive assembly. But the small lizard shoes and a pair of suède gloves lying on her lap were faultless. And new.

She wrote earnestly, pausing now and then to lift a flushed face and look around her. Then she bent over the pad and scribbled again. She was left to herself, for which she was thankful. She was on a "job" and she liked getting down to it. Nobody noticed her. Nobody would in a reception so full of smart society. The girl lifted her head again and noted a very fat matron in a huge black hat talking to Lady Brame at one end of the drawing-room.

"Oh, Lord," she said to herself. "There's Mrs. Byson-Byson. No reporter would be forgiven who didn't mention *her*. . . ."

The fountain-pen, held tightly by hard, determined little fingers, flowed on :

"Mrs. Byson-Byson was to be seen in a wonderful dress of coffee-coloured lace and a black hat. She wore her famous choker of yellow diamonds. . . ."

The head of the young journalist lifted again and a pair of very blue eyes rested a trifle grimly on the famous choker which clasped the fat red throat of Mrs. Byson-Byson, the American widow of a South African diamond merchant.

The bridegroom passed by, carrying a goblet of champagne. The young reporter sucked in her lips.

"Lord, I'm thirsty . . ." she thought.

As if in answer to this, Ian Kingleigh turned his head and saw the lonely figure of the girl in the black suit. He walked up to her.

"Have you had something to drink ? "

She stood up, smiling.

"Oh—no—thanks, awfully, Sir Ian—I would love a drink."

"Let me see," said Kingleigh with a thoughtful look at her. " Haven't we met before ? "

"Yes. I'm Joan Borrow."

"Joan Borrow," he repeated vaguely.

"Virginia's cousin."

"Good gracious me, yes. Of course you are," said Kingleigh. " You came to our dinner here—the night we celebrated our engagement."

"That's right."

"Of course," he repeated, and smiled at her in his kindly way.

She thought how tired and elderly he looked now that the wedding was over—as though it was too much for his strength. He wasn't supposed to be over-strong. She felt a sudden wave of sympathy for him. He was rather a dear, and so very kind. She hoped Virginia would make him happy. But would cousin Virginia make any man happy ? She was much too beautiful and spoiled. But she had such a fatal attraction for men.

"You seem to be very occupied, new cousin Joan," said Kingleigh. " What are you writing ? "

"Report of the reception," said Joan. "I'm on the *Hand Mirror*, you know."

"The *Hand Mirror*, are you? A most distinguished society journal."

"Humph," said Joan. "It tries to be. I'm sent round to all these shows and have to describe the che-arming dresses of all the females, until I get too dizzy and dazed to distinguish one from another. Honestly, I'm getting to that condition of mind when I can't tell tulle from georgette."

"Well, I'm sure I can't and never could," said Ian Kingleigh and laughed.

Joan laughed, too. A happy little chuckling laugh. Kingleigh decided that he liked Joan Borrow very much indeed. She was nice. Of course he remembered meeting her. And Virginia had told him she was a plucky child. Worked off her feet. Sent here, there, everywhere by the *Hand Mirror*. They kept her at it and only paid her a few pounds a week. She had to support herself. Her mother, Lady Brame's sister, had died three years ago. Weak heart. Her father was a victim of the war. Kingleigh recalled now that Lady Brame had spoken of Joan with some distress. She had wanted to make Joan an allowance. It seemed wrong for her niece to be living in digs alone, struggling for an existence. True, she spent occasional holidays with them—had stayed, often, at Wanderton before they gave up the Towers for good. But most of Joan's life was led on her own. She refused charity from her relatives.

"Such an independent, stubborn little thing," Lady Brame had described her niece.

Kingleigh, looking gravely at Joan this afternoon, could well believe that she was independent, if not stubborn. It was written all over the small face. He admired her for it. He liked pluck. The child had it. Any amount of character in the firm young lips, which were a fresh red, untouched by lipstick, and the squareness of a chin which had a fascinating cleft in it. An attractive face without being definitely a pretty one. Nobody could call Joan Borrow pretty, except that she had a pair of very blue, frank eyes with thick lashes; and a charming head of bright brown hair. Her nose was short and a little broad, which gave her a touch of "*gamin*". Her complexion, clear and fair, was faintly powdered with golden freckles. Her hands and feet were her chief asset. Small, narrow, well-bred, and she looked after them.

Men did not fall madly in love with Joan Borrow at first sight. Neither had she that fatal allure, that thing in these days called sex-appeal. But she was always cordially liked by people of both sexes. And the one or two men who had fallen in love with Joan did not fall out of love very easily. There was a very real charm about her in her serious and intimate moments. Those moments were few and far between. She was a thoroughly sensible and level-headed, practical little person. She had her job; her living to make. She made it—and brought a kind of gay courage to life which defied the hardships and disappointments of it. And there had been plenty of those. Only Joan knew about them.

Her relations—like the Brames, who knew her well and with whom she had spent so much of her time—did not know much about the real Joan. Lady Brame imagined that she was rather a hard little person. Virginia said Joan had " no sex " in her. Joan let them think what they pleased. She wasn't going to give herself away. But she knew perfectly well that she was capable of quite frightening emotions and passions. And she had been desperately in love with one man for the last three years. But she would have died rather than show it to him or anybody else.

Ian Kingleigh—a little shrewder in his conceptions of other people than a good many—fancied he detected sadness behind the laughter that lurked in the wide blue eyes of his wife's young cousin.

" Let me get you something to eat, Joan," he said in his kindly way. " A sandwich . . . a piece of cake ? "

" No, thanks . . . really. I must just finish my article."

" Oh, but it's unlucky, surely, to reject a bit of wedding cake."

" Will it mean I shall be an old maid ? "

" Certainly."

" I don't mind," said Joan unexpectedly. " That won't worry me. I expect I will be an old maid, anyhow."

" Nonsense," Kingleigh smiled at her.

She bent over her writing-block. And now some of the humour faded from the gay blue eyes. A fierce little feeling of misery swept over her. She had loved him for so long, and so faithfully. And he didn't care for her. For long days and long, long nights she had suffered this horrible ache; this blank, hopeless sensation. It never got less; never seemed to grow easier. Today it was worse than usual. That was because she was attending Virginia's wedding. The man whom she, Joan, loved so desperately was Virginia's lover. And Virginia had betrayed him. She had married Kingleigh. What Barry would suffer when he knew was too awful for Joan to contemplate.

But she couldn't stop thinking about it; brooding over it. Gina had married Kingleigh. Barry, who *worshipped* her, would come back from Ceylon and find her lost to him.

"The thing is," Joan told herself, "Gina oughtn't to have encouraged Barry as she did. He was so certain of her when he went out East last time."

Joan was not likely to forget that "last time". It was only two years ago. Barry had spent most of his holiday with the Brames. He was fond of Virginia's mother, and Joan knew that he had always had it at the back of his mind that Lady Brame would eventually be his mother-in-law. He and Gina had gone everywhere together; done everything. Dined, danced, seen all the shows; motored here, there, everywhere in the little second-hand car he had bought just for his leave, and sold again when he went back to Ceylon. He had spent more than he could afford on Virginia —deeply in love—anxious to amuse her.

Joan had dined with the Brames two nights before Barry went back. Barry, always amusing in his dry fashion, full of anecdotes of his travels and experiences out East, had kept them all entertained. To him she was just Virginia's "little cousin Joan". He liked her. She knew it. He had paid her the compliment of confiding in her that night of the dinner. He had told her what Virginia meant to him. Not that Joan needed telling. He revealed it in every look he gave Virginia. Even when he was "ragging" her in his fashion, there was an expression in his eyes which betrayed the fire behind the screen.

He had said to Joan:

"Virginia looks perfectly marvellous tonight—doesn't she?"

Joan had answered bravely:

"Yes, rather. But she always does. She's so terribly pretty."

And she had said that with genuine feeling. She was one of her cousin's most sincere admirers. Virginia *was* "terribly pretty" and most attractive. Who could deny it? But Joan wouldn't have been human if she hadn't also thought:

"If only *I* were half as pretty and attractive, and Barry thought so . . ."

That thought, however, was without bitterness, and in the months that followed Barry's departure to Ceylon, Joan sometimes wrote to him and gave him the news of Virginia that she knew he would like. She even took care to collect all the *Tatlers*, *Sketches*, or other journals which contained photographs of "lovely Virginia Brame". Virginia riding in the Row; or at a race meeting; or a Society ball.

She had tried hard to believe that he would gain his heart's desire and marry Virginia. But somehow Joan had always had a premonition that things would not go right for those two. She knew her cousin Gina so well. Gina was a delightful person—nobody could be more charming. But she was unstable and Joan could not imagine that she would wait faithfully for Barry and eventually settle down on a Ceylon tea plantation as his wife.

It was no shock to Joan to hear rumours of Virginia's affair with Ian Kingleigh and still less of a shock to hear from Virginia, personally, of her impending marriage. But her heart had sunk low for Barry, and because she loved him she almost hated Virginia for hurting him. Since they were children together Joan had regarded Virginia as the superior being—worshipped with the rest of the crowd—at the shrine of her beauty and charm. But that night when Joan had attended the dinner in celebration of Virginia's engagement, she had for the first time looked at her with some contempt. It seemed to her such a weak, shoddy thing to do—to shelve Barry because he had no money for Kingleigh and his fortune. If she had really been in love with Ian, Joan would not have minded. But she knew in her heart that Virginia still cared for Barry. She had prostituted their love—for the sake of money. It wasn't playing the game. Particularly did it seem dishonourable because she had kept Barry dangling on the end of the string and had been too much of a coward to tell him there was no real hope for him.

Sitting here, this afternoon, making her report on the

wedding, Joan tried hard not to think badly of Virginia. But the thought of Barry's heart-break haunted her. His grief would be hers. She knew so well what it meant to care for somebody who was beyond one's reach. She cared for him like that. Only, in her case, she had never had even a glimmer of hope, and Virginia had given him so much which made it harder for him.

Of course Virginia could not help her temperament. Virginia was not born to make sacrifices for any man's sake.

CHAPTER IV

JOAN became aware that the new Lady Kingleigh was fighting her way through the crowd, obviously trying to escape from her would-be admirers and reach her cousin.

Joan stood up, put the pad and pencil into her bag, and watched Virginia approach her. How lovely she was. That velvet suit was most effective. But she was very white. Her smile was not as wide and spontaneous as usual. It was set in a way which made Joan feel suddenly sorry for her.

" Gina isn't happy," she thought.

Virginia reached her.

" Joan—I want you a moment. My God—this crowd . . ."

" Let's get out of it," said Joan.

Virginia seized her cousin's arm and drew her out of the room across the hall into a small morning-room which was deserted. She closed the door behind her and stood with her back to it, breathing hard, shutting her eyes.

Joan said:

" What's the matter ? Aren't you well, my dear ? "

Virginia opened her eyes and Joan saw the torment in them.

" I'm all right, but I felt all of a sudden I couldn't stick it, Joan."

" Stick what ? "

" This business . . . my marriage . . . everything."

Joan looked at her squarely.

" Gina, for Lord's sake—you've only been married five seconds, my dear. I thought you loved Ian."

" I'm fond of him—yes—I do love him."

"Well—you've got what you want. You always get what you want. Why are you unhappy?"

Virginia put up a hand and caught at the pearls round her throat. She did not meet the gaze of Joan's steady blue eyes. Joan had always had that habit of looking at one squarely and directly. It made one feel uncomfortable.

"Oh, I'm not unhappy, damn it," she said between her teeth. "I'm perfectly satisfied."

"H'm," said Joan. "So it seems."

Virginia coloured and turned her tormented red-brown eyes upon her cousin again.

"Damn it," she repeated. "Joan—you know."

"You mean you're worrying about Barry," said Joan quietly.

"Yes, I am."

"It's a bit late, my dear."

"Yes, but I've been such a swine to Barry. I know it. I've been beastly. I oughtn't to have told him when he said good-bye, last time he was home, that I'd wait for him."

"Did you tell him that?"

"Yes."

Joan shook her head dumbly. She had not realised that Virginia had gone so far. It really was hard on Barry.

"I've been a little beast," repeated Virginia.

"Yes, you have," said Joan frankly. "But it isn't a ha'p'orth of good worrying about it now. The only thing is —you ought to have written and told him at the beginning of the affair with Ian."

"I hadn't the courage."

"Well, Barry will have to show all the courage now," said Joan. Then, when she saw Virginia's beautiful face twist, she added: "That was rotten of me. Sorry, Gina. I'm sure you are unhappy about it."

"I am—dreadfully," said Virginia, and shaded her eyes with her hand for an instant. "Joan, you say I've always had everything I've wanted. Up to a point—yes. But I really wanted Barry."

No amount of control could prevent the little stab of jealousy that pricked Joan's heart then.

"Well, Gina, *really*—how is one to understand you? If you'd wanted him so much as that you'd have married him."

"You don't look at things from my point of view. You

forget what a ghastly time Mummy and I have had. All these damned bills . . . the awful taxation—our investments going wrong—dividends being passed——" Virginia broke off with a gesture and walked away from her cousin to the window. " I *had* to marry Ian," she added fiercely, " besides, I'm very fond of him ! "

Joan wanted to say, " Oh, rot. . . ." But she desisted. After all, from Virginia's point of view she *had* to marry Ian . . . yes. And it was as well she was fond of him.

" I only hope you'll be happy, Gina," she said after a pause.

" I doubt if I shall."

" Well, you won't if you think about Barry. You chucked him—you'd better forget him."

" Chucked him," repeated Virginia. " That sounds rotten, doesn't it ? You are being a comfort, Joan."

Joan walked up to her and put an arm about her.

" I'm sorry, but you know me, Gina. I always say what I think."

Virginia laughed.

" Yes, you do that all right. You're such a funny, hard little thing."

" I'm not at all hard."

" Oh, you're up in arms for Barry. But then you've always had a soft corner for him, haven't you ? "

That was getting on to dangerous ground. Joan drew in her breath sharply.

" Well—try and forget it all and be happy," she said.

Virginia nodded.

" Ian's a dear—and marvellous to me."

" I think he's rather a dear. Be nice to him, Gina."

" Oh, yes. But what I wanted to tell you was this, Joan. If you see Barry when he comes home—tell him I—I *did* care—but I couldn't help myself over this. It was for Mummy as much as for myself. She would never have stood giving up her home and roughing it."

" No," said Joan.

There wasn't anything else to say. One couldn't argue with Virginia. She did love her mother—that was indisputable. And they were, financially, in a mess. They had both been unpardonably extravagant. But what was the use of analysing the affair now ? It was over and done with.

"If I see Barry, I'll tell him and soften the blow," said Joan.

Lady Brame's voice reached the two girls in the morning-room.

"Virginia—my sweet—where are you?"

"I must go," said Virginia, and bent and kissed Joan hurriedly.

"Good luck and don't worry," said Joan.

Virginia disappeared. Joan returned to the crowd and stood at the dining-room window, watching the bridal pair depart in the Rolls for Claydown Manor, Ian Kingleigh's country seat, near Worth Forest. The honeymoon was to be spent in Italy.

Virginia and her mother stood in a close embrace just before Kingleigh helped his wife into the car. Joan could see tears running down Lady Brame's delicate cheeks.

"Poor little Aunt Milly," she thought. "And poor old Gina. She did do it for Aunt Milly as much as anything, I suppose."

But that couldn't excuse her for what she had done to Barry.

Kingleigh, looking very happy, climbed into the Rolls after Virginia and waved a hand to the bevy of bridesmaids who were crowding round the car.

"Poor old Sir Ian, too," thought Joan. "He's had a poorish deal if Gina's going to fret for another man."

Lady Brame came back into the house, wiping her eyes. Joan met her.

"Can I do anything for you, Aunt Milly?"

"Dear Joan," said Lady Brame chokily. "Yes, do stay and dine with me and cheer me up, dear. The house will be too dreadful without my darling."

"Right—I'll stay, I'd like to. But I must go back to the office and deliver my report to the *Hand Mirror*."

"Very well, dear child, then come back again. Don't dress. I shan't change tonight. I feel too unhappy."

"This wedding business is as bad as a funeral," said Joan, smiling, and tucked her arm through her aunt's. "Cheer up, duckie."

"I'm really *very* happy!" said Lady Brame with a sob. "It's wonderful to think darling Gina has made such a splendid match. You know, Joan, dear child, I can tell you quite confidentially, I was afraid at one time that Virginia would marry Barry Elderton. A dear boy. I'm *devoted* to him, but not really good enough for Virginia—just a struggling planter——"

She broke off, blowing her nose daintily on a wisp of lace and cambric. Joan drew her arm away from her aunt. Her small figure had tightened. A fierce look replaced the sympathy in her very blue eyes. Not good enough for Virginia—Barry !

"She wasn't good enough for *him* . . ." thought Joan. And suddenly regret for his sake blotted out all other feelings. "Oh, poor, *poor old* Barry . . . if only this hadn't been done to you, of all men . . ."

In the same hour that she sat at a desk correcting the proofs of a report on the Kingleigh-Brame wedding—rushed through for the evening paper—the liner from Ceylon which included Barry Elderton in its list of passengers docked at Liverpool.

CHAPTER V

JOAN had a talent for writing and liked journalism. She enjoyed her work in spite of the fact that the life of a reporter is frequently a hard and exhausting one. And she was frankly bored at times having to attend one Society function after another and write fulsome articles about people in whom she had no interest and for whom she had little admiration.

She was much more in sympathy with the men and women in the office ; the workers of this world. In their lives were to be found the real heroism and sacrifice and kindliness. Everybody was nice to Joan Borrow. She was a general favourite. The editor of the *Hand Mirror* himself was her most ardent admirer. He had been a little too ardent lately. Last time they had lunched together he had asked her to marry him. In spite of her firm refusal he persisted in his devotion, and because he was a nice, very genuine person, Joan did not deny him her friendship. But more she could not give.

This evening, when she put her head inside his office,

which adjoined her room, and said "Good night," he called her in.

She walked into the room. Joe Halliday, the editor of the *Hand Mirror*, sat at a big desk which was littered with papers, attempting to make up a page and at the same time deal with an inefficient artist who stood meekly by, while his handiwork was criticised and condemned.

". . . the head's about four times too small for the body . . ." Halliday was saying. "You really must give me a better bit o' work than this, Smith. I'll see you later. Come in, Miss Borrow. . . ."

The timid and crestfallen artist clutched his disparaged sketch, seized a hat, and departed. Joe Halliday leaned back in his chair and took off his horn-rimmed glasses. He grinned at Joan. She liked that grin. It was good-humoured. He was rather like an overgrown schoolboy, this big, heavy man, six foot one and running to fat, in his thirty-fifth year. He had short-sighted eyes and a head of dark, thick untidy hair.

"Come and soothe me down, Joan dear," he said. "I'm all ruffled. That man Smith drives me frantic. He can't draw to save his life. The only thing he can draw with any inspiration or success is his salary. God knows why the Chartwood Press put up with him."

Joan smiled and seated herself on the arm of a chair.

"That's easily explained. Good artists are hard to find, and if they are good they're not going to waste their talents on the twopenny rags we publish."

"Twopenny rags be hanged!" said Joe Halliday, grimacing at her. "The *Hand Mirror* is a most worthy and intellectual production, and we have in this building a few other hundred journals, including several priced at one shilling, and don't forget it, Miss Borrow."

"Give me a cigarette, and don't be facetious with me, Joe. I can't stand it."

"Was it a good show?"

"Quite. Mr. Ebbwood phoned up to my room and asked me to let him have a copy of my report for tonight's *Evening Moon*."

"That's because Kingleigh's a big pot. Did the lovely Miss Brame look very lovely?"

"Wonderful."

Joe Halliday seized a pipe and stuck it between his teeth. He put on his horn-rims and regarded Joan critically.

"You do look a bit off colour, Joan dear."

"Well, I'm not," she said and flushed slightly, because she knew she was telling an untruth. She *was* off colour—Virginia's wedding had depressed her and she really didn't want to go back to that house in Greyes Street and dine with Aunt Milly.

Halliday sighed.

"I suppose you won't change your mind and marry me, Joan?"

She laughed and looked away from him.

"No, Joe—sorry!"

"Look here—I've been a confirmed bachelor for thirty-five years and you're the only girl——"

"Don't begin it again," she broke in. "Please, Joe. We're such good pals. Let's leave it at that."

Halliday's big, heavy face puckered with disappointment like a child's. He was an incurable optimist, however, and soon broke into a smile.

"I shall go on hoping."

"Don't," she said quickly. "Please, Joe."

"Won't you give me an ounce of hope, dear?"

"No, Joe."

"Why? You like me, Joan dear."

"Immensely. You're charming to me. But I happen to have learned from recent experience how wrong it is to give an ounce of hope when there isn't any."

"What do you mean?"

"Never mind," said Joan with a mind on which Barry weighed heavily.

"Oh, well—will you lunch with me tomorrow?" he asked her.

He looked so plaintive, with his short-sighted eyes peering at her through the horn-rims, she softened.

"Yes, I'll lunch with you."

"You're the nicest girl in the world, Joan dear."

"Bah," she said, and stood up and tucked a wisp of hair into her hat, just over the ear. "Bye-bye, Joe."

"Good night, dear," he said wistfully. He thought what a pity it was that Joan Borrow couldn't care for him as he did for her. Halliday had loved her from the beginning, three years ago, when she had first come on to his paper. Rather shy and reserved; a mere child of nineteen without experience of life and hard work. Just how pluckily she had faced things; how gallant she was in the teeth of unaccustomed hardship, Joe Halliday knew better than most people.

Joan went down in the lift, nodding here and there to an acquaintance. The big building swarmed with busy figures, passing in and out of the various rooms and through the corridors.

As she sat in the bus, riding home through the April dusk, she thought a little sadly of Halliday.

"Poor Joe. Isn't life a mess! A loves B—B loves C—C loves D, and so on in a vicious circle. In order to make things nice and happy, I should have been in love with Joe, or Barry should have been in love with me . . . and it's all just the opposite."

She reached home soon after five, and had a bath—one of the daily luxuries she did not deny herself—and changed from her black suit into a blue georgette dress with long sleeves. It was a beautifully cut frock which Virginia had handed on to her.

Just before she turned out the light in her room she walked to the mantelpiece and picked up a small framed snapshot of Barry Elderton; one she had herself taken of him in Cornwall five years ago.

Her spirits were very low this evening. She shook her head at the pictured Barry.

"Poor old boy. I wish this hadn't happened. It would have broken me all up to see you married to Virginia—but I could have borne that—if you'd been happy."

She wondered, as she journeyed to Greyes Street, when Barry would come home and what he would say and do when he did come. Nothing much, if she knew him. He would never show his feelings. He was like that. If he were hurt to the death he wouldn't let anybody see. . . . That made things so much worse.

She walked up the steps of No. 10 Greyes Street, and as she was about to ring the bell a taxi rolled up and stopped outside the same house.

Joan frowned.

"I hope Aunt Milly hasn't got anyone else to dinner. I don't feel like coping with people tonight. . . ."

A man stepped out of the taxi and put his hand in his

pocket to find the fare. And then Joan's heart seemed to give one great jerk and stand still and the blood rushed violently to her face. For she knew that tall, athletic figure ; knew it so well ; the shape of the handsome head ; the very gesture with which he dived into his pocket for change.

"*Barry!*" she said under her breath. "Barry. Good Lord! He's home!"

He paid the taxi-driver, turned and came toward her. As he recognised the small, straight figure his face broke into a smile and he hastened to her side.

"Hello! It's little Joan!"

She stood very still, breathless, staring at him. And she could tell at once, from the gaiety of his smile and the buoyancy of his voice, that he did not know about Virginia.

"He can't know," she thought. "Or he wouldn't look like that. He wouldn't be here——"

Then Barry Elderton stood before her, shaking both her hands with that warm, strong grip so familiar to her.

"And how's little cousin Joan? My dear—I do believe you've grown. It's good to see you again."

"Grown!" she repeated, and laughed because she could not help herself. But she was nearer tears than laughter. "Idiot!"

"How are you?"

"Awfully well."

"Still working hard?"

"Oh, yes, rather! And what about you?"

"I'm full of malaria, my dear, otherwise in very good form."

She looked at him. She had to look up. He was a very tall young man—a good head taller than she was. Yes, she could see he was in "good form", as he called it. Those rather penetrating eyes of his were bright and eager. He was full of humour, and browner than ever—such a dark tan that it made his eyes appear a curiously pale grey. She was not sure he looked very well. He was much too thin ; hollow in the cheeks. But that no doubt was the fever. He had told her in his last letter that he was "full of it".

"Ugh, it's cold in this infernal country," he grumbled, rubbing his hands and grinning at her. "No, I mustn't say that. I'm damned glad to be home. What is it the poet said about 'Now that April's there'? I'm no good at quoting.

You're the one for that, Joan. Well—here we are. Have we both turned up by accident or am I the only uninvited guest?"

He rattled on, while she slowly turned from him and pressed the bell. Her heart was beating so fast that it was painful. To see him again; hear his voice; deep, a little curt, he had a staccato way of speaking; to realise that he was here, before her, instead of a thousand miles away; brought her unspeakable delight, unbearable pain.

"I didn't send Virginia a cable or phone her," Barry was saying. It was his first mention of Virginia. "I wanted to surprise her. As a matter of fact I've a good many surprises for her."

"You're manager of the estate now?"

"I could have been, but I've quit."

"Quit—left Ceylon altogether?" said Joan in surprise.

"Yes. I'll tell you about it later. But tell me—how is Virginia? Do you know the little beast hasn't written to me for the last six mails. Is she ill?"

"No."

Joan did not look at him. Her heart was quailing; her courage deserting her. He didn't know. *Didn't know.* Oh, poor Barry. And the very voice with which he said those chaffing words "little beast" vibrated. . . . He had come back to England as madly in love with Virginia as he had been when he left her, two years ago. He was not the sort to change. He was the faithful sort. Poor Barry!

"Listen——" she began.

Then the butler opened the door. She swallowed hard and walked into the house. Barry followed, still chatting gaily. As he removed his coat he spoke to the butler, who was an old retainer.

"Well, Parks—here I am, back. You fit?"

"Yes, sir, thank you, sir," said Parks. "Glad to see you home again, sir."

He spoke with sincerity. The servants who had been with the Brames for any length of time all knew and liked Mr. Elderton. He was what they called a "nice gentleman" and he gave generous tips. Parks, who had a very human heart behind his well-trained impassivity, felt a little sorry for Mr. Elderton today. Everybody below stairs knew how keen he had been about Miss Virginia—that was—Lady

Kingleigh. He had practically lived with the family on his last holiday.

"I'll let her ladyship know you're here," said Parks; showed Joan and Barry upstairs into the drawing-room, and retired.

CHAPTER VI

BARRY ELDERTON stood in the centre of the room and looked around him. He was tired, cold, and he had a touch of fever which had attacked him in the train coming from Liverpool. But he felt only a tremendous happiness. It was a splendid thing to be back here in this country, the city that held the woman he loved; the woman he had loved since he was a boy of twenty-two. She had been predominant in his thoughts all through the months of isolation and hard work out in Ceylon.

He had worked with but one aim. To save money and make a home for Virginia. He was so certain of her. Why shouldn't he be? When he had left her on his last leave she had given him all the hope, the encouragement, that was necessary to his peace of mind. The fact that her letters had become few and far between and finally non-existent, these last few months, had worried him a little, but not much. He loathed writing letters himself, and Virginia he knew led a very full life. She was a popular young woman in Society. He was not an exacting man, and although he fretted a little because she left his letters unanswered he never for an instant suspected infidelity from her. He had known her and cared for her so long he never doubted that she would ultimately marry him.

In this very room she had said good-bye, in the winter of two years ago. He remembered every detail of that farewell. It had seemed to him he had reached the very summit of his ambitions when he had taken her in his arms and felt in the quality of her kiss, her embrace, something deeper than the careless affection which had existed between them in their extreme youth. She was in love with him, as passionately as he was with her.

He recalled the fervent beauty of her face upraised to his;

—B

the thrill of her arms and lips; the adorable and familiar way in which she screwed up her long, laughing eyes. The old thrall was upon him this evening when he stood here looking at all the remembered objects.

He paused before the fire-place and spread out his cold hands to the warmth of the electric fire. His eyes wandered restlessly around him. How well he remembered those two Sèvres jars; the ormolu clock; the exquisite little Queen Anne mirror; the miniatures against the creamy satin-panelled wall. One, a miniature which had been done of Virginia in her seventeenth year, caught and held his attention. That was an old favourite of his. He had often told Lady Brame that one day he would steal it. Virginia, in the glory of budding womanhood, with her dark, rippling hair tied with a bow at the nape of the neck; the long chestnut eyes looking gravely under the shadow of silken lashes.

And then Barry suddenly took his gaze from the miniature and became aware of two things. One, that the charming drawing-room was full of flowers—a great many magnificent spring flowers, golden and white—and two, that Joan had not said a single word to him since they entered the house.

He turned to her.

"The whole place is a mass of flowers. Has somebody had a birthday? What's the celebration?"

Joan, who was staring up at a seascape in an old gilt frame, blindly, without seeing it, felt herself grow hot and then cold. The dreadful moment had come. Barry *had* to know. She braced herself to meet his gaze. He looked so eager, so self-confident, she had little heart for the unhappy task which had befallen her.

"Barry," she said. "Look here, old thing, I'm afraid you're going to have rather a nasty shock. But it's no use beating about the bush. You've got to be told sooner or later. Virginia was married today. That's why there are all these flowers."

Silence. She saw a look of amazement, of incredulity, in his eyes change to something too painful to witness and she turned hastily from him. She felt so unhappy that she wanted to burst into tears. Poor old Barry. How was he going to take it? If only he had had some idea; if only Virginia had not been cruel enough to let him hope; if only he had not rushed here, straight from the boat, in that happy, confident fashion. She wished he would speak. But he did not for a long time. The room was so quiet that she could hear the soft ticking of the ormolu clock on the mantelpiece, and the scrape-scrape of a taxi grinding down Greyes Street.

All sorts of irrelevant things pushed a way into her head. She tried to remember the actual day when she first fell in love with this man. It was about three years ago. Oh, yes—the sixth of June—she did remember. Virginia's birthday. There had been a dance here. She had come to it. Barry was a good dancer, and Joan was not too bad herself. They had Rock 'n' rolled together; rather wildly; just for the fun of the thing, and Barry had caught Virginia's eye and called out:

"Bad form, this, but aren't we wonderful?"

Barry, in one of his ragging moods. But, for Joan, that Rock 'n' roll had been the beginning of everything. Clasped tightly in his arms, all the woman in her had been roused. She had always liked him; admired him; and she had realised at last that she was in love with him. She had gone home half thrilled, half frightened by the revelation. She had reasoned that it was a futile and stupid thing for a girl to fall in love with a man who loved somebody else. But she couldn't help herself. And she hadn't been able to help herself since then. She was older now; more experienced and much, much more in love.

If only she could help him. But she could do nothing to alleviate the agony that he must be enduring. He had lost the woman he loved and had wanted for his wife.

What comfort was there for him? What comfort had there been for her, all these years, caring for Barry? Unrequited passion was like an incurable disease; a cancer; eating the vitality, the hope, the love-life out of one until, mentally, one died. And sometimes it took a long time to die. She was so acutely conscious of her love for Barry today, when she saw him again, that she knew her own passion was not anywhere near dead. How long would it take his for Virginia to die?

Then she heard his voice. It was quite calm and steady.

"Joan—just a moment. Did you say Virginia was *married* today?"

"Yes."

"To whom?"

"Sir Ian Kingleigh."

"Ian Kingleigh. I don't know him."

"He—he used to be in the Diplomatic——"

"Oh, yes—I do know who you mean now. When did Virginia meet him?"

"Last Christmas."

"I see."

She looked at him now. She could not tell whether he had grown pale or not—because of the dark tan. But his face was as lacking in expression as his voice. He had been hit hard; and it had been a horrible unsporting blow, even a treacherous one. But Joan knew that Barry would not let a soul on earth know how badly he had felt it. That made things all the worse; his reticence, his terrific control. He went on questioning her.

"How long were they engaged?"

"Only a short time."

"But long enough for her to let me know, surely."

"Y-yes, I think so," she said, finding it very difficult to talk to him. She was much nearer breaking point than he was. He would not break. He never would. She was sure of that. And this thing must be like death to him; the death of his most cherished hopes and schemes of the past four years.

"Then why didn't she write?" he asked.

"Barry, I think, honestly, she was—afraid to."

"Afraid of hurting me, you mean?"

"Yes."

He laughed then, and Joan wished she had not heard that laugh. He said the one and only bitter thing she was to hear from him this night:

"By God, she went wrong on that, didn't she? She might have known it would hurt a bloody sight more for me to just turn up like this and find her married. *God!*"

Joan put a hand to her lips. They were trembling. Her eyes were full of tears. Barry turned to the fire and stared into it.

"Sorry, Joan," he added. "I didn't mean to use strong language."

"That's all right. I understand."

"Tell me a bit more about this interesting wedding, will you?"

His voice was not bitter now—only very weary. She looked at him through her tears and felt an aching longing to say something which would be of help; something to make things easier, but she knew that there was nothing. She remembered the message which Virginia had given her for him this afternoon before she went away.

"Barry," she said, "Virginia spoke to me about you just after the reception and she asked me to try and explain——"

"Explain?" he repeated, and turned round sharply. "Oh, that's all right, Joan. I want no explanation. After all, she had every right to marry this fellow if she liked him better than she did me. A woman has a right to choose."

"Yes, but listen, Barry. She—Sir Ian is a most awfully nice man and she is devoted to him, I think, but I think it was you she really loved."

The blood rushed violently to Barry's temples.

"Oh, my dear Joan—don't tell me that. It's quite absurd."

"No, listen," she said painfully. Heavens, how hard it was for her of all people to have to try and make feasible excuses for Virginia, when in her heart of hearts she despised her for letting this man down so badly. But she went on, desperately, in the hope that she could mitigate the blow for him . . . out of her love for him rather than her loyalty to her cousin.

"Listen," she said again. "You don't know anything yet, Barry. But before Aunt Milly comes in, I want to tell you a bit about things."

"Well—what?" he asked, his passion subsiding as quickly as it had flared up.

"Aunt Milly and Gina have had frightful bad luck lately with investments—they've had money troubles—you've no idea how bad—what an awful mess they've been in. Aunt Milly has been at her wits' ends and Gina simply could not let her face selling up this house and everything in it."

Barry stared at her.

"Do you mean things have been as bad as that? Virginia never mentioned it in her letters."

"No—but they were bad—frightfully so. I know it, Barry."

"So—it's a question of money."

"Well, Sir Ian is very rich and——"

"Don't bother to go on. I think I understand quite well, Joan," interrupted Barry.

"But—but it sounds so beastly mercenary," she stammered, clasping her hands together. "And it wasn't as rotten as it sounds. I mean—Virginia cares for Sir Ian, too."

"I hope she does. I shouldn't like to imagine her tied to a man she has married entirely for his money."

"Oh, no—she wouldn't do that."

He looked again at the exquisite miniatured face of Virginia. He was trying to realise that she was wholly lost to him and that his hopes of making her his wife were dead. Stone dead. But he could not really credit the fact just yet. His head ached abominably and he felt himself shivering. That damned malaria coming on again. How tired he felt. Rotten. He hadn't noticed quite how ill he did feel— till now. He couldn't stay here to dinner and face Lady Brame all the evening.

He tried to concentrate on what Joan was saying. A nice kid, Joan—awfully kind. She was trying to make things better. He knew it. But nothing could ever make them better—not even the knowledge that Virginia *had* to marry in order to save her mother and herself from a financial débâcle, and possibly still loved him. That didn't make things better. It made them a damn sight worse. He wished Virginia had married Kingleigh for love only.

He had loved her frightfully; since he was a boy. And it was all over. He had better get used to the idea. But he knew that he would never get used to it and that he would love her all his life . . . like a fool . . . because he was built that way.

"Barry," said Joan, coming nearer to him. "Please think kindly of Virginia."

"Good Lord, my dear, but I do," he said with a short laugh, pulling himself together. "I don't blame her. You say they were on the brink of ruin—well, naturally she had to save the situation, and if she liked this fellow—I believe Kingleigh's a very decent fellow, isn't he?—and he wanted to marry her and had pots of cash—who can blame her? I made a mistake, that's all. I suppose I attached more importance to her affection for me than I had any right to do."

"I don't think so," said Joan. "I think she cared and still does."

"We won't talk about that," said Barry. "Tell me—do you think she'll be happy with Kingleigh?"

"Yes."

"That's all right. Well, my dear, if you'll make my excuses to Lady Brame——"

"Oh, you aren't going before you see her; before dinner, Barry?"

"Yes, I must, if you'll forgive me. My infernal head's giving me hell and I've got a bit of a temperature. I'm going back to my hotel to bed."

"But Aunt Milly will be down any minute——"

"I'd rather get off, really, Joan. Give her my love and apologies, and all the necessary congratulations, will you?"

Joan stared at him miserably. He spoke easily and naturally; as though nothing had happened; and no great tragedy had befallen him. Yet she knew this must be the most tragic moment of his life. The bottom had been knocked out of his world. Her whole heart went out to him in admiration. He was taking it so gallantly. He was wonderful. This was all so like Barry. She was more in love with him tonight than she had ever been. Except for that one bitter criticism of Virginia because she had not warned him, he had not said one single word against her. "A woman had the right to choose," he had said. And yet a woman had just put an end to his dearest illusions.

"Oh, Barry," said Joan. "I'm so frightfully sorry—really I am."

He shrugged his shoulders and smiled at her. His grey eyes were very bright and very hard.

"You needn't be, my child. I'll get over it."

"That's a valiant lie," she thought. "If *he'd* ever given me hope—then married someone else—I'd never have got over it."

"There's one touch of irony in the whole damned business," added Barry. "I'm not quite so hard up as I used to be. I mean, poor old Uncle John died about six weeks ago, poor old blighter. That's why I chucked my job and rushed home. I've got a bit of cash now. Not that it would have been enough. I ought to have known that."

"Oh, Barry!" was all Joan could say in the face of this

new tragedy, and she wondered, had Virginia known that Barry was to inherit his uncle's money so soon, if she would have waited for him.

"Well—I shall run before I'm caught by Lady Brame. Bye-bye, Joan, old thing. I'm glad you were here to tell me all about it."

She walked with him to the door. She saw, as she stood close to him, how tired and ill he looked and how dead was his smile. Because she loved him very much she would have cut off her right hand—or more—to spare him the pain that he was suffering now. But she could not even let him know that. She managed to produce a smile of her own from somewhere and said:

"I'd like to see you again, Barry."

"Why not?" he said indifferently. The indifference cut her to the quick. "I'm at Brown's Hotel. I'll be there till I've settled up Uncle John's estate, anyhow. You still with the *Hand Mirror*?"

"Yes."

"Lunch with me tomorrow, if you'd care to, Joan."

"I'd love to," she said and wished her heart would not pound and hurt her so. Wasn't a girl mad to let her heart beat that way for a man who was broken to pieces over another woman?

"I'll call at the office for you—one-thirty. Good night, Joan."

"Good night. I'm sorry you won't stay. But I understand and so will Aunt Milly."

He went down the stairs, out of her sight, and found his coat and hat without troubling the butler, and let himself out of the house.

CHAPTER VII

IT was only when Joan reached the office on the following morning that she remembered she had done a dreadful thing. She had promised to lunch with two men today. Joe Halliday—and Barry.

The thought of lunching with Barry had held such precedence all night, there had been no room in her mind for

Halliday. She felt guilty and troubled as she took off coat and hat, smoothed her thick brown hair, and settled down at her desk. She knew that she would make an excuse to Joe and lunch with Barry, and she felt that she was treating Joe rather shabbily. But she could not help it. For two long years she had not seen the man she loved and he was, without doubt, a very unhappy man today. She could not turn down his invitation. She wanted to see him; do all that lay in her power to amuse and console him. Not that she could do much. She knew it.

"Lend me your comb, Joan," said Margaret Mackay, who shared the room with her. She was a plump, red-haired, Scottish girl with a jolly voice and laugh; several years older than Joan. They were very good friends. Miss Mackay—more commonly known in the office as "Mac"—was sub-editor of the *Hand Mirror*.

Joan walked to the window and looked down—a very long way down, it seemed—over the house-tops to the dome of St. Paul's. A wet, dismal morning. Pelting rain. Joan's forehead was creased. She felt restless and unlike work. There was a couple of articles to be written, and at midday a boring Society function to attend—a bazaar being opened by Her Grace the Duchess of Torlington. The *Hand Mirror* wanted a report on it. Joan wondered how soon she could get away and come back here where Barry was calling for her.

Why could she not stop thinking about Barry? It was so foolish. And she thought of Virginia, too; a little ironically this morning. What were Virginia's feelings—the day after her wedding to Ian Kingleigh?

"Oh, Lord, if she's human, she'll regret what she gave up when she flung Barry over," thought the girl who was in love with Barry.

A booming voice came through the communicating door.

"Miss Bor-row . . ."

Joan stepped into Halliday's room a little nervously. He gave her his most optimistic smile.

"Good morning, fairest. Isn't it a top-hole morning?"

"Don't be silly, Joe. It's pouring with rain."

"Ah, but I am lunching with a goddess."

Joan averted her gaze. Her cheeks coloured. How awkward. How embarrassing—when a man showed so plainly how pleased he was that he was about to lunch with her. And she must disappoint him. Difficult . . . and trying. No doubt he had been looking forward to it . . . just as she looked forward to her lunch with Barry.

"Joe," she said, "I'm so awfully sorry, but would you mind very much if I didn't lunch with you?"

Halliday's big face clouded. His eyes lost their sparkle.

"Oh, Joan dear, why?"

"I—it's like this—I—I've mixed my dates——" She stumbled over the explanation, conscious of being at fault. He came to her aid generously.

"That's all right, dear. You promised someone else? That's all right."

She drew nearer his desk, her heart warming towards him. He was always so decent to her. She was even conscious of an insane longing to tell him all about Barry Elderton; of the tragedy of his love for Virginia, and of her feelings for him. But that was absurd. Nobody knew about her love for Barry and she could never tell anybody.

"I'm so sorry, Joe," she repeated. "Perhaps tomorrow——"

"Surely—tomorrow," he said, brightening at once. Then added, grinning at her: "Who's the lucky fellow today?"

The colour burnt her face now, but she laughed.

"Nobody you know."

"Let me know if—well—if you ever fall in love with anybody—will you, Joan dear?" he asked wistfully.

"Certainly not," she said, laughing again to hide her confusion. "I shouldn't dream of giving myself away."

"Oh, well," he sighed, staring at the rough make-up of the paper on the desk before him. "I'm sure to wake up one morning to a hideous shock—to be told you're married and done for."

"'Done for' is good," she smiled. "Cheer up, Joe dear. My marriage is a long way off and less probable than a trip to the moon."

"Wait until somebody gives you the sort of heart attack you've given me!"

"Great stupid," she said; patted his arm and went back to her room.

Joan scribbled with a pencil on the blotter in front of her. She could not see very well because her eyes were misty and there was a little lump in her throat. She was remembering the pain in Barry's eyes last night. Her own pain; her own hopeless anguish of loving and wanting seemed to be mixed and mingled with his. She had tried so often to tell herself that she was young—very young—only twenty-three in a month's time; and at twenty-three one is not supposed to fall in love so badly that it is unremediable. Yet she felt that there could be no remedy for her—no release from the perpetual ache and smart of wanting Barry. It had gone on so long. And she was like him in that respect—she did not easily change. As a child she had been the same. She had been slow to place her affections and then they were concrete. Barry was the only man she had ever wanted as a lover. It seemed hard to accustom herself to the fact that he never would be a lover of hers. Yet never had she felt humiliated by her heart's persistent devotion to him. She was fiercely proud of it.

At half-past one she had got back to the office from the bazaar which was opened in Chelsea. She was ready and waiting when Barry called for her.

Margaret Mackay, lounging back in her chair, yawning through a set of proofs, looked with some curiosity at her friend when one of the lift-girls gave Joan the formal slip of paper announcing the arrival of Mr. Elderton. Joan was blushing. Miss Mackay could swear to it. Never before had she seen such a crimson flush on that small, determined face with its faint, attractive powdering of freckles. Joan was unusually smart this morning, too.

"Now then, what are you up to, my child?" said Miss Mackay. "Who's come to fetch you out, and why the new dress?"

"I've been to a very smart bazaar," said Joan, diving into her bag for a mirror and examining her crimson face. She hastily powdered her nose and pulled the small blue felt at a more rakish angle over her brows. She was glad she had bought this blue outfit. It suited her. The scarf knotted about her neck brought out all the colour in her eyes. She had to rely on the beauty of those eyes. . . . and she knew it. How she hated the shape of her nose. Hateful snub. And that big, wide mouth.

Joan went down in the lift and entered the waiting-room, wishing that her cheeks were not such flame-colour and that her heart would not beat so fast. But she ceased to feel anything but overwhelming love for Barry when she saw him again and he shook hands with her. She thought no more about poor Joe and his disappointment, or Mac and her teasing, or about anything . . . but Barry.

"How are you?" she said.

"Fine. How are you?" he replied.

They walked out of the big building together, up the narrow roadway and into the noise and turmoil of Fleet Street in the lunch-hour.

"We'll get a taxi," added Barry.

"I don't suppose he's even noticed my nice coat and dress and hat," thought Joan, the eternal feminine. Then forgot herself and looked anxiously at him. He had said he was "fine"—quite heartily. But that couldn't be true. He must have had a rotten night. He looked very brown after all her pallid colleagues in the office, but terribly tired.

"How's the fever?" she asked when they were in the taxi. Barry had told the driver to go to the Savoy Grill, because it was conveniently near, and he had an appointment with his solicitors in Holborn at three. That was a little disheartening. Joan had vaguely entertained a hope that he would ask her to spend the afternoon with him. They might have done a cinema or matinée. Not that she wanted the amusement . . . only to be with him . . . feel she was helping him to forget. She had told Joe she might steal a holiday and he did not mind, nice old thing.

From his corner of the taxi Barry surveyed his companion. It struck him that she looked unusually nice, and also what an amazing blue her eyes were. But he did not say anything. He was not the type to pay idle compliments—even to a woman he cared for. And this morning, certainly, he was not in a mood to flatter any woman. He was inclined to hate the whole of the weaker sex They were mercenary and faithless. Yes, he was in a much more bitter frame of mind today than he had been last night when he had first been faced with the shock of Virginia's marriage to Kingleigh.

He had had a bad night; scarcely slept; malaria and mental stress coming to torture him. It had not been humanly possible for him to stop thinking about Virginia— as Kingleigh's wife. And it had been damnable. The whole affair seemed more damnable now than it had done at first. Not that his bitterness was directed against Virginia personally. She was still the woman he loved and had wanted for so long, and she had had a right to choose. But he was at war with life in general . . . with the whole rotten scheme of things.

During breakfast he had contemplated putting Joan Borrow off. He really did not want to lunch with her or with anyone. She was a nice child. But he would rather be alone. And she was related to Virginia—therefore closely associated with her. He wanted to dissociate himself from Virginia.

Then—after breakfast—he reasoned wearily with himself that nothing mattered. Not a damn thing. He had said he would take little Joan out to lunch. She had been very nice and tactful last night. Why put her off? So here they were.

" Is the malaria better? " she was asking.

" Oh, yes. I'm all right," he said.

" You must take care of yourself, Barry."

" Oh, yes," he repeated indifferently.

Joan's fingers closed tightly over her bag. That indifference to her, to himself, to everything, hurt her. It meant that he was dreadfully unhappy. She dragged her gaze from the dark, tired face of the man—and remembered how bright and eager those grey eyes of his had been when she had first met him yesterday. They were changed and dull this morning. He said he was " all right." But he was not. It was obvious.

" How's work? " he asked.

" Oh, splendid," said Joan and talked hard about the *Hand Mirror*, the office, and her life as a reporter.

Barry regarded her with some curiosity. A queer little thing, Joan. Full of will-power and grit. He rather admired her outlook on life. It was so cheerful and sane. She was more balanced than most girls he knew—she was old for her age, of course. She had been through the mill since her mother died and she had left school. She had had a difficult time. It must be lonely for her, too. But she never whined. That was the one thing he remembered most about Virginia's young cousin. Her pluck. She never groused about her lot and she refused the charity of her relations. That appealed to Barry. He understood her dislike of whining and her love of freedom. He himself was like that. But it was much harder for a girl than a man to grin through life's disappointments and hardships. Her sex made everything more difficult. All the more credit to Joan for the gay courage with which she faced her existence.

She went on chatting to him about the office once they were in the grill-room at the Savoy and Barry ordered their meal. She thought that he seemed interested in details, and she was anxious to distract him. He asked her a lot of questions in that funny curt way he had of speaking. But his eyes, restless, tormented, roved constantly about the room. Joan, sitting opposite him, her own gaze riveted upon him with no interest in the rest of the community, wondered desolately if he was at all interested in her and her doings. Oh, the wandering, searching gaze of those grey eyes. As though he expected to see the ghost of Virginia arise from one of the crowded tables, and confront him.

But Virginia was on her way to Italy with her bridegroom. Joan knew it. Barry knew it. And she was sure that that unhappy thought dominated his mind. But neither of them mentioned Virginia's name during the lunch.

"What are you going to do with yourself this next month or two, Barry?" Joan asked him.

They had finished the meal and reached the coffee and cigarette stage. Joan had had a cocktail, but no other drinks. Barry had tonic-water.

"I'm dying for a whisky, but I daren't with this fever on me," he told her.

"I'm glad you haven't become a teetotaller," she laughed.

"Ye gods, no," he said. "You asked me what I'm going to do. Well, I don't know. I've got to see the lawyers and settle up my uncle's estate."

"You won't go back East?" she asked, trying not to care so desperately what the answer would be.

"I don't know. I haven't any plans. Everything is a bit upside down in my mind—all my ideas, I mean."

She knew what he meant. It was the only indirect allusion that he made to Virginia and what the loss of her as a future wife meant to him. But Joan could see how enormously the thing had altered his future; what a vital change it made in his schemes.

"You'll be comfortably off now, won't you, Barry?"

"Oh, yes, quite. I shan't have to work." He lit a fresh cigarette from the stump of the one nearly finished. Joan saw that he was smoking much too much and that he was a mass of nerves. "I shall certainly be in Town for a bit because there'll be a lot to settle up for my uncle. I shall have to sell his place in Hampstead and most of the stuff in it."

Joan looked at her plate, but her eyes were bright with relief. He would be in Town for a little while, anyhow. That meant she might see him.

"Next week," he added, "I may go down to the country with a pal of mine from Ceylon who wants me to play golf."

"That would do you a lot of good," she said.

"How do you amuse yourself?" He turned his roving gaze to her and smiled, and her pulses thrilled despite the inner voice that whispered: "Don't be a clot Joan Borrow."

"Oh, all sorts of ways. One of my best friends—Margaret Mackay—sub-editor of the *Hand Mirror*—has digs in Victoria not far from me. We go to the films or a matinée sometimes. When we've saved enough money we want to share a little flat."

"That would be better than digs on your own if you've got a pal you like to be with."

"Oh, yes."

"But it doesn't sound as though your life is wildly exciting, poor child."

"Oh, but it is!" she laughed gaily. "Think of the marvellous weddings and bazaars and At Homes I go to—for the sake of my work. I simply *live* with duchesses!"

Barry's lips relaxed into a smile.

"H'm. It sounds grim to me."

"Riotous living, *I* tell you, Barry."

"Amongst a crowd of women. Oh, Lord!"

"Don't you make any mistake. The Chartwood Press is seventy-five per cent male."

"Ah ha!" Barry drained his coffee-cup and his eyes twinkled at her over the rim. She was glad. She had not seen them twinkle like that for such a very long time. "Now we come to truths and open confession. Come on, Infant. How many lovers have you?"

She made a grand gesture.

"Thousands."

"No, really. Who's in the running?"

He watched a wave of crimson flood the determined young face—to the very roots of her bright brown hair. He thought, half amusedly: "Little Joan's in love with somebody . . . a damn nice kid, too. Hope he's a decent fellow." And she was thinking: "Oh, why, why does he ask me that in such a casual way? He doesn't care—of course he wouldn't care if I *had* a thousand lovers!"

How could she look him straight in the eyes and say:

"There's nobody—never has been anybody in my heart but you"?

She took refuge in a salted almond which she seized and nibbled with small, strong teeth.

"The divine passion isn't in my line, Barry. I'm much more intrigued with my work."

"Wise child."

"Quite so," she said, and sat back in her chair and smiled at him, very tight-lipped and secure because her love for this man was such a dead secret . . . a secret he would never know. "All the same," she added, "I've got a very good pal in my chief—Mr. Halliday, who's editor of the *Hand Mirror*. You must meet him one day. He's rather amusing."

"I'd like to."

He looked round the grill-room and wished that he had been more intrigued with his work out in Ceylon than he had been with his thoughts, his hopes of Virginia Brame. The damn thing hurt intolerably. He had nothing to look forward to now. What was the use of his uncle's money and his financial independence . . . without the woman he loved to share it? He had wanted a home with her; children. He adored kids. And she was on her way this very minute —to Italy—with her husband.

Joan saw his face grow harder; more strained.

"He's thinking of *her*," she told herself miserably.

But when he spoke it was about Joan.

"I'm sure you ought not to submerge yourself completely in work, Joan. A little relaxation will do you good. While I'm in Town, how about a few dinners and shows? There are one or two good things I want to see."

Her heart leapt with gladness.

"It sounds marvellous, Barry."

"You're on the phone at the office, aren't you?"

"Yes. Central 9000. Extension 41."

He took a note-book from his pocket and jotted this down. Joan's spirits rose considerably. Her eyes were such a starry blue when he looked at her again that he was struck afresh by the beauty of them. They transformed her whole face.

"I can imagine a fellow being crazy about this nice kid," he thought. And immediately followed the gloomy reflection: "I'll never be crazy about another woman in this life. Hell, I won't! It isn't worth it."

He was feeling raw today. . . . His pride as well as his passion was lacerated by the thing that Virginia had done to him.

He took Joan back to the Chartwood Press by taxi.

"I'm going on to old Tatham—the family lawyer. Thanks awfully for coming out to lunch with me, Joan. It's cheered me up."

"I'm so glad. I've loved it," she said.

He clasped her hand warmly for a second.

"So long, Infant. I'll phone you quite shortly if I may, and we'll have that riotous time we spoke of."

"I'd simply love it, Barry."

The memory of his friendly smile and that hope of meeting him again "quite shortly" carried her through the rest of the day's work and eased a little of the aching that was in her heart for him. She tried to imagine that he really was interested in her and that she *had* cheered him up, despite an inner conviction that nothing and nobody mattered to Barry after yesterday.

Well, she was not going to stop loving him whatever happened. She could not. He was in her very blood now. And it was much worse this time—much more real and devastating. She wanted to concentrate upon him; to stand between him and the loneliness, the depression into which the loss of Virginia had flung him. She could not very well do that. She would not be given the chance. She could only be with him for an hour or so in a day, and then, mentally, never close enough to comfort, to help. But it was something to know that she would see him again.

CHAPTER VIII

THAT telephone call from Barry did not come quite so soon as Joan wanted. At first she took it for granted that he was very busy—occupied with the solicitors and all the duties attached to his job as sole executor of John Elderton's will. As for the evenings—well, he had lots of friends and no doubt went out with them. Or he preferred to be alone. She did not know. She could only guess. At least she had not a single pang of jealousy. She was quite sure there was not a woman in Barry's life.

Then, as the days went by—one, two, three, four days, and no telephone call from him, her bright spirits began to fall, and she listened for the office telephone bell with a sick, nagging little pain at her heart. She was called up only too often—but never by Barry. She stopped hoping that it would be Barry and began to take up the receiver with a kind of dreary patience.

He had forgotten her. He was bored with her. She had bored him that day at the Savoy Grill. She leapt to all kinds of unhappy conjectures.

There was another woman in his life.

Well—what if there was? What right had she to be jealous? Obviously he knew other girls beside herself. A good-looking, attractive bachelor like Barry did not go about the world without making friends of both sexes.

He might meet some terribly pretty girl and marry her—on the rebound.

Joan went down into the depths of despair at such a thought. That would be ghastly. It would not have been so bad if she had seen him marry Virginia. She had prepared herself for that. But to watch him rush into matrimony with another girl—that would be too ghastly!

"Why, why aren't I devastatingly beautiful and fascinating!" she asked herself with a positive hatred of her own personal appearance. And not even Joe Halliday's unswerving devotion and attention could lift her from the slough of despond into which Barry's silence had pushed her.

One night as she lay in bed, thinking about him, she built up a fantastic picture of herself as a bad woman; a woman Barry might meet casually in his hotel or at a dance club, and with whom he might be amused for an evening. Perhaps that was what he was doing—finding amusement and oblivion in the arms of a woman like that. Joan, quite aware that she was being childish, wished fervently that she could be incorporated into such a person—and lie in his arms and comfort him. Yes, better that than never to lie in his arms at all.

Then, aghast at allowing her mind to stray into such wanton, impossible channels, she turned her face to her pillow and wept passionately.

Such moments of exaggerated emotions, however, were few and far between with Joan, and nobody at the office that following morning could have guessed that the busy, practical, cheerful Miss Borrow was capable of " wanton thoughts " about any man.

Then, one afternoon when she returned to the office from a wedding reception, Miss Mackay told her that Barry had rung up.

" Mr. Elderton phoned about half an hour ago, Joaney."

" Damn ! " said Joan with leaping pulses, and clenched her small teeth. Could anything have been more aggravating . . . to have missed Barry's call. She managed to question Mac calmly. " Any message ? "

" Only that he'd ring again."

" Right-ho," said Joan, took off her hat, and sat down at her desk.

Miss Mackay whistled under her breath and eyed her friend askance.

" Ah ha. So it's Mr. Elderton, is it ? What-ho ! "

Joan was thinking: " Perhaps he won't ring again. Oh, damn ! "

But he did. And she answered quite casually so far as Barry or Margaret Mackay, listening, could judge.

Could she do a dinner and show tonight ? He was so sorry he hadn't phoned before, but he had been so rushed. He'd booked seats for *Sonia*, the musical comedy at the Envoy Theatre. He had heard it was good. Would it bore her ?

" Oh, no, it won't bore me at all. I'd like it," said Joan.

"I like musical comedies. Right you are, Barry. At Taglioni's for dinner at seven-thirty. Bye-bye."

She hung up the receiver and dared not meet the sharp gaze of a friend which she knew was riveted upon her. She began to tidy up the papers on the desk.

Margaret Mackay asked no questions. She was much too tactful, but she wondered what kind of a man this Mr. Elderton was. Of course she knew about him. She had seen snapshots of him and had heard Joan speak of him. But she had never guessed that Joan was sentimentally attached to him. She had discussed him, always, as her cousin's admirer. Miss Brame had just married Sir Ian Kingleigh. Perhaps Joan was consoling the rejected suitor.

"I wonder," thought Miss Mackay.

Joan left her to wonder.

She also left Joe Halliday lamenting because she would not dine with him. But she did not care. She felt too absurdly happy. Barry had not forgotten, and of course he had been rushed with business affairs. He had not been chasing women. He was not like that. What a little fool she was. She went back to her digs in a state of excitement.

The only thing that spoiled her happiness was the thought that she could not afford a new dress and neither was there time to buy one. No—she must wear the old black lace. Well, it had been Virginia's once and very smart, and always looked nice.

Barry would not know it had belonged to Virginia or been worn by her. Thank goodness for that! She would succumb to one extravagance, anyhow, and buy a really nice shoulder spray to liven up the old dress. She stopped at a shop near Victoria Station and, with a delicious feeling of "don't care," bought a charming spray of pale pink carnations.

Heavenly prospect! A whole evening alone with Barry. She had never had an evening alone with him—only shared many with Virginia years ago.

The first thing that she saw when she entered her bed-sitting-room was a square white envelope with a foreign postage stamp lying on her table. An Italian stamp.

Joan picked up the letter, her lips tightening. From Gina. Somehow the sight of Virginia's delicate slanting hand, which brought so much of her personality with it, dulled the edge of Joan's happiness. What had the bride to say . . . she who should have been Barry's bride?

Joan opened the letter and read it. From the Hotel Angelico, Como, written two days ago, the eighth of April—soon after Virginia had arrived.

DEAR JOAN,—I am a little worried. I found a note from Eleanor Canfax waiting for me. She told me Barry was home. She saw him at Victoria Station. If you see him, let me know how he is. I can't forget him and I'm a little frightened. Because I *do* care for him still and if I've done him any harm I shall never forgive myself. Write and tell me he is all right and *please* tell him to try and understand and forgive me.

Ian is very good to me. Please burn this. I trust you, Joan.

Yours,
GINA.

Joan read this letter twice and then applied a match to it. Heavens, what a letter from a girl on her honeymoon—only married a few days and vowing she still cared for the man she had more or less jilted. The inconsistence of Virginia! And it was like Eleanor Canfax to have informed Virginia that Barry was home. Joan hated Eleanor. She interfered with other people's lives and found a malicious pleasure in creating difficult situations for them. Why couldn't she have left Gina alone?

The black lace dress—perfectly cut—brought back from Paris by Virginia a year ago—made Joan look slender and *soignée*. Her thick brown hair, combed smoothly back from her forehead, one big wave to the left side, shone with good health and brushing. She did at least possess an exquisite skin, and her arms and throat, slim and youthful, were milk-white. She had outlined her lips with red, but her lashes, naturally black and luxuriant, were untouched. Wistfully the blue eyes looked back at her.

"I hope *he'll* think you will pass in a crowd, anyhow. . . ."

She put on her black velvet coat with a shabby imitation fur collar—oh, the need of new clothes!—and brightened up the whole effect with that fresh pink shoulder spray, and a double row of pale pink pearls which toned with it.

Barry was waiting for her outside Taglioni's; walking up and down the pavement, enjoying the mild spring night. Joan saw him long before he saw her, and thought how nice he looked in his dinner jacket, the white collar, and shirt-front accentuating the dark tan of his face. She was glad, too, to notice less evidence in that handsome face of the strain and fatigue. He had the old familiar greeting for her.

"Hello, Infant. Here you are, then. Nice of you to come."

"Nice of you to ask me, Barry."

"Aren't we smart!" He smiled and ran a critical gaze over her. "That's a very attractive dress, my child."

Joan sailed, mentally, to the stars. He had noticed the dress and thought she looked smart. Well, that was more than she had hoped from Barry. Thank heavens he did not know who had worn that dress before her!

She found him in a very good mood once they were seated at a corner table in the warm, charming restaurant which she discovered was a favourite haunt of his. He had been out every night since she last saw him, he told her, with a lot of fellows home from the East.

"I hesitate to tell you, at your age, that I returned to my hotel last night, slightly tight," he grinned at her.

"Oh, Barry—what a confession. That's what you do when you get together, you men."

"Not always, but last night we were celebrating. There's a damn good fellow who was out in Ceylon with me—a man named Hungerford, and he was being married today, so we gave him a grand bachelor's night to buoy him up."

"Oh, Barry!" she laughed.

He examined the menu and wine-card and they discussed food and drink. Then he lit a cigarette for her and one for himself.

"I'm feeling full of beans, as you see," he said. "I've got rid of the fever, and riotous living suits me."

She wondered how much of this was bluff. A good deal, if she knew Barry. He did not really like "riotous living," although he was the type to enjoy going out with a lot of his pals. Probably he had flung himself into a good deal of dissipation just to forget . . . forget how unhappy he was.

She remembered the letter from Virginia and the message for him. But she could not give it to him just yet. He was in such good spirits. She would not banish that smile from his lips, whether it was bluff or not.

When they were drinking coffee he said one particularly charming thing:

"You know, Joan, you're a great little pal to a man. You've got such a keen sense of humour, my dear, and you do understand a fellow. I've been friends with a lot of women, but I've never found any of 'em quite so reliable as you. It's amazing, considering what an infant you are."

"Not so much of this infant. I'm twenty-three next month," she laughed, thrilled by his praise.

"You've grown up a lot since I was last home. I remember you as a real kid in the old days."

"Well, one has to grow up, Barry."

"You're still a baby to me," he ragged her.

"Grandfather," she jeered back.

"That suits me. I feel rather a grey-beard."

"Well, you don't look it."

"That's something. Look here, we must make a move. This show begins at eight-thirty."

Joan felt nearer to him than she had ever been when he took her arm and walked with her down the street through the soft April starlight. The contact with him vibrated through her. She felt tongue-tied, emotional with happiness. He found her more "reliable" than any other woman in his life. She wanted to be so; wanted him to go on finding her that—always there—when he needed her.

Why did she love him so much? She could not tell. But she glanced shyly up at the straight, attractive profile of the man and was amazed that Virginia should have barred herself from Paradise.

The musical comedy *Sonia* was not out of the ordinary, but there were plenty of good tunes and good dancing and a pretty chorus. Barry seemed to enjoy it thoroughly.

"This is the sort of thing you dream about when you're out East," he told her in the interval. "I like that waltz song. Can you hum it, Joan?"

She hummed it—blissful because she was quick at picking up a melody and he appreciated it. She would not have thought *Sonia* very good if she had seen it under normal circumstances, but tonight it seemed the finest show she had seen in her life. Barry's presence, his companionship, magnified all the good points; made her impervious to the bad ones. She hung on his criticisms; agreed with him, or argued against him, both quite happily.

She was absurdly jealous when he picked out a tall, willowy chorus girl with black hair and large dark eyes and whispered:

"That's a damn pretty girl."

And then was equally pleased because he added:

"But I couldn't go and take these girls out to supper like some fellows do. They've no brains. They'd bore me stiff."

Joan thought:

"Well, I *have* got a few brains. I hope I don't bore him."

She did not. He found her an invigorating and charming companion. He had not realised until tonight what a delightful person Joan was to go out with. Sympathetic, amusing, appreciative. She looked awfully nice; quite pretty in evening dress. Her hair smelt nice, too. He did like a woman to be well turned out. She was quiet, as well as amusing. He liked that. He hated a noisy woman. Altogether it was a nice, quiet, entertaining evening. Different from the rag with all the fellows last night. Nicer, in a way He was happy in the company of men, but it was soothing after the lonely years in Ceylon to go out with a girl like Joan.

He would not let the evening end. He took her on to supper at a night club. She wondered if it was because he wished to prolong their evening; or merely to escape from his thoughts; because he dreaded going back to the hotel and remembering. . . .

She looked at several of the couples dancing on the small circle of shining floor in the centre of the room and wondered how many of them were lovers; how many married. There wasn't a woman in the room she envied . . . or one in the world for a matter of that. She was with the only man on earth who mattered. But she wondered, emotionally, what her sentiments would have been if she had been married to Barry. Just married today; or yesterday. If, instead of going back to her lonely digs, she was to go back to his hotel . . . *their* hotel . . . back to his kiss, his embrace. . . .

The poignant ecstasy of that thought hurt until she could not endure it. She turned her gaze from the thin, dark, restless face of the man, and thought:

"Oh, don't be more idiotic than you can help!"

"It's been a great evening," said Barry.

"Lovely," she said.

"We must do it again, my dear."

"I'd like to."

"I'm not going to play golf. The fellow I was going with has got lumbago, poor devil. I shall stay in Town for a bit."

Her heart sang.

"Oh, good," she said quite casually.

"Today's Friday," he said. "You don't work at the office on Saturdays, do you?"

"No."

"How about a day in the country tomorrow?"

She hardly dared answer. It sounded so awfully good. Too good to be possible. Was he doing it because he really did like being with her, or just to drown his sorrows, and pass the time? She did not know and it would not do to probe too deeply into whys and wherefores with Barry.

"It would be heavenly," she said. "The country—this time of the year!"

"I'm rather fond of Oxford," he said. "My uncle was born there, you know, and used to take me up there when I was a small boy. How about motoring up to Oxford? I'll get hold of a car—and we'll have some lunch and go on the river."

"It sounds simply perfect to me."

"Right," he said, and beckoned to the waiter for his bill.

Joan sat still. She had not delivered Virginia's message. And she could not; could not bring herself to mention that name which must inevitably blot the perfection of this evening; perhaps destroy the promise of tomorrow. A whole day—up at Oxford—on the river—with Barry.

In the taxi, driving Joan back to Victoria, Barry was conscious of gratitude towards her. She was a dear and had been awfully decent to him. London was not quite so intolerably lonely as it might have been—without Joan.

Impulsively he slipped an arm around the small, slim figure in the black velvet coat.

"It's been a terrific evening," he said again. "Can you remember that waltz song from *Sonia*?"

She held her breath. His arm about her was such

exquisite delight and she was so afraid he might take it away. She trembled a little, but managed to sing the first two bars of the waltz song.

He whistled it with her—his long legs stretched out—feet on the opposite seat—arm tightening unconsciously about her shoulders. This was all like a drug; a kindly opiate; this sort of thing; dulling the pain that never left him, day or night; intolerable and bitter need of Virginia.

"Jolly good tune, that, and you've picked it up amazingly well."

"I'm a genius," she said, and giggled helplessly, quite aware that her emotions were rapidly getting beyond her control . . . because she was so close against his side in the dusk of the taxi. Oh, if only it were a thousand miles to Victoria, instead of one and a half. They were horribly near the street now.

"Well—here we are," she said with a frantic effort at nonchalance, and drew away from him.

Suddenly he pulled her back against him.

"Good night, Infant. You've been a dear to me and put up with all my boring conversation. Thank you——"

Before she could prevent it he had kissed her. On the lips. The first kiss she had ever had from him. She would not have been human if she had not responded to it. Her heart throbbing madly, she clung to him for an instant and her lips were warm and fervent under his. It was a more fervent kiss than Barry had intended. He was a little astonished and stirred. He put both arms around her and kissed the top of her head.

"Nice child," he murmured.

Joan was thankful when the taxi stopped. This wouldn't do. He was only saying good night in the way any man might say good night to a girl he liked and had been out with. Nobody attached any importance to a harmless kiss these days. But she must not let him guess that it tore all her emotions to shreds. She drew away from him; glad that he could not see the colour of her cheeks nor feel her heart's frantic beating.

"Good night, old thing, and lots of thanks," she said.

"I'll fetch you tomorrow in whatever bus I rake up," he said, stepping out of the taxi after her. "Here—let me see you to the door."

She pulled the fur collar of her coat well about her face to hide it from him. She was shivering from head to foot.

"What time?" she asked.

"Oh, we'll make an early start. Half-past ten suit you?"

"Quite."

"Good night," he said, and returned to the taxi.

He drove to his hotel, still a little astonished at the unexpected fervour of the embrace with Joan. How soft and small she was to hold, and her lips were very fragrant and disturbing.

"Damn it, I oughtn't to have kissed her like that. It was caddish," he told himself. "I mustn't do it again."

CHAPTER IX

JOAN had yet to learn the folly of looking forward to anything too much. She was young, and optimism and enthusiasm are the heritage of youth. Those who are older and wiser know the significance of that ancient proverb: "Man proposes—God disposes," and do not set too much store upon future events.

Joan's mind before she slept that night dwelt ecstatically upon the thought of tomorrow, Oxford, and a long golden day with Barry. But when she awakened it was to hear a steady driving rain against her window pane and that horrid gurgling of water in drain-pipes—a sound only too familiar to the Londoner.

Joan sprang from bed, pushed the hair back from her eyes, and looked out upon chimney-tops that were wet and slippery with rain. The sky was sullen grey, heavy and oppressive, without promise of a break.

She felt sick with disappointment. Of course it *would* be a day like this; cold, wet, dreary, instead of a sunny April morning which lured one to the country and the river. It might be mid-January instead of spring. All hopes of a lovely day at Oxford with Barry crashed for Joan. She thought bitterly: "Isn't it just my luck!" She was not on the telephone, but of course Barry would wire her—put her off. She would not even see him. She could not even ask him here. If she had had a home of her own—a little flat to which she could ask him—it would have been all right. But how could a lone girl invite a man to her bed-sitting-room?

Not that this room was unattractive. Many of her own possessions had transformed it; given it her own atmosphere and she had, in crazy moments, spent more than she could really afford on things that delighted the eye of a connoisseur.

It was a big room. Joan had put up with being at the top and the back of the house because it was the biggest which Mrs. Fletcher, who ran these furnished suites, could offer at the price. The furniture was plain and unobtrusive. Over the mantelpiece Joan had hung one lovely reproduction of a Van Gogh in a grey frame. Except for that, the green distempered walls were unadorned. The divan bed during the daytime was covered with a lovely piece of old embroidery which had belonged to Joan's grandmother. The well-worn and faded green Axminster carpet had been such a tribulation to her that she had saved up for one beautiful Persian rug and bought it. On her desk—the interior of which was as untidy as befitted a literary lady—stood a piece of Bristol glass and a Waterford jug, gleaming crystal in the gloom. On the mantelpiece there were two photographs; one of her mother, the framed snapshot of Barry, and a shagreen cigarette-box which Joe Halliday had given her.

Nothing, however, could take from her the memory of last night; of the first kiss which Barry had ever laid upon her lips. She found her pulses thrilling every time she remembered it. He had been so awfully nice; and she really did think she had distracted him from the unhappy thought of Virginia, and made him forget for a little while. But it was all so transient. He was bound to go away from her soon. It seemed so futile to hope for anything more.

Ten o'clock found her walking up and down the room, smoking, restless, wretched. Half-past ten came. She could not smoke any more because she had run out of cigarettes. This was the hour when Barry had promised to call for her. But of course he would not come now. A horrible telegraph boy would bring a horrible telegram. She stared out of the window. Unceasing rain! It looked as though it would go on for ever.

"Damn!" said Joan, seated herself at her desk, and tried to concentrate on an article which she had promised to write for one of the women's magazines at the Chartwood Press. The editress of the paper had suggested for this article the title: "*Common Sense in Love-Affairs*".

"You're a nice, practical person, Miss Borrow," Joan was told. "You ought to be able to write this very well. I want it pointed out that it is much more sensible for a girl to look at love prosaically and not to let her romantic or sentimental feelings run away with her."

Joan's sense of humour was tickled even in the midst of her disappointment when she reflected upon her subject. It was really rather funny. How little do people know one another. At the Chartwood they thought her "nice and sensible". Well, perhaps she was in a way. But this morning she felt quite unfitted to lecture young women and suggest that they should be prosaic in their love affairs. She was not in the least prosaic about her own. She was absurdly, exaggeratedly miserable because she expected the man she loved to cancel their appointment.

"He'd grin, if he could see me," reflected Joan. "I expect he is rather relieved. He only issued that invitation on the impulse of the moment."

The thought of Virginia leapt to her mind. She must answer Virginia's letter. She felt guilty, too, because she had not even delivered Virginia's message to Barry. She set aside the article and began a letter to her cousin, then abandoned that after the first sentence. She really could not write affectionately and pleasantly to Lady Kingleigh. Lady Kingleigh, indeed! She must have been crazy—when she might have been Mrs. Barryclough Elderton. How could she have treated him so shabbily? And Barry was so awfully nice about it.

Somebody knocked on the door.

"Come in," said Joan and prepared herself for the horrible telegram.

There was no more astonished person on earth than Joan when the door opened and Barry himself walked into the room. For a second she looked speechlessly at the tall figure in the grey tweeds, with hat and stick in his hand. He smiled at her and looked round the room.

"Hello!" he said. "Can I come in! I'm sure I've shocked the entire household by asking to be shown up here. The maid looked scandalised, but I really couldn't talk to you down in the hall and the maid said there was no public sitting-room. This is a very charming room, Joan. Delightful in fact."

He walked in before Joan could recover from her astonishment. But her eyes were like stars as she regarded him. Her heart beat fast. The whole aspect of life was altered. It could rain cats and dogs outside for all she cared. Her bed-sitting-room was heaven. Barry was here. It didn't seem in the least wrong that he should be here.

"How are you?" was all she could say when she found speech.

"Not too bad."

"Had a good night?"

"So-so. I never sleep very well. I used to sleep very badly out in the East. It's a filthy day. I didn't even bother to hire a car. Oxford's off. Hardly the weather for the river—what?"

"No," said Joan with a laugh. "One could scarcely sit in a punt and put up a sunshade."

"It feels perishing cold to me," said Barry, standing with his back to the gas fire and his hands behind him. "But I honestly don't mind the grey skies. It's such a change from Ceylon."

Joan's quick eye roving round her room discovered a frightful thing. The framed snapshot of Barry on the mantelpiece. Heavens! What a give-away! She had not dreamed he would ever enter this room. It would betray too much—only two photographs in her room—one of him and one of her mother.

Barry nodded towards the desk.

"That's a nice bit of Waterford, my child! By the way, is it very shocking, entertaining a bachelor in your bed-sitting-room? Turn me out if you don't like it——"

"Good heavens, I don't mind," laughed Joan. "I may lose my reputation with Mrs. Fletcher and Ethel, but who cares?"

"I'm quite safe," said Barry. He gave her a cigarette, lit one for himself, and grinned at her through the smoke.

Joan almost wished that he was not quite so safe. But she sat on the edge of her divan and wondered how long it would be before he discovered his photograph. Not very long, for he turned, admired the Van Gogh, and said:

"You've got plenty of taste, haven't you, Infant?" Then he examined the two photographs.

"That's your mother, isn't it? I think I've seen that before. Awfully pretty woman she must have been. Good Lord! That's me! Now where the devil was that taken?"

Her cheeks were flaming.

"Oh, don't you remember?" she said casually. "On the links near Padstow. You know—when we were all down there five years ago. . . ."

He shook his head at the snapshot.

"Of course! I look very young and enthusiastic. How we do change! Did you take it?"

"Yes."

"You were only a kid."

"Seventeen."

"That was rather a cheery holiday, so far as I remember," said Barry. "You and the Brames and myself. I have distinct recollections of a slight row with Lady Brame because Virginia and I went out in the car, ran out of petrol and didn't get back till long after dark."

"I remember that," said Joan.

Yes, she recalled Aunt Milly's wrath and trepidation because her darling girl stayed out so late and so long with Barry. And Joan herself had felt nothing more than envy of Virginia—even in those early days.

Barry spoke of Virginia quite calmly this morning. But Joan wondered just how unhappy he was behind the nonchalance. She also wondered what he thought about seeing this enlarged and framed snapshot of himself in her bedroom. But he made no comment on it.

Barry was by nature too modest to attach any importance to the presence of the snapshot. He was, perhaps, a little flattered; wondered why she had bothered to put the foolish snapshot into such a nice frame. Then he forgot about it and discussed his handicap on the links in those days.

"Virginia was beginning to play very good golf just before I went to Ceylon last time," he remarked.

Joan tried not to feel a pang of jealousy.

"Yes, she was awfully good."

Barry looked at the end of his cigarette. He had a sudden tormenting vision of Virginia and their old delightful comradeship. She had been a marvellous companion—looked so lovely—did everything so well—how he had loved her! Would he ever get used to the thought that she had married another man?

Instinctively Joan read his thoughts; saw his lips tighten and the brightness of his eyes fade out. She knew he was thinking of Virginia. Why must he think of Virginia when he was here? Because she was herself in love with him she resented the shadow of Virginia which was always and would be for ever between them.

Barry glanced at her. She sat on the edge of the bed smoking, brown head bent a little. She looked rather nice in that blue thing, he thought. The child had extremely nice ankles and he liked a woman who was well shod. He had thought about her once or twice since last night. Their good-night embrace had been slightly disturbing. But that sort of thing must not happen again.

"Well, Joan, I don't quite know how we're going to spend this sunny day," he said cheerfully. "I'm sorry about Oxford."

She looked up at him.

"So am I."

"I think we'll have to chuck the idea of the country and do it the next fine day when you can get away from the office."

"That would be nice," said Joan. But a prospect so vague was not comforting.

Barry looked at his wrist-watch.

"Half after eleven. H'm. What are you going to do?"

Joan had no answer to that question because there was only one thing she wanted to do—stay with him. So she shook her head helplessly.

"Well, look here," said Barry. "I want a hair-cut and I also want to visit my bank manager and suggest that he gives me an overdraft on the strength of the money I'm coming into once poor Uncle John's estate is settled up."

Joan nodded. Of course. He would find so many things to do which would not include her. Naturally. She must try and get into her head that Barry was not wrapped up in her and that she was only a very small factor in his existence.

"I must do some shopping," she said brightly and quite untruthfully.

"Well, I'll tell you what I suggest," said Barry. "Supposing we have a spot of lunch somewhere—say one o'clock at the Hungaria Restaurant, and then amuse ourselves as best we can on a wet day in Town. . . ."

Hope revived in Joan.

" That sounds very nice."

After all, she thought, there were so many attractive things to do in London on a wet day. Barry might suggest a matinée. She liked to sit beside him and see a show and hear his views and exchange opinions with him.

Then Barry said:

" I don't know that I feel like stuffing in a theatre. This head of mine is so dicky. And I simply loathe cinemas. I tell you what I do want to do. I want to have a look at the National Gallery—haven't been there since I was a boy. Would it bore you frightfully ? "

Joan nearly laughed aloud. Oh, how funny! Idiot that she was, hoping for a glamorous hour or two in the softening atmosphere of a theatre, and Barry suggested the National Gallery! How typical of a man who was not in love. And what indisputable proof that he was not in love. She could imagine it—patrolling staidly through those enormous rooms, solemnly leaning over the barriers, regarding the primitives with gloom—or the Dutch school with a necessary show of enthusiasm. As a matter of fact she liked the Dutch school. She liked good pictures. But she did not wish to go through a process of education with a man whom she loved wildly and absurdly.

She greeted Barry's suggestion with apparent delight.

" I'd love that! The last time I went to the National Gallery was with my father one school holidays."

Barry heaved a sigh of relief. That was settled then. And how should he know that he had made quite the wrong suggestion! He merely thought Joan was most amiable and easy to get on with. He wanted a woman like that when he was a mass of nerves and irritation—raw from the most lacerating blow that life had ever dealt him. He had no wish to see shows that were all about love and passion. Such things were a snare and delusion and best regarded with a cynical eye. The æsthetic pleasure of a picture gallery appealed to him in this particular mood. Of course he was selfish, but a man usually is in his dealing with a woman with whom he is not in love.

Frankly, Joan enjoyed the lunch at the Hungaria a good deal better than the afternoon that followed it, but she told herself that she was lucky to be with Barry at all. In a measure she liked to see his enthusiasm when he found a picture that particularly appealed to him. She was beginning to know him so much better and she was a little surprised to discover quite a high degree of culture in him, and intelligence and learning above the average. It increased her admiration of him. She had thought of him as a sportsman, more of athletic than artistic taste. He was always amusing. She grew slightly weary of accompanying him through endless galleries in the solemn and sacred silence, but now and then they shared a humorous moment. He dragged her away hurriedly from a group of students gathered around an enormous Raphael, listening to the fervent lecture of a pallid young man with horn-rimmed glasses.

" I don't think we can bear that," whispered Barry, taking her arm and leading her into another room.

" I'm sure we can't," said Joan and laughed.

" Not bored ? " he asked her.

" Not in the least," she said and wished that she did not resent the feeling that he showed a great deal more enthusiasm for the pictures than he had ever shown for her. Unfortunately she had very distinct recollections of his ardent interest in her cousin Virginia. She could not imagine him being content to spend two solid hours in this gallery with Virginia when there was a limit to the time they could be alone together.

How futile to compare his treatment of Virginia with his attitude towards herself. She must not do it. She was only making herself unhappy. Things were as they were and nothing could alter them.

Such is the perversity of human nature and the varying emotions of a woman in love that when Joan came out of the National Gallery with Barry into the April dusk and foresaw an ending to their day together she wished she could have the two hours of pictures all over again. Deep depression descended upon her as they walked through the crowded street together.

" You'd like a spot of tea, my dear, I'm sure," said Barry. " And then I must leave you. I found a note waiting for me when I dropped into my club just before lunch, from a woman I know—a pal of mine who was married to a man who had a bungalow near mine in the East when I first went out there. They were very kind to me when I was a youngster. Ralstone's dead—died of fever up country—and Pat Ralstone lives over here in Town with her married sister. They heard I was back and asked me to go and dine there tonight. I like Pat. She's a woman of thirty-four or so and extraordinarily nice. I think Virginia knew her—met her and poor old Tom before he died some years back. Didn't you ever meet them?"

Joan said no. Her depression increased. Absurd, of course, not to take it for granted that Barry had women friends other than herself. But she hated this Pat Ralstone for taking Barry from her tonight. She would go back to her lonely digs and spend an evening by herself. She had made no appointments because she had taken it for granted that she would have a long day up in Oxford with Barry and not get back to Town until late. The wet weather had spoilt everything. He wouldn't have seen Mrs. Ralstone's invitation if they had had their day out in the car. But not for worlds would she let Barry know what she felt.

"It will be nice for you to see old pals from the East," she said during tea.

"Yes." Then he added: "I've enjoyed this afternoon."

"So have I."

"What are you doing tonight?"

"Oh, I'm going out with a girl at the office," Joan lied for pride's sake.

"Tomorrow," said Barry, stifling a yawn, "we come to the Sabbath, which is undeniably the dreariest day on earth in London. Now if the sun will only condescend to shine we might take a car and go into the country, if you'd like it and have nothing better to do."

Up soared Joan's volatile spirits again. The outlook ceased to be so black and she ceased to regard the unknown Mrs. Ralstone with such gloom.

"I think it's really too early in the year for the river," went on Barry. "But we might have a look at the country and the sea. I tell you what. I was at prep. school at Rottingdean. We might have lunch at Brighton—it's only a couple of hours in the car—and go on to Rottingdean for tea."

Joan was happy again. She left Barry and went back to Victoria telling herself that tomorrow the sun *must* shine or she would go quite crazy.

Barry found his thoughts dwelling upon Joan several times during the evening with Mrs. Ralstone and her sister. He thought what a cheery, companionable child she was. Not such a child either. A young woman on her own, facing a none too joyous existence with any amount of fortitude. There was a very real charm about Joan—particularly when she smiled and those very blue eyes of hers flashed with amusement and looked like stars. He was not quite able to forget either how sweet she had been to kiss last night. She was quite the nicest girl he had ever known, except Virginia. So far as character went, no doubt she was nicer than Virginia—not nearly so selfish—much more steadfast and faithful. But one doesn't love a person because of what they are or what they do. One just loves—and there it is. Virginia had made his heart beat and filled his life, during their associations together, in a way which no other woman could ever do. He would never love another woman like that—never again lay himself open to be hurt like that. Besides, something in him was dead; had died in the hour when he had come back to be told that Virginia was married to another man.

He wondered, had he never known Virginia, if he could have loved Joan. Who knows? She was charming and companionable and he liked her and had known her a long time. She might make an excellent wife and mother. He had wanted children—Virginia's children!

He trod savagely on the entire thought of love and marriage and ceased to think of Joan.

CHAPTER X

JOAN had her day with Barry after all. The weather relented and Sunday was fine and fresh if not warm. Joan found herself seated beside Barry in a hired two-seater—a fast Buick—on the road to Brighton, and the spring morning seemed to her the loveliest she had known. Once they had left the outskirts of London behind them and were close to

Redhill the country looked enchanting. Fresh green hedges; green trees bursting into leaf; blue skies and little white clouds scudding across the heavens in a fresh April wind.

Joan snuggled under the rug in the Buick and surveyed the landscape with an ecstatic look in her eyes. Barry drove well and fast and they seemed to spin past an unending trail of cars all bound for Brighton this gay April morning.

"Scared?" Barry asked her, grinning, every time he accelerated and shot ahead of a more sedately driven car.

"Not in the least. I've got no nerves," was her answer.

"We'll be in Brighton by one, and then after lunch we'll go to Rottingdean. Not cold, are you?"

"Not a bit," she said, and was pleased because he was thoughtful for her comfort.

She asked him if he had enjoyed his dinner with Mrs. Ralstone last night. She could talk about Mrs. Ralstone without a pang now, when she was out with Barry, happy and secure in the knowledge that she would be with him all day. His answer was eminently satisfactory.

"Oh, all right. But I liked Pat better in the old days out in Ceylon when Ralstone was alive. She's changed."

Joan was too discreet to probe deeper into the matter. It really did not matter to her why or how Mrs. Ralstone had changed. But it was obvious that Barry was not *épris*.

How foolish she was. Why hunger for this concentration upon herself by a man who was not and never would be in love with her? Why hope for the utterly impossible? But she could not stem the ever-increasing tide of her own love for Barry and let it rush on recklessly to whatever end fate had in store. She intended to live for the present and make the best of what she was given. She meant, anyhow, to enjoy her day out with Barry and to amuse him as best she could. She could, at least, devote herself to him, and she did.

No man, unless devoid of all natural feeling, can be impervious to the attractions of a charming girl who is concentrating upon him, and Barry was no exception. Virginia had dealt him a bitter blow from which he might never recover. But he was still a creature of flesh and blood with normal, human tendencies. Joan was delightful to him; sympathetic, easy to get on with, quick to share a joke and exchange an opinion. He found himself soothed and amused in her presence and it was obvious to him that she was putting herself out to be especially nice to him. He had only to express a wish and she fell in with it at once. He thought it very sweet of her and told himself that he had a very real friend in this nice child. But at the moment it did not enter his head that she was in love with him and had been for years.

They lunched together at the Albion in Brighton and sat afterwards for some time, drinking coffee and smoking their cigarettes in the loggia with its big glass windows which looked out upon the Palace Pier. There was plenty to watch; a kaleidoscope of moving vehicles, figures, colours. This part of Brighton was congested on a fine spring day.

Joan did not know Brighton, but Barry was full of recollections of his childhood here.

"My uncle used to bring me in from prep. school at half term," he told her. "Lord! The pennies I've poured into those slot machines on that pier."

Joan dwelt on the thought of the little schoolboy rushing on to the pier with his pocket full of pennies. She felt rather sentimental about it.

"You must have been quite a nice little boy, Barry," she said.

He smiled at her.

"Quite the reverse. I was a hateful little beast—always getting into rows."

"That's quite as it should be," said Joan.

"Come on—I'll show you my prep. school," he said, rising and stubbing his cigarette end on an ash-tray. "That is, if it will amuse you."

"I'd love to see it," she said.

They drove along the Marine Parade, away from the pier, towards Black Rock. The sea was amazingly blue and the waves, whipped by the fresh breeze, were white-crested with foam. Undaunted by the cold, there were quite a number of people on the beach or out on the water in boats. It was a gay, invigorating scene and Joan liked it. London, Victoria, and her bed-sitting-room seemed a long, long way away. She did not want to think about going back. Yet half the day had gone already. How terribly quickly time flew by when she was with Barry. Much too quickly!

Barry drove away from the sea, through the winding main street towards his school, which was farther inland. He seemed to enjoy seeing the old sights, and Joan shared his pleasure. He was such a boy still, whatever life had done to embitter or disillusion him.

Here was the tiny tuck-shop where he used to buy halfpenny buns. Here the playing field where he first won his cap and colours and played in the eleven.

"Cricket was the only thing I ever was good at at school," he told Joan modestly. "I failed dismally in the classrooms, I tell you."

She laughed.

"I don't believe it. You're much too well educated. But I won't argue the point."

He sat in the car outside the gates of his old school, lit a cigarette, and stared round the familiar precincts. Then he felt suddenly depressed. A wave of melancholy swept over him and destroyed the pleasure of revisiting these haunts of his boyhood again. What ecstasy can a grown man experience comparable to that he knew in the playing field, for instance, when he has just made the runs needed to win the match . . . or when he boarded the train, homeward bound for Christmas "hols". . . . Pure and simple pleasures, unequalled by any in later years when rapture is invariably linked with sorrow and dimmed by the complexities, the problems of the mature.

Inevitably Barry's thoughts turned to the woman he had loved and lost. Depression settled on him. Joan, glancing at his darkened face, felt her own bright spirits fall. She knew . . . somehow she always knew when he was thinking of Virginia. The glory of the April day passed for Joan. But she tried to distract him.

"Did you like your Public School better than this, Barry?"

"No, I don't think so. In fact I'm sure I didn't."

"Do you approve of Public School system?"

"Not particularly. There's a great deal which warrants alteration and improvement, but I suppose it's as good a system as any other and turns out for the best in the long run. After all, it's only a question of disciplining the young and instilling a spirit of honour and sportsmanship into 'em. As long as that end is achieved, the means don't much matter."

"What a Jesuitical philosophy!" she laughed. "Do you apply it to everything?"

"To nothing." He gave a brief laugh. "I'm not really a philosopher, Joan. I just take life as it comes . . . these days."

These days! Since Virginia had let him down. Not so long ago, thought Joan. She was silent and subdued when Barry turned the car and they drove back to the village for tea. After that, the April day began to wane, and they drove back through the dusk to Brighton and up the hill on to the Dyke. It was quite dark when they reached that most beautiful and inspiring part of the Sussex Downs. Behind them, below them, glittered and winked the lights of the town; of Portslade and Southwick along the sea coast to Shoreham. Overhead the sky seemed very vast and blazing with stars. The spring night was cool and clear.

Barry went on past the golf club and then stopped the car on the side of the road farther along and switched off the engine.

"This is worth looking at for a moment, Joan."

"I agree," she said.

She sat back, silent and contemplative, lifted suddenly from the depression into which Barry's melancholy had flung her. It was so beautiful, so immense, this great cauldron-like dip of the Downs . . . the deep valley below them was misty in the darkness . . . the stretch of water a crystal-clear mirror for the stars between two huge green globes which looked like the smooth breasts of a giant goddess who has lain herself down upon the earth, offering her warm vital curving body to the embrace of the night.

"This part of the Dyke always pleases me," he said. "It's rather magnificent, isn't it?"

"It's lovely . . . a dream," whispered Joan. "I've never seen it before."

"I wanted you to see it, and it's all on our way. I can cut through to the London road from here."

"I don't want to go back," she said impulsively, and wished desperately that she could get out of this car with Barry and walk with him hand in hand over the starlit Downs into space. . . .

But he had no glamorous reply for her. Typical of Barry, a practical thought had come into his mind and superseded any other.

"We want some more petrol. Don't forget to remind

me, Joan, when we come to another pump, otherwise we'll run out and be stranded on the road."

Joan would not have minded being stranded on the road with Barry, but naturally he would not welcome it.

"Yes, right-ho," she said, and told herself to stop being romantic about the Downs and this hopelessly unresponsive but adorable man who was with her.

He pitched a half-finished cigarette out of the car and then turned and looked down at her face. It was rather a dreamy and absorbed young face seen in this light—a very bewitching light. Barry felt a sudden sensation of tenderness for her. He put a hand out and took one of hers.

"Well, enjoyed the day, Infant?"

The unexpected caress made her heart thrill. She nodded mutely. How warm and strong Barry's fingers were. He had the nicest, brownest hands of any man she knew.

"You've been very nice, my dear," he added. "I seem to have done everything I wanted to do . . . most selfish of me. But what about you?"

"I've done just what I've wanted."

"And now for the homeward journey, eh?"

Again a mute nod from Joan. Barry wondered what she was thinking about. It was not like her to be so quiet. She had taken off her scarf and her hair was ruffled, like a child's, over her head. How young she was, he thought. Yet there was an expression in her eyes which was not at all youthful. It was mature; unhappy. Why was she unhappy? He did not want her to be. He liked her so very much and she had been so nice to him since his home-coming.

He forgot that he had made up his mind not to give way to any emotional impulse towards Joan, and putting out his other hand, he touched her soft cheek.

"Joan, you aren't unhappy about anything, are you? You looked so sad just then. Tell me . . ."

Horrified that she had betrayed herself, she answered in a jocular voice:

"Good gracious, no, Barry, I'm full of beans."

"I envy you, then."

"Why—aren't you?" She tried to joke with him, although she was trembling at the touch of his fingers against her face and hair. They had crept up to her hair and pulled at it gently, caressingly. Lord, but it was difficult to control oneself under conditions like these. She wanted him to go on playing with her hair . . . adored it . . . and dreaded it . . . because she did not know how far she could trust herself.

"I can't say I'm wildly happy, Joan, but you know why," he said after a pause. "I try not to let the damn thing get a hold on me, but there it is . . . isn't it?"

"Yes," she said, gritting her teeth. Hadn't the same sort of feeling "got hold of her" . . . had had a hold for years and years. Since she was a child of seventeen, she had loved this man devotedly and there was no getting away from that fact. . . . Particularly not now that his hopes of marriage with Virginia were dead and she, Joan, had been so close to him . . . mentally closer than she had ever been before.

"Take my advice, Joan," said Barry. "Never fall in love. It doesn't pay."

"Perhaps not," she whispered.

"I wonder if Virginia is happy," he said in a grim voice. "Did you think she was going to be?"

Joan shivered. Not for a long while had he mentioned Virginia so directly. Perhaps he had felt he could not until now. It spoiled everything . . . the beauty of the night . . . the thrilling caress of his restless fingers threading through her hair. But she knew that she must give her cousin's message to him now. She must . . . in fairness to Virginia.

"I had a letter from Gina yesterday," she said.

His hand fell away from her hair. She grew cold and did not look at him. He stared down into the impenetrable valley of the Dyke.

"Oh . . . well . . . what did she say?"

"I think she is . . . quite happy."

"More than quite, surely!"

"It's hard to tell."

"But she must be happy," he said stubbornly. "Would she have chucked me for Kingleigh just because he had money? She must be in love with him."

"I honestly do not know," said Joan, with dry lips. Her whole being revolted from the conversation. "Except that she is frightfully upset about you."

Barry twisted in his seat, and Joan, looking at him now, saw that his face was an ironic mask.

"Upset about *me*? Why? What for? She married the

other fellow . . . jolly good luck to her . . . but why be upset about me *now* ? "

Joan's heart beat rapidly.

" Don't you understand, Barry . . . she . . . she was devoted to you . . ."

" Must have been," he interrupted.

" She was," said Joan. She could not bear his sarcasm . . . the outward proof of the inner hurt. " And she asked me in her letter to beg you to try and understand and forgive her."

" There isn't anything to forgive. I've told you, a woman has the right to choose, but I can't understand . . . that's all. After all we were to each other . . . all those years."

" I know," said Joan helplessly. " I know how much you cared."

" I more than cared. I adored her," he said. " And the chief mistake I made was in imagining she loved me."

Joan stared miserably into space. She was trembling, unhappy, nerves all on edge. Everything was spoiled by this ending to her " day ". She could not bear the way his voice had vibrated when he had said " I adored her . . . ."

" Damn Virginia," she thought. " Oh, damn, damn everything. Why couldn't he have adored me? I'd have died for him."

" What else did she have to say ? " Barry asked.

" Nothing much . . . but, you see, Eleanor Canfax had written out to her and said she had seen you not looking too fit . . . and so . . ." she paused, stammering.

Barry laughed.

" Miss Canfax had a finger in the pie, did she ? I never liked that young woman. I used to tell Gina not to trust her. And so she told Gina I wasn't looking fit. That worried Gina, did it ? "

" I suppose so," whispered Joan.

" She didn't think I was going to cut my throat or blow my brains out, did she ? "

" Oh, *Barry* ! " said Joan, and could bear no more. She hid her face in her hands because the tears sprang to her eyes and rolled hotly, swiftly, down her cheeks.

Barry seemed oblivious of her presence for a few moments. His hands were clenched in his lap and he was staring up at the stars, his lips twisted into a smile that was without a vestige of humour. Virginia pitied him. . . . Eleanor Canfax pitied him. They were a little afraid for him. That was all these women felt about the affair. He was the poor mutt who had made a mistake and been kicked out for the other chap, and Virginia, secure and no doubt happy in her marriage, watched a little anxiously, a little contritely, because she had ruined his life. At least she must be thinking she had ruined his life and broken his heart. And everybody else who knew them would think of it. That infuriated him . . . gnawed at his pride until he could not bear the nagging pain of it. He was not going to let any woman, even Virginia, whom he adored, *pity* him.

He turned to Joan and became aware that she was in tears. He spoke to her almost roughly:

"Joan, you're not crying over *me*, are you?"

She did not answer, but her slim body shook with sobs which she could no longer control. To see her thus . . . brave, cheery, sensible little Joan . . . baffled him for a moment, and at the same time irritated him. Damn it, he would not be cried over. He would show her and everybody else that he did not depend upon Virginia or any woman on earth for his happiness. He put an arm around Joan.

"For heaven's sake stop crying, you silly infant. Don't be so absurd. What's the matter? I'm quite all right. I don't care a damn about anything—honestly."

Impulsively she turned to him and hid her wet face against his shoulder. It was so good to feel that warm arm about her, too good to last, of course. But she gave herself up to the sorrowful ecstasy of the moment. Half-laughing, half-crying, she said:

"Neither do I, Barry . . . not a d-damn about a-anything."

"Don't you, you funny little thing?"

"No," she lied.

"But you were crying over my woes."

"Perhaps . . ." came from Joan in a muffled voice. Then she relapsed into silence and held her body almost taut because his hand was ruffling her hair again and she did not want it to stop; wished with exaggerated emotion that she could just die here in the crook of his arm before he took it away.

Something seemed to grip the man by the throat; the

beauty of the night; of the quiet, starlit downs; and the curve of the girl's lovely young body lying against him. His own intolerable hurt was merged into a strange, fierce desire to rise above it; to take life with both hands and mould something new out of it. All his life he would love Virginia because he could not easily change, but he would not let the loss of her crush him body and soul. He needed a woman in his life; a companion; someone with whom he might share his worldly goods, his physical and mental existence. He wanted children; a son. Very well, he would not let this thing that Virginia had done put an end to all those desires.

He liked this girl whose slight, exquisite body trembled to his touch; whose hair smelt sweet against his nostrils; whose skin was soft and cool. He had always liked her. And she was crying because of his sorrow. He felt an immense tenderness for her and knew that he had reached a curious emotional crisis which might alter the whole shape of his destiny.

It seemed to Joan a very long while before he spoke to her again. But his fingers continued to play with her hair. He sat very still. After a moment she raised her head and looked out of the window of the car. The stars were all blurred through her tears. She thought:

"I love him much too much. I'm only hurting myself. Why don't I cut it out and refuse to see him again?"

Then Barry, suddenly and unexpectedly, bent his head and kissed her on the mouth. It was not the fleeting caress that he had given her in the taxi the other night. It was a deeper, more insistent kiss. There was a quality in it almost of desperate passion. She could not understand or analyse. She just went to pieces in his arms, clung to him, one arm curved about his neck, shut her eyes and kissed him with all the pent-up passion of years in her lips.

He did not release her when that long kiss ended. He put both arms around her and held her very tightly. She kept her eyes tight shut and her small face was rapt and white in the starlight. He looked down at her with astonishment and tenderness combined and smoothed her hair back from her eyes.

"Do you love me?" he asked abruptly.

She felt crushed by the curtness of that question and the

knowledge that her secret was no longer her own. But she knew that she must tell him the truth, after that embrace which had passed between them and shattered her control.

"Yes," she whispered.

"Since when?"

"Oh, a long, long time, Barry."

"I didn't know. It never entered my head."

"Why should it?" She tried to laugh and draw away from him, but his arms held her back.

"No . . . stay where you are. Joan, listen. Tell me something . . . I want to know . . . how long you've cared for me like this."

"I won't tell you."

"Yes, please. It isn't just idle curiosity. I want to know . . . for a deeper reason."

"I can't talk about it . . . measure it by time . . . in cold blood, Barry," she said, and took one of his hands and hid her eyes against it. He was shocked to feel the warm moisture of tears against his palm and drew it away.

"No . . . you mustn't. I'm not worth that. My God, what a life this is. I never dreamed that you . . ."

"Forget about it, Barry," she whispered. She felt crushed by a burden of shame and grief. He refused to take his arms away from her and she felt his lips against her hot forehead.

"I don't think I want to forget it, Infant. But I do want you to answer this question. Do you *really* care for me?"

"I should have thought it was horribly obvious."

"No. It hasn't been at all until now."

"Barry, I've been in love with you for years, like a complete idiot."

"Good Lord! I can't think why."

That was so ingenuous of him that she had to laugh, even while she surreptitiously wiped away the tears that rolled down her cheeks.

"Neither can I."

"I've never done a thing to deserve it. It's very sweet of you, my dear."

"Sweet of me—to love you? Don't be an old ass, Barry darling. It isn't at all sweet. I just couldn't help myself."

"You're such a dear," he said in a low voice, and kissed her on the lips again. "And I never knew . . ."

"Thank goodness. I hate you knowing now."

"But I'm glad to know. After all, what have I left but you?"

That made her heart leap. For she had never dared hope that she could mean even so much as that to him. She pressed her wet, flushed cheek against his shoulder.

"You've got some money, luckily."

"Money isn't everything."

"No. How right you are!" she whispered. "There are other things in life which mean so much more."

"Look here, Joan," he said. "Isn't there any other fellow that means anything to you?"

"Not a single soul. It's always been you."

"I'm very touched, my dear."

She said nothing, but thought once again, wildly:

"I wish I could die before he takes his arms away. This will end very soon and he'll say it's better that we don't see each other much in future and I shall smile and agree and then go home and break my heart in two. Oh, why must it end?"

She heard him say:

"Look at me a moment, poppet."

She looked up obediently. She could just see his face in the shadows; dark, thin, with eyes full of a kindliness that had never been there before for her.

"Answer me this. Are you quite, quite sure of your love for me? As sure of its lasting as anyone reasonably can be, I mean?"

"Good heavens, yes. I loved you before you first went out to Ceylon."

"You were such a kid. . . ."

"But now I'm not. I'm quite old and experienced."

"Old! Not yet twenty-three," he laughed.

"Well, I do know, Barry. I've proved it to myself in a thousand different ways."

"Very well. Do you by any chance think you'd care to be married to me?"

The question was such a shock that she drew away from him and stared . . . her cheeks hot and red in the darkness.

"*Barry!*"

"Well . . . do you ? "

"Barry, it isn't very fair . . . to ask such a question . . . when . . ."

"Damn it, I'm not asking it as a joke. Answer me, Joan."

She gulped.

"It all seems so crazy. Oh, very well. Yes, of course I would like to be married to you. Doesn't any woman want to marry the one and only man she cares for! But when your affair with Virginia started I just knew it was all hopeless . . . about me, I mean . . . and I tried to put you out of my heart in that way. Only I couldn't."

"Dear little Joan . . ." He squeezed her hand hard with his. "How terribly sweet of you. I honestly never guessed. . . ."

She pulled her hand away. Her heart was racing, her throat dry and hot and aching with misery.

"Don't drag any more confessions from me. I'm wretched enough. Forget about it all—let's go home—*please*. It hasn't been a joke all these years and I can't stand much more. Let's go . . . please!"

But he took her in his arms again.

"Joan, listen. I like and admire you tremendously . . . more than ever after this. Joan, will you marry me?"

She stared up at him, breathless, dumbfounded. That strange, curt proposal of marriage from Barry was the last thing in the world she had expected, and it stunned her mentally. He added:

"I'm not jesting. I want to marry you—at once—if you will—if you really would like to be married to me, although I'm an irritable, selfish swine and I can't think why you like me."

She shook her head dumbly. Was the world coming to an end or was she crazy or he out of his mind? The earth about her seemed to be rocking a little, and the stars were all blurred; merged into each other. Barry was asking her to marry him and was not joking. Asking her to marry him *at once*.

She found her voice; very small and shaking.

"Barry . . . you're mad."

"No. I mean it. Will you marry me, Joan?"

"But why, *why*?"

"Because I think it would be a good plan."

"But, Barry," wildly, "you don't love me. Virginia . . ."

"Virginia's out of it, my dear," he broke in grimly. "She didn't want me."

"But *you* don't want *me*."

"I do in lots of ways."

"Barry, this means so much to me—for the love of God, be truthful with me. You aren't in the least in love with me, are you?"

"Not in love as you understand it, Joan. No. I'm going to be truthful. It's best for both of us. I'm never going to be in love, wildly, recklessly, with any woman again. It isn't there. That sort of feeling died . . . when Virginia married the other man. But I'm very fond of you, Joan, and getting fonder, damn it . . ." He laughed a little dryly. "You're so very sweet to me, my dear. We have a lot in common and we're excellent pals. We might make quite a success of life together. Who knows?"

She sat very still and quiet in the circle of his arms. Her heart beat so fast that it hurt her. What was she going to do about this? She had known before he said it that he was not in love with her. But she was in love with him—dreadfully in love. Was marriage to him going to be worth while . . . knowing that? Knowing that she must always, inevitably, be second best and that Virginia would remain the one real love of his life?

"It's all very sudden and unexpected, I know," said Barry. "But I generally make up my mind about things very suddenly. Joan, I'm being absolutely frank, my dear—perhaps brutal. But the position is this: I'm fond of you. I want a wife and companion and kids. I'll do everything in my power to make you happy. But it doesn't seem a very fair bargain, so for Lord's sake turn it down if you resent it."

For a long, long while Joan was silent. She turned the thing over and over in her mind. And one fact stood out above all others . . . the fact of her love for this man which nothing could destroy. It was a bitter pill to swallow . . . the knowledge that he was only "fond," and still hungered in his heart for another woman. Bitter to reflect that probably this would never alter, and that, if she married him, he might even live to regret having taken the step. That would be unbearable to her. She said huskily:

"Barry, are you sure you want to give up your freedom?"

"Oh, yes," he shrugged his shoulders. "It doesn't mean much to me these days. I'd like a home and children, as I've said before, and I don't want to wait till I'm forty and then be sorry I was a damn fool enough to lose my opportunities just because Virginia failed me."

Joan dug her teeth into her lower lip. He wanted a home and children. He did not say "wife" this time. But of course the others came first. Why should he particularly want a wife? She was astounded that he should offer her marriage, so soon after his *débâcle* with Virginia.

"Well, do you think you could put up with me for good and all, Infant?" she heard him ask with a humorous note in his voice.

She was defeated by a sense of despair. He sounded so casual and so prosaic. And to her this thing was a matter of life and death. But such emotion as that must be crushed right out if she was going to accept Barry and make a success of things with him. She must realise that she, personally, did not mean so much to him as the factors she stood for. A companion, a home, a mother of his children.

She closed her eyes very tightly. Barry's children. Rapture lay in that thought. She had never thought it possible. She had never thought any of this possible. Yet he was opening the gates of heaven to her. The gates of hell, too, she told herself wryly. It would be hell as well as heaven to marry the man one adored, knowing that he was not in love, and that he was taking one on the rebound from an unhappy affair with another woman. Wouldn't she be a perfect little idiot to accept him?

"Think over it well—sleep on it if you want to, my dear," she heard him say. His fingers touched her hair and neck. "I don't want you to make a mistake."

"But it's you, not me," she stammered. "I know *my* mind . . . but do you know yours?"

"Yes," he said quietly. "I'd like to marry and make a home with you, Joan. You're quite the dearest thing I know and much too nice for me, really."

Then she flung her arms about his neck and pulled his head down to hers; pressed her cheek against his, breathless and trembling.

"Barry, Barry, don't say that—when I love you so much."

"My dear," he said, much moved by her passion and more so by what he knew to be her sincerity, and hugged her close. "I'll do my best to make you happy. We'll have some good times together. But do you want me . . . knowing how I feel?"

"I may be seven times a fool," said Joan in a muffled voice. "But I do want you, terribly, darling, even though I know just how you feel. But if I marry you, try and love me a little."

"I do now," he said. "Well, is it all right?"

"If you mean will I marry you, yes, damn it," she said with a weak laugh.

He kissed her twice, with passion. But the earth and the stars rocked for her, and not for him. With melancholy he surveyed the wreckage of his own emotional life which had been for so long dedicated to Virginia. She seemed to be here, now, mocking him a little, with those long, alluring eyes of her . . . making him remember the dizzy heights to which he had climbed when he held her in his arms.

He could not climb to those heights now, holding little Joan against him, sweet, responsive though she was. That was the tragedy of it. But he would be awfully good to her. If he could make her very happy, that was something. And after all, she stirred him quite considerably and filled some of the aching void which Virginia had left.

Joan lay against him silently, full of delirious happiness. She was going to marry him. She would be his wife. It would be worth while whatever the price she paid in the future. She wanted nothing else in the world. She envied nobody else. Yes, one person. Virginia! Virginia whom he had loved and would regret to the end of his days. But she would not think of Virginia now, and anyhow, she was Lady Kingleigh . . . beyond Barry's reach. Feverishly Joan clung to her happiness.

"I do love you, my dear," she whispered.

But Barry did not hear. His reply to that made her laugh. It was so like him to spoil the emotional moment . . . not that anything could really spoil it for her tonight.

"We must push on and get some petrol. Come along!"

CHAPTER XI

THE drive back to Town, following upon Barry's unexpected proposal, was far from being as romantic as Joan might have wished. She remained in a delirious state of excitement and rode on the very crest of happiness. But he, like any man not particularly in love, was fretted by trifling annoyances.

They could not find an open garage or pump for miles and he was afraid they would run out of petrol. When they did find the pump, Barry had no change and neither had Joan. The lad who worked the pump kept them waiting an unjustifiable time while he changed a pound note. Joan sat close to Barry, laughing to herself. What did she care? But Barry complained. He complained even more bitterly when they found themselves one of a stream of cars returning from Brighton to London, unable to speed ahead and inconvenienced by the dazzling headlights of vehicles coming from the opposite direction. He gave vent to little explosions of wrath every now and then:

"Blast that man . . . why can't he dim . . . oh, for Lord's sake, why can't the damn Morris go on or let me get on . . . *look* at that chap—he ought to be shot, cutting in like that. . . . Oh, hell, what a crawl. We'll be in Town at midnight going at this pace. That's the worst of this road on a Sunday evening. . . ."

Joan listened and sympathised, but the light of ecstasy never left her eyes and it is doubtful whether she noticed any of the annoyances. But she reflected:

" Poor darling Barry . . . he isn't the perfect lover by any means. If he was he wouldn't care if we did reach London at midnight, or at dawn if it comes to that!"

Still, she could not expect him to be the perfect lover. He had just told her that he would never feel like that about any woman again. She had taken him on, knowing it, so it was not the slightest use being critical within an hour of promising to marry him. She must just regard the situation with a good deal of humour if she was going to be happy. And she *was* happy. Frightfully so. After all the repression, the heart-ache, the hopelessness of loving him, it was a miracle to know that she would belong to him, on any terms.

She was neither conceited nor stupid enough to tell herself that she would make him fall in love with her once she was his wife. She knew she could not achieve anything of the sort. It would be no use trying, with a man of Barry's temperament and set ideas. But she determined to make him a good wife; keep his affection. And she would have her moments when he was stirred to something more than affection for her. He would have moods . . . be difficult . . . and never would she get away from the knowledge that she took second place to Virginia. Many women would not have taken on marriage under such conditions, but Joan faced the whole position calmly and without flinching. She knew quite definitely that she would rather be second in his life than nothing at all.

Once, just before they reached London, speeding down the wide smooth road past Croydon Aerodrome, Barry put out a hand, laid it on her knee, and said:

"I'm an irritable brute. Sorry, Infant. But I loathe these sort of journeys, don't you?"

The warm pressure of that hand against her knee compensated Joan for the whole drive. She put a hand rather shyly over his. It seemed so wonderful, so strange, that she had a right to do this now.

"I haven't minded it, Barry."

"You're an amiable child. Well, seeing as how we're engaged, hadn't we better celebrate and have a spot of dinner somewhere?"

"That would be great."

"Don't change. Let's go to Soho as we are."

"I'd like that. I'm not very attached to smart restaurants."

"No, I don't suppose you are. Well, they bore me, and I much prefer a rattling good meal at a place like Varini's . . ."

He mentioned the name of a small restaurant in Shaftesbury Avenue, where the food was especially good. Joan felt a queer little pang when she heard it. That was Joe Halliday's favourite spot for a meal and she had often lunched with him there. Poor old Joe. She could not help realising that this engagement of hers was going to be a blow to him. In spite of her many refusals, he had never really lost hope of winning her one day. Well, he would have to recognise defeat this time. But she was sorry for him because she knew what a dark day it had been in her young life when Virginia had first told her that she was going to marry Barry.

Her thoughts swung from Joe to Virginia. Sudden, fierce exultation swept over her. Thank *God* Gina married Ian. It had given Barry to her. She ought not to feel like that. She ought to wish that Gina had married Barry—for his sake. But she really could not be as angelic as that. She was so ecstatically happy and at peace with the world tonight because Barry had asked her to marry him, she could not regret the tragedy that had given him to her. There might be a lot of heart-burning and discontent for her in the future, but the present, at least, was glorious.

She entered Varini's with Barry and swept Virginia from her mind.

Dinner was a success. Barry was in good spirits and said one or two very nice things to her.

" You've got the prettiest eyes I've ever seen," he told her. " And the longest lashes."

" And what about my snub nose ? " she laughed, her cheeks flaming, and the " prettiest eyes ", like blue jewels, sparkling at him.

" It's rather a nice nose. I don't mind it," said Barry. " Well, let's drink to our future."

He raised his glass. He had chosen hock. It gleamed like pale liquid amber translucent in the tall thin goblets. Joan raised hers. They touched glasses.

" Here's to the success of our future together," said Barry with a crooked little smile which was curiously tender.

Joan said, with all her heart in her voice :

" God bless you, Barry darling."

He drained his glass, set it down and grinned at her again, like a boy.

" Lord, what a business. I feel frightened to death."

" What of ? " she laughed.

" What I've done. Do you realise that I've let myself in for matrimony, young woman ? "

She wished that he would not jest about it, but she knew that he must, because he was Barry. She answered gaily, hiding just a small heart-ache.

"I've let myself in for something, too, old boy."

"You have, my dear—you're quite right. I shall be the devil to live with. Sure you want to do it?"

"Quite sure," she said steadily. "Are you?"

"Positive. I'm charmed at the idea of having such a nice wife. A clever little beast you are, too . . . my little journalist. You must quit that office, by the way. Give immediate notice tomorrow."

Her heart-beats quickened. So it really was an end to the life at the Chartwood Press; an end to her lonely existence in her bed-sitting-room and a new life to be shared with Barry. She soared up to the stars again; forgetting to grieve because he was not a more ardent lover.

"I must stay there till the end of April, Barry."

"It's the first of May in a fortnight's time," he said, leaning back in his chair and regarding her thoughtfully. "Shall we get married on May Day?"

"And dance round the pole together," she said with a tremulous laugh.

"I shall get tight out of sheer fright."

"Barry, you *are* a brute!"

"Don't get cross, I'm only ragging you."

"I know."

"Well, shall we get married on May Day? I'll get a licence and fix it up."

Joan looked at the thin brown face opposite her; into the light grey eyes that were smiling at her, and thought:

"Oh, I wish he didn't look so tired and so sad behind that smile. I can't believe he wants to marry me. I *can't* believe it's true. . . ."

"What about it?" he asked.

"Yes, I . . . I see nothing against it," she stammered. "Only I won't have much time to get clothes."

"My dear, you can't afford a large trousseau, I know, and I'm going to have a little money to play with once this will is proved, so let me buy what you want in Paris. I'm sure that's the right thing to say, isn't it?"

"Quite correct," said Joan with a shaky laugh.

"Where shall we go for the honeymoon? I warn you, I shan't be any good on a honeymoon."

"We needn't have one," said Joan valiantly.

"Oh, yes. You need a holiday after working in that

damned office for years. We'll quit this country, Joan, for at least a month, and go abroad."

"Barry, how marvellous that sounds."

"No fashionable resorts in the south of France, mark you. I'm not good amongst the idle rich."

"Barry, you ought to know by now that I don't want a Society life. I've been a reporter on Society weddings and functions for so long that I loathe the very sound of a title. No—if you want to know what I want—let it be a very small place where we shan't meet anybody. That is—if it won't bore you."

"Oh, it won't bore me if I can get a game of golf or something," said Barry cheerfully.

"That wasn't at all the right thing to say, my funny lover," thought Joan, grimacing. But she laughed.

"Let's go where you can play golf, then, and I'll be your caddie like I was once down at Padstow."

She realised too late her mistake in mentioning Padstow. But she saw the smile fade from Barry's eyes and turned from him to stare miserably round the restaurant.

"What an idiot I am. He's thinking about Virginia now."

Virginia was so closely associated with his memories of that holiday at Padstow. Yes, he was thinking of her . . . of the wild, crazy way in which his heart had beaten whenever she had been extra nice, or said an unusually nice word to him; of his frantic desire to please her, to obey her slightest command. Well, that was all over . . . irrevocably so. He was going to marry " little cousin Joan." He could not love her like that. No, and it didn't pay to love a woman so blindly, either. One only got a kick for it. He felt glad, relieved in a queer sort of way that he was wiping out the past and going to settle down with this nice child who seemed to love him very sincerely. But he wished to heaven he could forget Virginia and the way he had felt about her.

"I'm starting one of my infernal heads, Joan," he said abruptly. "I think our celebration must break up, my dear. I'm going back to bed."

"Of course," she said. She looked at him anxiously. "Are you all right?"

"Oh, yes. It's the malaria again. I get it every time I come back from Ceylon. I don't take much notice of it, but I think I'm better in bed. What time is it . . . quarter-past nine? It's rottenly early to break up the party and send you home."

"Not in the least. I'm perfectly happy," she said.

He took her in a taxi back to Victoria. Just for a moment he held her in his arms and kissed her on the lips.

"I'm glad we've fixed things up. You're very sweet to me. But I feel rather a swine . . . I seem to have so little to offer you, dear."

She held him close to her; shut her eyes and kept his lips against hers for a moment. Then she whispered:

"I don't ask anything that you can't give, Barry darling."

"No . . . but I feel a swine. . . ."

"You needn't. You've made me the happiest woman in the world."

"We'll make something of life together, I dare say." He smiled and stroked her hair. "I'll see you tomorrow. I'll phone you up at the office. We've got to go and buy a ring and do the thing properly."

He laughed. But she could not speak. She was too profoundly moved; speechless with great happiness. Then, when she realised they were nearing her digs, she gave him a convulsive little hug and whispered:

"I do love you so much. Good night, *darling*."

"Good night, sweetheart," he said.

It was the first time he had ever called her that; the first lover's endearment she had ever heard from his lips. It thrilled her inexpressibly and gave her infinite hope.

CHAPTER XII

WHEN Joan walked into Halliday's office first thing that next morning to break her joyous news to him, he commented upon her appearance before she had time to speak.

"Joan dear, what's come over you? Rockefeller left you half his fortune or something? You're all glowing, my dear."

She laughed and seated herself on the edge of the desk. She looked down at him a little embarrassed and sad because she was going to wipe that jolly, cheery grin from his good-natured face.

"I feel all glowing, Joe dear."

"Well—is it a fortune?"

He held out a packet of cigarettes to her. She took one and he lit it. An office-boy opened the door and thrust a tow-coloured head inside.

"Get out," said the editor of the *Hand Mirror*, and added under his breath: "And stay out, for heaven's sake. There's no peace in this office. Now, Joan, dear child, what's happened?"

"I'm going to be married, Joe," she said quietly.

Halliday sat back in his chair. The light left his big, jovial face, as she had expected. But he smiled gallantly.

"Not really, dear?"

"Really and truly."

"What a shock. Who to?"

"Barry Elderton."

"Elderton! You mean that fellow from Ceylon who was going to marry the cousin who married Kingleigh the other day."

Joan's lashes hid the expression in her eyes.

"Yes."

Halliday twisted his lips and stared at her.

"But, Joan dear, you've always told me that Elderton was . . ."

"Was frightfully devoted to Gina. Yes, he was. But now he's going to marry me."

"Well, I can't but say he's made a wise choice, this time, Joan dear, but do you care for him?"

"I adore him, Joe."

She said it so simply and unashamedly that Halliday felt something tighten in his throat. He looked away from her, out of the editorial window at the tall chimney-tops and the scudding white clouds of a windy April day. He thought:

"Hell and damn! I've lost her for good and she adores him. The lucky blighter. God help him if he doesn't make her happy." Aloud he said: "Joan dear, you know how much you mean and always have meant to me. Well, I want you to be terribly happy, because you deserve to be."

"No, I don't."

"I say you do. Is this fellow going to make you happy?"

"Yes, frightfully, Joe."

"Then I'm glad. I'm certain he must be crazy about you. Any man would be."

That brought the colour to her cheeks and the inevitable ache to her heart. Crazy about her. No—Barry, funny old lover, wasn't that. He wanted to be certain of a game of golf if they went to a lonely place for their honeymoon, poor dear. But she was not going to tell Joe of the queer understanding between her and Barry, so she said gaily:

"Well, I'm engaged, anyhow, and I want you to know Barry and like him. I'm not going to lose you as a pal, am I, Joe?"

He wanted to sweep her off the desk into his great arms and hug her. Dear little Joan, with her starry blue eyes and brave, sweet mouth and a store of common sense and intelligence in her little mind. Damn this Elderton fellow. The lucky swine. Halliday put out a big hand and laid it on hers.

"Of course you'll never lose me, Joan dear. I hope to meet your future husband and be great friends with him."

Tears suddenly sprang to Joan's eyes.

"You are a dear, Joe."

"We must send out for a bottle of champagne and bring in Mac and drink your health," he said. He raised his voice: "Hi ... Mac ... Mac!"

Miss Mackay entered the room, clad as usual in a brightly flowered cretonne overall with enormous pockets, in which reposed cigarettes, powder-box, comb, matches, pencils, and a variety of "things for use", as she told people. The inevitable cigarette hung from her lower lip and she carried a proof sketch at which she was gazing in despair.

"That infernal man can't draw!" she wailed. "The heroine's arms are supposed to be round the hero's neck in an abandonment of love, and she looks as though she's strangling him."

"Well, come here and listen to me," said Halliday. "Joan's gone and abandoned herself to love and we've got to have some fizz at twelve o'clock on the strength of it."

He grinned at Miss Mackay. But he felt so depressed that he wished somebody would strangle him. He had lost Joan. He had never had her, but he had lost what was within his grasp and now was beyond it ... hope.

Joan met the gaze of her friend Mac. Mac regarded her dubiously.

"Joan, you aren't married or about to take a week-end with one of our directors or something shameful?"

"No," she smiled. "But I'm engaged . . . to Barry Elderton."

"Good Lord," said Mac. "Bang go all our plans for sharing a flat."

"I'm afraid so."

Miss Mackay shook her head, then walked up to Joan and patted her head.

"Tragedy," she said. "But I congratulate you. I suppose you're madly in love, and the young man's madly in love with you and you're going to be happy for ever and ever."

"Of course," said Joan.

Then, very self-conscious and not quite certain whether she was very happy or unhappy, she hurried out of Joe's room into her own to take off her things.

The editor and the sub-editor exchanged looks. Halliday stubbed his cigarette end on a tray already littered with ends.

"Hell," he said.

"Poor old thing," said Mac sympathetically.

"I don't mind if she's happy. But who is this fellow Elderton? Does anyone know him?"

"Joan's often spoken to me about him. She has had a snapshot of him on her mantelpiece in her room for years. She must be very attached, only I thought he was crazy about Miss Brame."

"Well, he's a fool if he isn't crazy about Joan."

"I hope he is, but I have a feeling that most of the passion is on Joan's side."

"God forbid, Mac. How could she hope to be happy?"

Mac shook her red head.

"I don't know. But I hope she will be, as she's one of the nicest——"

"Shut up," broke in Halliday gloomily. "I know it."

"We shall miss her here, shan't we?"

"If this fellow doesn't make her happy I'll break his neck," said Halliday. "Mac, you must have lunch with me today and cheer me up, or I shall pitch myself into the Thames."

Mac held up both hands.

"Suicide of well-known editor ... what a bit of publicity for the Chartwood Press."

He glared at her.

"Little comforter."

Her lips softened. She came up to the desk and patted his shoulder.

"Joking apart, I am sorry, Joe, and I'd like to have lunch with you."

In the adjoining room the telephone-bell rang. Joan answered it and some of the light in her eyes died out.

"I'm not very fit," said Barry's voice, "and I think I'd better stick in bed, my dear, till the fever's gone and my temperature down. We must put off buying the ring till tomorrow if you don't mind."

"Of course I don't mind," she assured him. "But can I do anything for you ... see you ..."

"You can't very well ... in the hotel. I'll be all right. I'll phone you tomorrow."

"I understand," she said.

"So long, my dear."

"So long," she said steadily and put up the receiver. She sat with elbows on the desk, chin on her hand, staring at her blotter. There had been so much she wanted to say. Tender little things. She would liked to have said: "Good-bye, my darling, *my darling*...." But he wasn't like that and wouldn't like that sort of thing on the phone. He dreaded and avoided displays of emotion. That was Barry ... the new Barry created by Virginia. In the old days he would have got out of bed, with a temperature, with anything, recklessly ... just to see Gina for five minutes.

Joan swallowed hard. She *must* stop expecting Barry to behave like that with her. What had she to grouse about? She would see him tomorrow. And she could not very well call upon him at the hotel when he was in bed. It wouldn't be proper.

She tried to laugh and be philosophical. But she was forced to realise that she was not very much closer to this man she loved, now that she was engaged to him, than she had been before. He was miles apart from her. He always would be. That something that she wanted from him, hungered for, belonged to Virginia and to the past.

"Oh, damn," said Joan.

While Joe Halliday and Miss Mackay lunched together, both believing that Joan would be with her fiancé, Joan had a solitary meal at a Lyons restaurant and read over the report she had made, that morning, of the bazaar opened by the Duchess of Chelway in aid of a children's hospital. But her mind was on Barry and not upon the report. After lunch she went out and searched a big book-shop for a book that he might like to read, should his head improve and the fever die down, tonight. She found two novels by authors whom she knew he liked and sent them to his hotel with a short note. She wrote two notes. The first ended up:

"You are never out of my thoughts, I love you so, my darling, darling Barry . . ."

But she tore that up.

"It's no use giving way to sentimentality with a man who isn't in love with you and is marrying you on a friendly basis. Cut it out, Joan, my girl!"

She wrote another note which she sent with the books, and finished:

"Hurry up and get fit. I've had a glorious morning all amongst the duchesses. Hooray! My love to you, dearest.
"JOAN."

The answer to the note and the books was gloriously unexpected.

Joan did not go out that evening. At eight o'clock she ate the usual small, solitary meal in her room and then seriously attacked some sewing. She was not over-fond of the needle but she had a trousseau to prepare in a very short time—happy thought—and she felt that while she might buy most of the necessities, she would at least make one pair of pyjamas. She found a pattern and bought the material at Marshall's that afternoon when she left the office. She was gorgeously extravagant. But what did money matter . . . she wanted something really alluring for her wedding.

She told herself that she must not dwell too much on the thought of her wedding because she was certain to be disappointed. She could never be as lovely and *soignée* and alluring as Virginia . . . *damn it!* She must just take what came and make the best of it. It was no earthly good expecting Barry to make much fuss of her.

She wondered if he liked the books she had chosen and if he was better.

She sat curled up in an arm-chair, hair very untidy, face flushed, and dress discarded for a camel-hair dressing-gown. A boy's dressing-gown, purchased at Jaeger's for warmth rather than allurement. The gas fire did not give out any too much heat and the April night was chilly.

Somebody knocked on her door.

"Come in," said Joan. Her wrist-watch said eight forty-five. This could only be Mac or one of the other girls in the office, or Mrs. Fletcher.

She was speechless with surprise and pleasure when Barry walked into the room. She sprang off the chair, dropped the sewing, and put both hands to her untidy head. Panic-stricken she stared at him.

"Good heavens . . . what a shock! And look at me . . . far from properly attired!"

"Shall I go away again? Were you just going to bed?" asked Barry.

He smiled at her. He looked tired and there were dark circles under his eyes—marks of the fever that had attacked him all day—but he seemed in good spirits.

"No, please don't go away. That is if you don't mind my peculiar garb," she said.

"It looks all right to me," he said, and regarded the slim, small figure in the brown woollen dressing-gown with affectionate amusement. "I felt better tonight so I decided to get up and come and thank you for the books and your nice note. It was charming of you, but you're not to spend your money on me, Infant."

"But I—I wanted you to have something to r-read." She was flushed and stammering and starry-eyed. He looked at the heap of white on the floor.

"Good Lord, what's that? I feel scared stiff . . . coming into a lady's room and seeing things like that all over the carpet."

"You fool," she laughed helplessly. "It isn't anything yet. It's only a few yards of material."

"Can I help you sew?"

"And ruin my lovely stuff. No, thanks."

He wandered about the room in his restless way. He liked the soft light of the one amber-shaded lamp on the table. He liked the room, altogether.

"I mustn't stay, Joan. But I thought I'd put my head in and say good night and thank you for the books. I read one and liked it very much."

Joan's blue eyes danced at him. What did it matter that she had been disappointed this morning because she would not see him? He was here, now, in the flesh, being extremely nice and appreciative. Was there anybody in the world like him? Nobody for whom she would exchange him, anyhow; her queer, undemonstrative, prosaic lover!

"I'm glad you came," she said.

"I shouldn't mind settling down for a long yarn, my dear, but it's your bedroom and...."

"Heavens, aren't we conventional!" she laughed.

"We have to be, when the reputation of a nice young thing like you is at stake."

"Nice young thing ... Gawd!" exclaimed Joan.

"Do you know, you look about fifteen in that dressing-gown with your mop of hair," he observed. "I think I must break the engagement. It's too much like baby-snatching."

"Will you be *quiet* about my youth," she said, stamping her foot.

"Temper," he grinned.

"I'm not so young and you know it."

"I know you look extraordinarily attractive and that this is no place for me," he said unexpectedly.

Her heart began to pound.

"Sit down and have some coffee."

"No. I mustn't stop, really."

"Why not?"

"Because I'm in an amorous mood."

Joan giggled helplessly, but every nerve in her body was quivering. She said:

"Don't be so *silly*."

He came across the dim-lit room and caught her in his arms. She went limp at once and put her arms about his neck, her eyes adoring him. Barry, in one of those queer fierce moods which came upon him suddenly and as suddenly departed, kissed her throat, then slipped a hand under the thick warm dressing-gown and caressed her shoulder. It was cool and smooth and he realised not for the first time what a lovely skin the child had, what a lovely body. He said :

" You're rather sweet, do you know that ? "

Joan put up a shaking hand and caressed his head. She was quite white and her eyes looked enormous.

" I love you ! I love you ! " she said, and forgot to be prosaic.

He kissed her, tightening his hold, and for a moment of unrestrained passion, covered her face and throat with kisses. Then when he felt the frantic beating of her heart and heard her passionate repetition, " I love you . . . I love you . . ." he drew away from her and the mad moment passed. He was controlled again.

" This won't do at all, Infant."

Joan, quite lost to time and space, lying against him with her eyes shut, remained speechless. She could not tell him all that she felt ; could never tell him what his arms, his lips, roused in her. It was almost terrifyingly intense . . . this emotion. She had never been held or kissed like this by any other man but Barry. She was supremely glad now of her past reticence with other men . . . of the virginity which she could give to this one man.

" I must go, dear," he said, and kissed her gently on the hair and let her go. " I went quite crazy for a moment, I'm afraid."

She pulled herself together and smiled.

" That's all right, darling. So did I."

" Tomorrow," he said. " I'll fetch you from the office at lunch time and we'll get that damned ring."

" That damned ring." So like Barry. She laughed but was on the verge of tears ; still emotional, thrilling from his kisses. But he was quite calm again. She was a little bewildered by his facility for rapid change of mood. She had wanted to stay in his arms for ever.

" If you must go . . ." she said.

" I must, my dear. And forgive me for losing my head. You looked such a kid and so sweet just now. . . ."

" What is there to forgive when we're engaged and I love you," she said impulsively.

He felt suddenly ashamed. He knew that he did not love her in the way she loved him and that for him the moment of passion had been a purely sensual thing. For her it had been much more. He did not want to hurt her. But he could not and would not play the lover often and he knew it. He wanted companionship from her more than the other thing.

He put an arm about her shoulders.

"Don't love me too much, dear. I don't deserve it."

"Can I love you too much if I'm going to be your wife?" she asked wistfully.

"Yes, you can. You mustn't. I'm so afraid of hurting you."

"Don't be," she said. Some of the glory left her eyes. She knew what he alluded to. That wretched second place she took in his heart. In his arms just now she had forgotten it and possessed him so entirely in her own mind. But she was forced back to earth—to the knowledge that she would never possess him in the way Virginia had done. She took his hand and put it against her hot cheek.

"That's all right, darling. You won't hurt me. And I can't stop loving you and you don't really want me to, do you?"

"No," he said, with that swift, charming smile which always made her heart ache with love for him. "I'm a selfish swine and I don't think I do want you to stop loving me."

"I never will," she said.

"Good night, sweetheart," he said, and left her.

She sat down on her bed after he had gone, hid her face on the pillow, wept passionately. She knew that she loved him too much. He was right. She would get hurt in the end. She was bound to. But she did not care. She could not give him up now, and if she could have his love, his passion, even for a little while, as she had had it tonight, life was worth living . . . while it lasted.

BOOK II

CHAPTER I

THROUGH the beautiful gardens of the Hotel Angelico, which is isolated on a promontory between Cadenabbia and Tremezzo, Virginia Kingleigh strolled down to the water's edge and seated herself on the low marble balustrade to wait for her husband. When he came they were going by motor-boat to Como.

It was the first day of May and in the bright, hot sunshine the vivid blue of the sky seemed to blaze down into the deep, glittering blue of the lake. All along the shore at this time of the year the azaleas were bursting into flower. When Virginia first came she had been enraptured by the brilliant beauty of these pink and flame-hued blooms which looked like vivid splashes from a painter's brush fringing the sapphire water.

She put up a sunshade and sat idle for a moment, drinking in all this beauty through half-shut eyes. This morning's mail lay unopened on her lap. She felt too hot, too lazy to open them, and in spite of all the loveliness and the luxurious warmth which caressed her body through the thin silk of her dress, she was bored. Yet Lake Como and the Hotel Angelico in the Italian spring should be a paradise for married lovers.

The trouble was that Virginia and Ian were not lovers; and this was not the sort of honeymoon it should have been. The love, the passion, the enthraldom were all on his side. She was merely the passive recipient of his worship. That seemed a tragedy because Ian was such a dear and so awfully good to her. Anything within reason that she asked he gave her. But she could give so little in return. Her body, her companionship, yes, but nothing mentally. And it was the real Virginia whom he wanted, of course. She knew that; grieved that this honeymoon must be a disappointment to him although he would never tell her so.

In England she had tried to believe that she could put Barry out of her mind and be entirely happy with Ian. But she knew as soon as they reached Italy, and their honeymoon began, that she had made a terrible mistake.

She had loved Barry. She still loved him. She regretted

what she had done—and would regret it to the end of her life.

It was not that she disliked Ian, because he was so essentially nice and charming as a husband; no woman could dislike him. But she was utterly indifferent to him as a lover and, in a queer, half-conscious way, resented the fact that she had given him all that she had meant to give Barry.

She realised the futility of such resentment and of regrets. She had burned her boats and incidentally she had saved the financial situation and ensured her mother's peace and comfort. But that could not more than partially compensate her for losing Barry. She was ashamed, also, of the manner in which she had treated Barry. For, after all, they had been intimate friends for four years and she had given him her word. He must be suffering, too. Virginia, weak, selfish though she was, hated to think that she had made Barry suffer. Yes, she felt miserable and restless and longing to see him again and revive the old delightful comradeship grew stronger every day. But she had forfeited the right to see him. The ties between them were broken. She, herself, had destroyed all the dreams they had built up together.

She tried to console herself with the idea that one day in the far distant future she and Barry would come together again. They must. She could not bear it to be otherwise.

She drew a heavy sigh and turned to the letters on her lap and glanced through them. One from her mother; several sent on from Greyes Street. Bills. And one from cousin Joan. Virginia wondered how Joan was and if she had seen much or anything of Barry in Town. She opened Joan's letter.

For a moment she stayed very still, staring down at the letter, not very long and written with obvious haste in Joan's untidy small writing.

So still she sat, her white figure might have been carven of marble there; and her face as white as her dress. She could not quite credit what she read for the first few seconds.

"My Dear Gina,—I feel you ought to know I am being married to Barry on the 1st of May at a register-office in Town. We have seen a lot of each other since he came back from Ceylon and I can only say I hope that I shall make him as happy as he will make me.

"It's all turned out in a queer way, hasn't it ? I do so hope *you* are happy, my dear.

"Ever, JOAN."

"P.S.—I have no idea what our future plans are, but we shall be away for a month and then probably have a flat in Town."

Virginia raised her eyes from the letter and stared blindly across the blue, shimmering water.

Joan's news seemed to stun her at first. Then the numbness passed and she began to think again. She put down her sunshade, fumbled in the brocade bag in her lap for a cigarette case—found a cigarette and lit it. Every nerve in her body was jumping and the pupils of her eyes were very big and dark.

Joan and Barry, married . . . *Joan and Barry*. She could hardly believe it. The 1st of May. That was today. She almost laughed. While she had sat here grieving for Barry, regretting the choice that she had made voluntarily, Barry and Joan were getting married in London. It was an ironic jest. No—not a jest—a frightful calamity.

It was the last thing in the world Virginia had expected. With the most exquisite selfishness she had hoped to keep Barry's love even though she had thrown it away for Ian and financial security. But now she had lost him altogether. He had married Joan.

Virginia became conscious suddenly of a thwarted, furious sensation. She tore Joan's letter in pieces and laughed aloud.

She wondered, suddenly, how Barry and Joan would manage on the little he had. They were going to have a flat in Town, Joan said. That was queer. Why weren't they going back East ?

It had not taken Barry very long to recover from the blow she had given him. Virginia felt bitter and injured about that. Then she told herself that was not true. He had thrown himself into this affair with Joan on the rebound. No doubt Joan had been nice and kind to him and he had responded to her sympathy. Any man might have done the same.

She opened her mother's letter. Perhaps there was more news about Barry and Joan. Joan had been pretty curt about it. Virginia found herself hating Joan violently in this moment.

Lady Brame had plenty to say about the affair. Feverishly Virginia scanned the long letter. One paragraph in particular held her attention.

> Of course, my darling, it was the best thing that could happen. So nice for dear Joan to settle down with a nice husband—I'm sure poor Barry will be an excellent husband. . . .

Virginia felt that the " poor Barry " was significant.

> And of course they will not be badly off, as John Elderton died recently and Barry has come into the money. I am going to give Joan a small cheque for her wedding present, and if I were you I would bring back some nice little thing from Italy for their new home. . . .

Virginia lifted her eyes from the letter and now her usually pale face was red and her whole body was shaking.

So Barry's uncle had died. Barry had come into the money. She knew that meant about two thousand pounds a year. And they had not expected the old uncle to retire to another world for years and years. That piece of news shook Virginia. She knew, in the depths of her heart, that she would never have given Barry up could she have foreseen that he would come into John Elderton's money this year.

The whole thing was a wretched, horrible mistake. She felt cheated, and most of all she felt ashamed of what she had done to Barry—to herself—to the man she had married.

Through a queer haze she saw the tall, distinguished figure of her husband, in white flannels, coming from the hotel towards her. He had waited for the English newspapers to arrive. He carried one under his arm, and was glancing through *The Times* as he walked. He put this down, smiled, and waved a hand in greeting as he neared her. She sat very still, feeling suddenly tired and cold even in the hot sunlight. All her nerves were jumping. She thought how attractive Ian was when his grave face relaxed into that tender and eager smile reserved for her. But she could not love him as she had loved Barry. The pity of it all! The futility of regretting now ; when she was face to face with her mistake. Not since the hour when she had decided to give up Barry and marry Ian had she suffered like this. But it was not much good allowing herself to suffer. She had better make the best of it and be kind to Ian because he was deeply in love with her.

"Any exciting news, my dear?" he asked as he reached her.

She answered in a low voice:

"No—none."

"You're rather pale, dearest. Is the sun too much for you?"

"Perhaps."

"Do you want to take this trip to Como?"

"Oh, yes. I'm all right."

He looked anxiously at the lovely face under the big white hat which she was wearing. She was afraid that he was going to question her, fuss over her, and felt she could not bear it. She was on the verge of tears. To save herself from such a disaster, she turned the conversation round to him.

"You don't look up to much yourself, this morning, my dear Ian."

Kingleigh smiled.

"I didn't sleep well last night. Too hot."

"Do you think this place suits you?"

"Oh, yes. Why not?"

"You haven't been sleeping well, I know."

He seated himself beside her and looked at her with kindling eyes. Her solicitude was very refreshing. He was not going to spoil her honeymoon by telling her the truth about himself. But he knew perfectly well that he was a very sick man. The doctors had warned him in London about that dicky heart of his. It had been the pain—gnawing and nagging—that had kept him awake last night. He would have to go slow. Well, he was lazing here in the sunlight and Virginia seemed to love the lake. They would stay a little longer.

He took her hand and pressed it.

"I'm quite all right, my dear. Heard from your mother?"

"Yes."

"And no excitements?"

"None...." she turned her face from him and looked at the glittering lake. A beautiful slim motor-boat, flashing white in the sunlight, was cutting through the blue water towards them. She added; "Here comes our boat, Ian."

He put out a hand and pulled her on to her feet.

"Put up your sunshade, darling. The sun is so hot."

She gave him her vague, sweet smile. She looked not at him, but at her wrist-watch. Midday. At this very moment, little doubt, Barry and Joan were being married.

CHAPTER II

JOAN came out of the register-office with a slim platinum circlet on her marriage finger and a certificate in her bag, feeling very like most brides. Excited, slightly embarrassed, and extremely happy.

Joan Borrow was no more. She was Joan Elderton. The thing that had been a dream for so many years—it had seemed a very hopeless dream, too—had come to pass. She was married to the man she loved better than anybody or anything in the world. She had cause to be happy, and not even the memory of Virginia could dispel the little triumphant, exalted feeling that thrilled through her this morning.

Barry came out of that register office feeling, probably, quite unlike most bridegrooms. He knew no exaltation, no particular excitement, and somewhat diluted happiness. The memory of Virginia was only too brutally insistent and vivid for him in this hour.

Since his boyhood he had loved her and meant to marry her. It seemed to him amazing and slightly crazy that he should find himself married to Joan. He really believed that he had died to himself and to all real thrills of life in the hour that he had learned that Virginia had let him down. He would never again experience the "first fine rapture" that he had known with and for her. On the other hand, he knew quite well what he was doing when he tied himself up to Joan for life. He was going against the coward's inclination to creep into a corner and die. He was pulling himself out of the wreckage of things and he was going to make something out of what was left. He would make a home for himself and for Joan. She was a dear and charming companion, and in the fullness of time, no doubt, she would give him children, which he wanted.

It all seemed a bit cut and dried and cold-blooded seen from this point of view, but he could not help that. It also seemed a little unfair to Joan. But he had been frank with her. She knew what she had taken on. She cared for him enough to take the risk and make what she could of life with him. All the same, he was sorry for her, in a way, and for himself, too. For this was not at all the marriage he had planned.

Neither of them had wanted a fuss. The wedding had been quiet enough in all conscience. Two witnesses only. Miss Mackay—Joan's friend from the office. Geoffrey Calthrop, one of Barry's pals from the East who happened to be in Town and available. They were even avoiding a wedding breakfast. Barry and Joan were going straight to Victoria now, to catch the eleven o'clock boat-train to Dover, and crossing the Channel. Paris for a night and then the south of France and a small island off the coast known as the "*Ile des Fleurs.*" The Island of Flowers. Barry knew it. He had been there once in his youth and had always meant to go back. It was, he told Joan, small, as beautiful as its name suggested, and deserted except for the few peasants who lived upon it. It was a place very rarely visited by English or American tourists because it was, so to speak, "right off the map." There was only one small boat a week to and from the island, no shops, and one tiny hotel.

When Barry had told Joan about it she had gasped and said:

"But you'll be bored! There's no golf!"

He had laughed about that and answered:

"I know, but if we get bored we can move. But we'll endure it for a week. It really is beautiful at this time of the year, and I'm sure you'll like it. You're fond of flowers."

Joan knew just how much she would like it. For days before her wedding she dreamed about the *Ile des Fleurs* and the man she loved, and she was amazed and touched that he, who confessed himself an unromantic man, should choose so romantic a spot for their honeymoon. It seemed to her a good augury for their future happiness and she set out this morning with the most passionate and sincere intention of making him happy. Of her own contentment she was assured.

There was so much to make her happy today. Everybody had been extraordinarily nice. A shoal of telegrams had reached her at her "digs" early—because she was being married at ten o'clock in order to catch the boat-train. It seemed to her that everybody on the staff at the Chartwood Press wired her good wishes, and they had combined to give her a beautiful present. A canteen of stainless cutlery. Joe Halliday had called personally to wish her luck and give her his present—an enchanting Lalique bowl. He had said:

"Don't forget me altogether, Joan dear. Let me hear from you, and you know I shall never fail you if you want me at any time."

She had told him that she knew that and promised that she would never forget him.

Aunt Milly had sent a handsome cheque, but confessed herself grieved because Joan was not going to have a more fashionable wedding which she, Lady Brame, might have attended and been in her element. But Joan, like Barry, shrank from the idea of publicity.

She was glad, however, to have dear old "Mac" there; Mac, glorious in a new dress and hat bought for the occasion; and Geoffrey Calthrop, who was an amusing man of middle age, kept up a running flow of jokes and maintained a cheerful spirit for which everybody was thankful.

Being a confirmed bachelor, Calthrop thought his friend Elderton quite crazy to launch into matrimony. But when he was introduced to Joan he liked her and told himself that Barry was not such a fool after all. This girl was obviously a sensible, intelligent, and rather charming creature. Not strictly pretty; but most attractive eyes and smile and had a sense of humour. Calthrop considered it most important that a wife should have a sense of humour. She would probably need it in the course of her career as a married woman!

Joan, of course, looked her very best today. Nothing beautifies a woman so skilfully as happiness, and she radiated it. She had a lovely colour; eyes like blue stars and a becoming dress. Most extravagant she had been about her "going away" dress and hat, since she was to be married in them. A "couture" dress of dark blue satin; a chic little hat to match; sapphire and diamond clips and an ermine coat which Barry had given her for a wedding present. They had agreed on a channel crossing instead of flying. Both liked the sea. This morning the sun was shining, but a stiff breeze blew lustily down the London streets and the Channel was going to be rough and cold, so Joan was thankful for her coat. It was a very lovely one. Barry had chosen it with her.

"Any woman would look nice in it," Joan had said happily after Barry had bought it for her.

"Well, you look nice in it, anyhow," he had said in his curt, dry way, but that was praise enough to bring the starry lights into Joan's blue eyes.

He was really being marvellous to her this morning, she thought tenderly. He had even remembered to bring her flowers, as a bridegroom should. A great dewy bunch of violets in their frame of dark green leaves. They were fragrant and sweet, pinned to her furs.

When they were in the Pullman, and the train had steamed out of Victoria, and they had waved good-bye to Geoffrey Calthrop and Miss Mackay, who was holding a handkerchief to her nose, unusually affected by the farewell to her best friend, Barry and Joan looked at each other across the small table and grinned like self-conscious children. But there was no attempt on the bridegroom's part to be sentimental at the moment. He said, quite bluntly :

"Thank God that's over, and may I never have to get married again."

"I should hope not," Joan laughed. "But really, Barry, you are a coward. We had the most peaceful and secluded wedding. You ought to have figured in a Society 'do'. . ."

"I'd rather be shot at dawn. Look here, my dear, do you mind if I order a drink?"

"Go ahead," she laughed again.

"It's a bit early, Lord knows, but I need a stimulant."

"What about poor me?"

"I believe you actually enjoyed the whole thing, you little devil."

She regarded her wedding ring proudly.

"Certainly I did."

"Well, do you want a brandy and soda?"

"No. I don't think I need fortifying."

"I shall have a whisky."

"At eleven a.m. My goodness, these men from the East!"

Barry gave his order to the waiter who came along the swaying Pullman.

"Smoke, Infant?" he said, and handed her a packet of cigarettes. She took one and he lit it for her. Their eyes met. Her heart gave a leap and the blood rushed to her cheeks. She experienced an instant of the most intense happiness. She thought :

"Can it be true? I'm *his wife*. He's *my husband* . . . Oh, I'm so happy!"

But she kept her ecstasies to herself because she was not going to risk his being irritated by her. Whatever happened, he must not get sick of her. Let the overtures come from him. It was better—much better that way.

Barry, not being really in love with this newly-married wife of his, although he felt quite astonishingly pleased with life, and looked forward to his honeymoon, was more concerned with practical reflections than with ecstasies.

Cigarette between his lips; eyes screwed up; he examined the two books of tickets and a roll of French notes he extracted from his coat pocket.

"Let's see . . . yes, all here. Calais, Paris, and then through Cannes and Le Trayas and down the coast to the *Ile des Fleurs*."

Joan, watching him with glowing eyes, snuggled into her soft fur coat which was a constant source of pleasure, and said :

"Think of hot sunshine and an Island of Flowers, Barry."

"Not a bad thought either, my child. Commend me to an English May for cold, wet, windy weather."

"When we get back it'll be June."

"Yes. I'm not sure we oughtn't to take a cottage in the country instead of a flat in Town."

"I'd like that."

"As long as we get near a golf course," he grinned

"Oh, you and your golf!"

"Now, don't start hen-pecking me, Mrs. Elderton."

The form of address thrilled her deliciously.

"Darling!" she said.

"What a name to call a defenceless man," said Barry, and took refuge in the drink which was placed before him.

CHAPTER III

BARRY knew of a quiet and excellent hotel in Paris just off the Rivoli, and it was there that they spent their wedding night.

"We'll do the thing properly and have a magnificent meal somewhere and go to a show," Barry said when they reached their destination. "Anything you like, but don't ask me to dance. I'm no good at it, and they only give you a floor the size of a lozenge in the night clubs here."

Joan did not want to dance. She was much too exalted in mind and body to care what she did so long as she was with him.

They had a small and quite charming suite; two bedrooms and a bath. It all seemed very comfortable and typically French; thick lace curtains framed by pale rose taffeta ones, thick rose carpets, pale grey furniture; low luxurious-looking beds with cunning little lights on the gilt head-boards; and an atmosphere of heat that was too much even for the man from Ceylon.

"You can't breathe!" he said, threw open the windows in his room, and strolled through the communicating door into Joan's room. She was busily unpacking.

"Never satisfied, are you, my lamb?" she smiled.

"Quite right," he said. "Although I'm really rather satisfied with my better half."

She lifted a flushed and radiant face from the suit-case.

"Mean that?"

"Yes," he said, and held out a hand to her. "Come and kiss me, Infant. You're so damned good-natured. I grumble at everything and you never lose your temper."

"Wait till I do!" she laughed, and suddenly clung to him, took his arms and put them around her. "Oh, Barry, darling, I'm so happy!"

He kissed the top of her head.

"I'm glad."

"I do so want you to be, too."

"I am, my dear."

She hid her eyes against his coat for a moment, trembling slightly. She thought:

"I wonder . . . or is he being—just nice ? Does he think about Virginia ? *Does he ?*"

The emotional moment passed for the man. He patted her head, released her, and walked back to his room. She looked after him, her heart aching with love for him.

"I'll come and unpack for you in a second."

"What a dutiful bride," he called back.

She drew from folds of tissue-paper the white silk pyjamas; the famous pair on which she had worked half the night in order to get them finished. She laid them on the bed beside her house-coat. The old camel's hair dressing-gown had been abandoned for this new, alluring one of pale green padded silk. Across the bed she laid the pale blue cocktail dress she was going to wear tonight. Beside it, a velvet evening coat, and of course a set of lovely "undies," of sheerest stockings, and blue satin shoes. It had been so thrilling in London, buying those things—more expensive clothes than any she had allowed herself before. All for her wedding-day.

"Joan, the seductress!" she grinned to herself, and then walked into Barry's room and helped him unpack, which was very domesticated and satisfying to her feminine heart.

They spent what was undoubtedly the happiest evening of Joan's life, and Barry was a great deal happier than he had expected to be. Joan was a perfect companion. He wanted an amusing companion; someone who would not be too emotional or ask too much of him, and she did not fail him. His one dread was that he might fail her. She was so "decent" to him, he told himself, and he wished he were not so dried up; so cynical. He wished there had never been a Virginia in his life these past four years.

He did not allow himself to dwell on the thought of Virginia, and possibly the evening would have been an unmitigated success but for one unfortunate incident. They went on to a famous night club in the Bois de Boulogne, after seeing the show at the Casino. There, as luck would have it, Barry ran up against a married couple he had known out East. The woman was a talkative, tactless creature and as soon as Barry introduced Joan as "my wife," she exclaimed:

"Oh, so *this* is the wonderful Virginia, Bill and I heard so much about in Nurwaraylia, is it, Barry?"

Dead silence. Joan felt as though somebody had stabbed her. Barry went scarlet, but she dared not look at him. Then he said dryly :

"No—this is Joan, who was Miss Borrow."

"Oh, I see," said the lady; realised her mistake and drifted off.

Barry sat down again at his table opposite Joan. For a moment neither of them spoke. Her heart beat slowly and uncomfortably. She felt herself wishing, wickedly, that Virginia was dead and buried. She raised eyes, from which all light had flown, to Barry's face and saw at once how the incident had affected him. His lips were set; his face grim.

"Oh, damn," she thought miserably. "That's spoiled everything."

It had spoiled a great deal—for him. He felt savagely angry with the woman who had dragged all his thoughts back to that best-forgotten past. Now every nerve was jarred by the memory of those long, lonely years in Nurwaraylia when he had given his whole heart and mind to Virginia; talked of her, worked for her, wanted her sometimes until the ache was intolerable; built up a thousand dreams and schemes around her.

The bitterness of remembering. The mental torture he had endured that first night in London after he had heard of Virginia's marriage was not yet dead. And not yet could he bring himself to think of Virginia, in Italy on her honeymoon, without a bitter pang. Yet he had thrown himself into marriage with her cousin Joan. And here he was in Paris, on *his* honeymoon . . . with a woman who adored him.

He looked at Joan and saw how her face had changed. He guessed that this had hit her on the raw. His lips softened. He leaned across the table and touched her hand.

"Don't be depressed, my dear," he said, trying to speak cheerfully.

"I'm not," she said, and smiled at him.

"She is a dear," he thought.

They neither of them referred to the incident, but it cast a shadow over the rest of the evening.

It was half-past one in the morning when they finished supper, left the night club, and drove back to their hotel. In the taxi Barry put an arm about Joan.

"What a marvellous night!" he said.

She nodded mutely. It was a wonderful night. Paris, in a white blaze of moonlight and canopied by a sky that was sewn thickly with stars. A still spring night, milder than it had been in London. The Arc de Triomphe was black and splendid, silhouetted against the pale, moonlit heaven.

"Enjoyed the show, didn't you, Joan," said Barry.

"M'm, very much."

"And the food."

"Rather."

She was trying so hard to meet him on his own ground and crush the tremendous desire to pull his head down to hers and make love to him crazily. Then suddenly, of his own accord, he turned and put his lips to her mouth. He said nothing. But the passion of his kiss assuaged some of the longing in her heart which seemed to ache and hurt with love for him. She knew by now that he rarely said pretty things, or in fact anything at all in these moods. And he did not want her to speak. So she kissed him back, dumb and quiescent in his arms, and hoped to God that now, at least, he would forget Virginia.

Later, when he came to her room, he found her crying. Against her will—all her resolutions to be gay and cheerful and philosophical about the position into which she had stepped with both eyes open—she dissolved into tears once she was in bed. Possibly because she was tired. It had been a long and fatiguing day.

Then Barry gathered the trembling little figure in the white pyjamas close to his heart, and for once broke through his own reserve.

"Don't cry, Joan, sweetheart," he said. "Don't, my dear. I can't bear you to cry. Have I been a brute to you?"

"No, no—no, of course not!" She clung to him passionately and pressed a wet, flushed cheek to his. "I'm an idiot, Barry darling."

"You're a very nice idiot," he whispered against her tumbled hair. "I'm sorry about that business tonight—it was unfortunate——"

"Forget it—I've forgotten it," she broke in. "Forget everything except that I love you and try and love me a little, my dear. Oh, do, *do*!"

"I love you a lot," he said in answer to that pitiful cry.

In his heart he wished to God that he could forget everything else, but knew that even now, with Joan in his arms, he was thinking how different it would all have been . . . with Virginia. It was a damnable thing, but he could not love this girl as he had loved that first, idolised woman in his life.

He tasted the salt of Joan's tears against his lips and felt the tragedy of the thing from her point of view. And suddenly he closed his mind to everything but the sweetness, the passionate surrender of her in his arms. He whispered:

" Don't cry any more now. Kiss me. I want you to love me, sweetheart."

She gave herself to him without reserve in almost bitter ecstasy, and knew that for a few hours at least he wanted her, and she belonged to him as the other woman never had done.

CHAPTER IV

DURING that month of their honeymoon Joan and Barry grew to know each other very well indeed. The four delightful weeks of intimacy and companionship could not make Joan love Barry much more than she already loved him. They merely confirmed all her previous convictions that he was the one and only man in the world for her.

He was inclined to be selfish; he was moody; he was in many ways difficult. She never quite knew what to expect from him. There were hours when he seemed to need every ounce of love that she could give him; when his own passion rose to her level—and she felt absolutely content— happy that she possessed and was possessed by him. There were days, too, when their comradeship seemed without a flaw. They were in sympathy with each other; shared many tastes and views in common and seemed always to have a great deal to say to each other without growing bored.

Joan was always the same, unvarying, tireless in her efforts to amuse and satisfy him; sweet-tempered and willing to give in to him. She realised that this was a little stupid of her; that it did not do to spoil any man to such an extent. But she could not help herself and it seemed that Barry was not easily spoiled. He was amazingly kind and considerate to her on most occasions and showed a charming anxiety not to hurt or disappoint her.

There were, of course, days and nights when Joan felt that he did not want her at all; when he seemed to withdraw from her love and loving into a tight shell of reticence. On these occasions any attempt on her part to be emotional, or to force him to be so, would have been fatal and Joan knew it. She used the exquisite tact and unselfishness of a woman in love and asked nothing. She was content to wait until the dark, difficult mood left him and he became lover as well as companion again. But during those short spells of reluctance on his part to display any physical or mental desire for her, she suffered. She was bound to suffer, since her own passionate affection for him was always at high pressure.

She felt then that she was divided from him; no use to him; even that her presence fretted him. And on these occasions she took it for granted that it was the thought of that other love of Virginia which separated them. A bitter pill to swallow, but she swallowed it and said nothing, and stepped back into the second place, waiting for Barry to change. Her one dark and secret dread was that one day he might fall into one of his black moods and never change; never want her again. She sometimes tormented herself with that fear. Then when she lay in his arms again and he wanted her and all that she had to offer, she was profoundly and ecstatically happy. The whole thing seemed well worth while, no matter how many the blows to her pride, her vanity, her deep and absorbing passion for him.

In reply to a letter which Joe Halliday wrote, asking her if all was well, she answered:

"Absolutely and entirely happy—so much so that I wonder how long it will last. . . ."

It was a satisfying fact for Joan that by the time her honeymoon was nearly over, Barry's black moods seemed less frequent and his affection for her more marked. That was the surest and most thrilling sign of her success with him. She had set out to make a success of this strange marriage; she meant to achieve it, and it seemed that she would. The shadow of Virginia seemed to fade farther and farther away. Barry never mentioned her. The subject had not been brought up since that night in Paris. Joan could not, of course, know what was going on in his mind, but she guessed, instinctively, that he was not brooding about that unhappy affair. He seemed too cheerful and pleased with life for that.

The four weeks in the south of France did them both good. Joan had needed a holiday from the office for a long time. Her thin face filled out; her body took on new, lovely curves. She bathed every day, and her face and arms and legs tanned in the hot sun to a beautiful golden brown which Barry told her was "distinctly pleasant to behold".

He himself benefited by the change and rest. He had not had one attack of fever since he left England. He also put on weight and his face lost that tired, strained look that he had had before his marriage.

The *Ile des Fleurs* was as enchanting as its name promised it would be. Joan and Barry explored every inch of it; were dressed practically all day in bathing costumes; and spent a lot of time lying on the warm beach sun-bathing after a dip in the water, which was the clear, deep blue of the Mediterranean, and beautifully warm.

There were quaint white fishermen's cottages on the shore all round the island; one straggling cobbled street with a few tiny shops for provisions; and the one solitary hotel in which Barry and Joan were staying. This was the most pretentious building on the island—and about the size of an English village "pub"; Joan found it adorably pretty with its peach-coloured walls; green jalousies; and masses of white and yellow roses climbing all over it. Their bedrooms opened on to balconies from which they could see the beach and water and the browny-green curve of the coast five miles opposite them. It became a habit with them on Sundays to stroll down to the quaint, primitive quay, amongst a crowd of peasants, most of them fisherfolk, and watch the ferry come in with the mail, fuel, and food for the islanders. This was always an occasion for a *fête* and general rejoicing.

Joan need not have feared that Barry would grow tired of the island; its isolated position and lack of amusement. He seemed to welcome the isolation; and, like one tired in body and mind, surrendered all will-power and gave himself up to the luxury of idleness.

The nights were superb, when the whole island seemed

enchanted; ablaze with moonlight and surrounded by a calm sea which was a mirror for the stars, and the hot, still air was rich with the scent of a million roses.

Once when it was too hot to sleep and the sea looked like a smooth sheet of silver in the clear moonlight, Joan and Barry, by mutual consent, left the hotel in bathing costumes, took their towels, and went down to the shore for a nocturnal swim. They were both good swimmers and the water was deliciously cool and smooth. They swam far out, turned back and emerged, two dripping, glistening figures in the white light, and sat side by side on the beach, which was still warm from the sun, and smoked a cigarette.

"I feel glowing all over," said Barry. "It was a grand bathe, Joaney."

"Grand!" she echoed, and began to rub her hair briskly with her towel; the cigarette between her lips.

"Let me do it for you," said Barry.

She laughed and bent towards him.

"Go on, then!"

He applied the towel vigorously to her thick tangle of wet brown hair. She protested in a smothered voice:

"Darling, you're suffocating me!"

He let the towel drop and grinned at her.

"I'm no good as a lady's maid. Joan, you look rather a pet, all wet in the moonlight like this. Your arms and neck are like bronze, they're so sun-burned. Heavens, child, you'll never be able to wear an evening dress again."

"What's it matter?" she said happily.

"Not a hoot, my dear."

She stretched her arms above her head and gave a little shiver.

"It's getting chilly. Let's run in."

"You haven't caught cold, have you?"

"Lord, no. But I think it's time to get back to bed. It must be nearly one a.m."

"Think of doing this in England—Brighton, eh?"

"Don't, Barry, it would be freezing."

They stood up and he looked round with appreciative eyes. There were palm trees fringing the white, sandy shore. It was like a tropical island, this *Ile des Fleurs*. It appealed to him, and Joan loved it. He knew that. She looked awfully happy and well with her brown face and shining eyes and he knew that he was a great deal fonder of her now, three weeks after marriage, than he had been at first. He wondered if their delightful comradeship and this peaceful state of affairs would continue. No doubt they would—if he let them. It lay in his hands. He was positive of Joan's love. It was himself that he did not trust. For he knew, only too well, that the thought of Virginia was by no means eradicated from his mind; neither had he recovered from the bitterness of losing her.

But he had been much happier with Joan than he had expected to be, and he felt tonight that there was every chance of making a success of things with her. He told himself that it would be so, providing he did not see Virginia again. He must never again come in contact with her. Well, he never would. She was married to Kingleigh and they were not likely to run across each other now.

Joan flung her towel over her shoulder and threw away her cigarette-end.

"Race you to the hotel," she said.

"Good God, I'm much too old and decrepit to run——" began Barry.

But Joan had sped on and he would have been ashamed not to follow. He was not going to let a slip of a girl beat him. Good Lord, hadn't he won the quarter at the school sports in his last term? He used to think himself a hell of a fellow at running.

But Joan had the start and the advantage and his pursuit of her failed ignominiously. He called after her as her slim, half-naked figure vanished into the hotel:

"Ssh—don't make a row——"

She laughed, did not stop, and rushed up the wooden, uncarpeted stairs two at a time. Barry, panting, followed her. She turned and faced him in her bedroom.

"Got you beat!"

"Little devil," he said, half annoyed. "I haven't any wind left."

"Out of condition," she laughed breathlessly.

"Don't you jeer at me, my child. I'll get even with you."

"How?"

The lamps were not lit, but the moon poured through the open, unshuttered windows, and lit up her glowing face and made her look extraordinarily provocative. Barry looked at the slim, clean lines of the young figure and felt his blood stir. The possession of his wife was still a new and rather enchanting thing despite the fact that he was not in love in the way that she was.

"How are you going to get even with me, honey?" she asked him.

"Like this," he said, and catching her round the waist with one hand, peeled off her tight wet swimming suit with the other.

Her laughing face grew warm and passionate, but she tried to hold him off; her fingers pressed against his wrist.

"Shy of me?" he said.

"Yes, a little . . ." Then her cool bare arms went round his neck and she pressed her warm cheek against his. "Oh, darling, darling, *darling*, I *do* love you so!"

"I like you a bit myself," he said huskily, and lifted her right up into his arms.

She wondered, later, when he lay asleep, supine, warm, breathing deeply and regularly beside her, just how long this tremendous happiness would endure, and whether Barry really loved her more now than he used to.

She was still too stirred, too ecstatic after his embrace, to close her eyes and sleep. But it was always the same. Barry flamed, suddenly, into these passionate moods, and as suddenly the flame flickered out. She tried to accustom herself to it; to realise that he was like that, temperamentally. But at times it troubled and saddened her. It seemed so obviously a sign that his passion was entirely physical and that he did not share her mental rapture, that elation which was so much of the mind as well as body. Perhaps all men were the same. She did not know. But she would have liked him to hold her in his arms a little longer and tell her all the fond and foolish things which are of such tremendous importance to a woman.

She never dreamed of speaking to him about this. Her one dread was that she might make him tired of her, or irritate him by too much love. But it was inevitable that she should feel that it was because he did not care for her in the way she wanted that he was so undemonstrative, and his moments of passion so brief. Inevitable, too, that she should hurt herself by thinking:

"With Virginia he would have been different."

Tonight she was restless, excited, unable to sleep. She envied him his calm slumber. She could just see the faint, dark outline of his head beside her, and she watched him silently, with that ache of the heart that he could not appease, just because her body was satisfied.

CHAPTER V

BARRY and Joan came back to England from their honeymoon and stayed two nights in Town. They had half made up their minds, out in France, to start life in the country, and London was so fine and warm the first week in June that it finally decided them in favour of the country.

They agreed to look for a cottage in the neighbourhood of Horsham. It was lovely country all round that part of Sussex and there was Manning Heath Golf Course for Barry; Brighton less than an hour away if they wanted the sea; and London within easy and agreeable reach.

"We'll stay at some little country pub, my dear, and wander round Horsham in the car and find something attractive which we can rent," Barry said. "We won't buy because you know what a restless devil I am, and if you buy a place it's a millstone round your neck if you do want a change."

"I quite agree," said Joan.

"We might take a trip out East later," he said.

"That would be marvellous fun," she said.

They separated, the morning after they arrived in London. Barry had an appointment with his solicitor and business concerning his uncle's estate. Joan found plenty to do alone. She went round to her old "digs" in Victoria where her few belongings were stored, and arranged for Mrs. Fletcher to keep them a few weeks longer until she was settled. It gave her a most delightful sensation of happiness to go back to that dreary house under the existing conditions. Now that she was Barry's wife and had belonged to him for a month, she wondered how she had ever endured those lonely, depressing years as Joan Borrow, reporter on the *Hand Mirror*. She deliberately made herself recall the torture she had gone through when her cousin, Virginia, had first told her that she was going to marry Barry when he came back from Ceylon next time. The unhappy nights when she had wept herself sick and blind—loving Barry without hope.

After all the pain and hopelessness it was heaven to be as she was now. She told herself that that was the way to appreciate a thing; to suffer and want it for years before one got it.

Of course she had to go down to Fleet Street and call at the Chartwood Press. It was rather pleasant to go into the big, busy, noisy building and see all the familiar faces and realise that she was no longer a struggling reporter, but Mrs. Barry Elderton—the wife of a man she adored.

She walked into Halliday's office looking so radiant that Joe was dumb for a moment when he saw her. He sat back in his chair and gaped at her. Then he exploded:

"Joan dear . . . *you* . . . oh, my *dear*!"

She was touched by his evident pleasure at seeing her again. He sprang up and clasped both her hands tightly.

"Dear child—how lovely to see you again."

"It's nice to see you, Joe."

"How are you?"

"How do I look?"

He shook his head as he scrutinised the brown, glowing face, and read the happiness in those very blue eyes which still seemed to him the most beautiful in the world.

"My dear, you look as though you've walked straight out of paradise into this dusty old office."

"So I have!" she laughed.

"Then it's a success, dear?"

"It certainly is!"

He dropped her hands and sighed.

"I'm glad, Joan dear, but I've missed you like hell."

She looked round the room. She felt almost ashamed to show her great happiness to this man who had loved her. She said:

"I've often thought of you all. Is Mac all right?"

He nodded toward the communicating door.

"In there—just the same."

"I must go and chat with her. And my successor?"

"Rather a pretty little girl."

"Ah ha!" said Joan.

Halliday's big face grew very grave.

"Ah, no, my dear. Nobody can ever replace you."

"You mustn't say that, Joe."

"Well, I do, Joan dear. But I'm quite satisfied to see you so happy. May it last. Husband fit?"

"Very. We're house-hunting down in Sussex tomorrow."

Margaret walked in. The same old Mac, thought Joan. Cretonne overall; bundles of papers; cigarettes; grouse about the artists. She greeted Joan with enthusiasm.

"My dear, how nice to see you. And how is our little bride?"

"A much-married woman," said Joan, laughing.

"She looks all right, doesn't she, Joe?" said Mac.

"Well, I don't think Elderton beats her," he said.

"Come and yap with me, Joan," said Mac. "It's an age since I last saw you and I've missed you, my dear."

They had all missed her. Joan was touched and gratified. She left the Chartwood Press feeling thoroughly pleased with life. It was a marvellous existence at the moment and the best thing of all was this going back to Barry. They were meeting for lunch at Brown's Hotel where they were staying.

Some of the elation cooled down a little when she walked into her bedroom and found Barry marching up and down with a face like thunder.

"Oh, my dear, what *has* happened?" she exclaimed.

He turned to her, frowning.

"Oh, I've had a filthy morning with old Tatham."

"But why?" She took off her hat, walked to the dressing-table, and combed her hair.

"My uncle's will. He's left all kinds of instructions with Tatham about investments. I can't explain—you wouldn't understand."

"I might." She looked at him anxiously.

"Well, anyhow, I don't approve of a lot of it and it seems I'm tied hand and foot. The snag is that I can't get hold of much ready cash and with the stock market in the state it is both here and in the States, we look like being hard up for a bit."

Her face cleared. Was that all? Money meant so little compared to other things. She had been afraid, for a moment, that he was annoyed with her, personally.

"Darling," she said, "I don't mind being poor. Will we be very poor?"

She sat on the edge of the bed, took off her shoes and changed her stockings, which had laddered. Barry hunched his shoulders.

"No. Not exactly poor. I've got my own money—my savings from Ceylon—and we shall have a couple of thousand a year in time. But my uncle's made everything so difficult. He always had crazy ideas about investments and trusts. I've been arguing with Tatham for an hour and a half. If the whole country doesn't go to pot, we shall be all right—in time. But we'll have to go slow."

"What's that matter?"

"I don't care about it much," said Barry shortly.

Joan sat still for a moment and stared at him, then at the floor. Her cheeks reddened a little. Of course—Barry, not being in love, would mind about the financial side of things. The ecstasies of the morning fell a bit flat as she reflected upon this. She walked across the room to the window out of which Barry was gazing. She laid a hand on his shoulder.

"Darling—I'll be very economical and it doesn't spoil things for me a bit. Please don't let it spoil them for you."

His eyes softened. He patted her hand.

"Nice old thing . . ."

She rubbed her head against his arm.

"I'd be perfectly happy in a garret with you, Barry."

He said:

"I'm not built like that, I'm afraid, my dear."

She bit her lip. Was that so? Or was it just because he was not in love? Would he have minded having to economise with Virginia? *Damn the thought of Virginia*. Would she ever be able to kill the gnawing sensation of jealousy that accompanied it?

She smiled up at Barry.

"Cheer up, darling—I expect things will turn out all right."

"Oh, yes," he said.

He did not offer to kiss her and she did not ask him to. She felt none too happy during lunch. But Barry seemed to recover his spirits.

"What the hell's it matter? I'm an evil-tempered brute, Joan. Sorry, sweetheart. Let's go to the cinema."

"But you loathe pictures!" she said, happy again just because of that "sweetheart" and the tenderness in those queer light-coloured eyes of his.

" But you like 'em. . . ." He felt remorseful, afraid that he had hurt her by his bluntness just before lunch. But fond though he was of her, he could not truthfully have said he could share a garret and poverty with her and be happy. That was the sort of thing one only felt about one woman once only, and never again.

He was charming to Joan for the rest of that afternoon, and she was entirely content once more when they came out of the Plaza Theatre and returned to their hotel.

When Joan was changing for dinner, still in her house-coat, busily manicuring her nails, Barry came into her room in a lover-like mood which enchanted her. He bent and kissed the nape of her neck.

" You're brown as a quadroon maid, my Infant."

She put up a hand and stroked his hair, her heart beating fast, her eyes shining.

" Do you like your quadroon maid ? "

" Very much."

He was half dressed; black trousers, boiled shirt, collarless; thick dark hair standing on end, waiting for comb and brilliantine. Joan adored him like that. He looked such a boy. She stood up and leaned against him, threading her fingers through the untidy hair.

" You're not disappointed in me, are you ? " she asked in a low voice.

" Why should I be ? "

" I mean—do you find marriage frightfully irksome ? "

" A bit," he teased her.

" No—really. Can you bear it ? "

" I rather like it."

" My dear——" Her heart beat very fast indeed and she clung to him closely, her arms about his neck. " I'm an awful idiot about you, honey. I'm so sensible and prosaic and unsentimental with everybody else but I go all to pieces with you."

He held her close and kissed her eyelids.

" That's all right, funny old thing—go to pieces with me. I really don't mind."

" I don't bore you ? "

" Good Lord, no. I'm so afraid I bore you. I'm not nearly as nice to you as you are to me."

" You are."

"I'm not. I know it. But I feel a lot I don't say to you."

"Do you?" she asked wistfully.

"Yes—honestly. Look here, Joan, I'll tell you this much —I enjoyed every moment of our honeymoon on the *Ile des Fleurs* and I really don't know why I ever doubted that I'd be happy with you. You're an ideal wife and companion."

That from him was praise indeed. She thrilled to her finger-tips.

"I'm so glad, Barry."

"When we arranged to get married," he continued, stroking her hair with his right hand, "I told you I could never love you in the way you loved me. You know why . . ."

"Yes . . ." she held her breath. And for an instant the memory of Virginia was between them; and there was a sharp pain in her heart, like a knife, cutting her.

"Well, my dear, that business is over and done with, and I never think of it now. *She* is married to another fellow and you're my wife. If it makes you happy to know that I'm damn glad I married you—well, there it is! I am."

"It makes me terribly happy to know it . . ." The tears rushed to her eyes; the first tears she had shed since that first night of their wedding in Paris. "I just adore you."

"We're going to make a good thing of our lives together, dear," he said, holding her closely.

"Barry, go on feeling that way."

"Why, sure," he said softly, mimicking the American accent.

"Nothing will change you now, will it?"

"What can?"

"Oh, I don't know——" The tears suddenly rolled down her cheeks. She felt weak and emotional. "I suppose I care for you so much, Barry, that I'm afraid."

"Of what?"

"That one day you won't want me—that you'll be sorry you married me."

"Never. You mustn't cry, old thing. I'm not worth all the love you give me."

"You are," she said passionately. "I think you are, anyway. Only supposing . . ."

"Well?"

"Supposing you ever saw Gina again," she burst out.

An instant's silence. She fancied she felt his arms relax. Had she? Or was it imagination? It was stupid to mention

Virginia, but the thing tumbled out . . . the thing that was permanently secret torment and dread to her.

Then he said quietly:

"I don't want to see Virginia again. It's better I shouldn't."

Her heart gave a sick twist.

"That means you still love her, then," she said in an anguished voice.

It was very stupid indeed. But she could not help herself. Barry took his arms away from her.

"For God's sake don't let's talk of her," he said with sudden violence. "I've done with that business. I don't want to remember it or the fact that I loved Virginia. I don't love her any more. She belongs to Kingleigh and I belong to you."

Joan looked at him with big, unhappy eyes. She only half believed him. She thought that he was lying in order to make her happy. If he did not love Virginia any more, what would it matter to him whether he saw her or not? She was mad to have this sort of conversation, anyhow. It was destructive to their peace; their closeness. She felt suddenly terrified and flung herself into his arms again.

"Nothing on God's earth matters so long as you love me a little," she said in a stifled voice.

"I love you a lot, my dear . . . but you mustn't make yourself unhappy about the past."

"I'm a fool. . . ."

"You're a dear. Dry your eyes and kiss me. . . . You mean much more to me that I ever dreamed you would, and nothing is going to spoil things for us now."

"Oh, I'm glad, I'm glad, my sweet," she whispered.

He took fire from the passion of her lips and the sweetness of her trembling, straining body. She gave herself to him and felt that he was giving himself more completely than he had ever done; that mentally as well as physically he was close to her tonight. Her ecstasy was complete. The shadow of Virginia grew so faint that it became negligible.

Before he left her to complete her dressing, he held her very close to him and said:

"Thank you, darling—you *do* mean a hell of a lot, you know."

He had never called her "darling" before. She closed her eyes and gave him a last, convulsive little hug.

"So do you. We are a disgraceful pair. We shall be late for dinner."

"Damn dinner," he said cheerfully, and walked back to his room.

She felt that that was the greatest compliment he had ever paid her.

They were late for dinner, but neither seemed to care very much. They decided to dine in the hotel. As they walked through the lounge a page came up to Joan.

"Please, madam, you are wanted on the telephone."

"On the phone—me!" Joan looked at her husband in surprise. "Now I wonder who——"

"Lady Brame is the name, madam," said the page.

Joan knit her brows.

"What on earth can Aunt Milly want? If you'll excuse me, Barry——"

"Of course," he said, opened an evening paper and turned to the Test Match result, which seemed to interest him more than Lady Brame's telephone call.

Joan answered the telephone, a little frown puckering her brows. It was so extraordinary—Aunt Milly phoning her up at this time of night.

"Hello—is that you, Aunt Milly?" she said, picking up the receiver in the call-box.

"Hello—is that Joan?" came a faint voice.

"Yes, it is."

"Oh, Joan, my dear child, I'm so *glad* to have caught you. It's the fourth or fifth time I've telephoned today. Haven't you had a message from me?"

"No—none."

"How careless of them. Joan, I've been wanting to get hold of you, my dear, but I thought you were still abroad on your honeymoon, and I hadn't the heart to spoil it with my sad news."

"Sad news!" echoed Joan. "But what, Aunt Milly? What's happened . . . ?"

"Poor darling Gina . . ." came the faint voice with a break in it.

Joan's heart gave a queer twist.

"Nothing's happened to Gina, has it?"

"To her, no. But to her husband, poor dear Ian——"

"What?"

"Oh, Joan—it's too tragic, my dear. He's dead!"

Silence a moment. Joan's heart beat very fast now and her cheeks felt fiery hot.

"Ian—dead?" she repeated stupidly. "No—it's impossible."

"It does seem so. Too awful—and they had only been married a few weeks."

"But how—where—how did it happen?"

"In Italy. Of heart. He had a very weak heart. Virginia never dreamed . . . nor did I. The doctors there said it was angina. He must have suffered dreadful pains at times, poor man, and never let her know—dear, brave Ian. It was a ghastly shock for my poor Gina. So terribly sudden . . . I can't go into details on the telephone, but Gina will tell you everything."

Joan swallowed hard.

"But, Aunt Milly—when did it happen?"

"A fortnight ago. The funeral is over. Gina's home with me, of course."

Joan's head was whirling. Ian Kingleigh dead and buried. Good heavens, it seemed incredible; such a brief while ago that she had attended the reception after Gina's wedding and Ian had brought her a drink; spoken to her in that kindly, courteous way of his. She had thought at the time that he looked tired and ill; but never imagined that any fatal disease was threatening his life. Poor old Ian! Poor Virginia! This meant that Virginia was a widow; a widow after three weeks of married life. It was ghastly.

". . . must come round tonight." She became aware of her aunt's voice again. "Don't refuse, dear. It's Gina's special wish. She won't see anybody, but she has particularly asked to see you. You will come, won't you?"

Joan stammered:

"I—I must see—my husband—I——"

"Yes, yes, of course—it seems so strange to think of our little Joan with a husband, and dear Barry, too. Perhaps Barry will come and talk to me while you are upstairs with Gina."

"I don't suppose he will," said Joan wildly, then added: "I'll come, of course, if Gina wants me. Good-bye, Aunt Milly. . . ."

She hung up the receiver. Her hand was cold and shaking

although her cheeks felt hot. A queer cold hand seemed to be clutching her heart. She walked slowly back to the lounge, where she had left Barry. She dreaded facing him; telling him this news. It was the last thing in the world she wanted to tell him—that Virginia was a widow. Had been a widow for a fortnight. And, of course, the horrible, hurtful question leapt to Joan's confused mind like a flash:

"*Would he have married me when he did if he'd known that two weeks later Gina would be free?*"

Barry was still studying his paper. He looked up as she approached him and smiled.

"I say, Joan—not a bad score—hello—what's wrong, Infant?"

He had seen the look in her eyes. Her face was quite white. He regarded her anxiously.

"Have you had bad news, old thing?"

Bad news, yes, bad from every point of view, she thought. A tragedy for Ian Kingleigh; a tragedy for Virginia; and a tragedy for Barry and for her. She answered dully:

"Ian Kingleigh's dead, Barry."

"Kingleigh!" he exclaimed.

"Yes. Virginia's husband. Apparently he had a 'heart.' He died of angina in Italy two weeks ago. It's all over and done with. The honeymoon ended with a funeral—horrible, isn't it? . . ." She moistened her lips with her tongue, nervously, avoiding his gaze. "Virginia is home and asking to see me. Aunt Milly insists that I go round tonight."

Silence. Then Joan had to look at Barry. When she saw his face it told her nothing. It was expressionless. Stony. Too stony. It was a mask—hiding something. What? She did not know. But she told herself, in agony, that that same thought had leapt to his mind. If he had waited; if he had known Virginia was free again; *would he have married her?*

Then Barry spoke; quite casually.

"What a tragic business. Let's have our meal, my dear. We're frightfully late."

Nothing; no outburst from him; no hint as to what this news meant to him. Of course—it was so typical of Barry to hide everything he felt. She walked beside him into the restaurant. Her own face was set and without life in it. She thought:

"Oh, damn, *damn!* Why need this have happened?"

Upstairs, half an hour ago, she had lain in his arms and his lips had been fervent and demanding upon hers. She had felt that he was wholly her lover. He had told her that he did not love Virginia any more; that he belonged to her, his wife. She had come downstairs with him, radiantly happy, confident of their future happiness.

And now it was all swept away; all the hope; the confidence; all her ecstasy. They had both thrust Virginia outside their scheme of things. But she had thrust her way back; unwittingly, but surely. Through her tragic and sudden loss of her husband she had found her way back into their lives. Barry had wanted to finish with her; she, Joan, had felt that it *was* all finished; because Barry belonged to her and Virginia to another man. But the death of that other man had altered things . . . reopened the past. It was not finishing. It was just beginning again.

Joan felt as though a horrible blight had suddenly settled upon the flower of her happiness; destroying the freshness, the bloom of it. Virginia was no longer safely tied to another man. She was free again and therefore accessible. And Joan knew that Barry must remind himself of that fact. *God*, how awful, if he regretted his haste in marrying her.

Yet he said nothing and he gave her no real reason to believe that Kingleigh's death had altered his feelings in any way. He was charming to her during dinner; attentive; showing no more than ordinary interest in Kingleigh's death. Joan talked about it also, attaching only ordinary importance to the tragedy.

"So terrible for Gina," she said, not daring to meet Barry's eyes. She stared at her food which she left untasted.

"Yes, a dreadful affair. Of course you must go round to Greyes Street if she wants you, Joan."

"Yes, I will. Aunt Milly wondered if you——"

"No, I shan't come," he broke in quickly. "I'll go round to the Club if you don't mind, my dear. I'll get a game of bridge."

"Yes, all right," she said.

"I shan't be late and I don't suppose you will be."

"No—I shall just see Gina for a bit and come back."

"Don't tire yourself out," he added. "You look fagged as it is."

"Oh, no—I'm all right," she forced a laugh. She looked

at him. He smiled at her and lit a cigarette. But she fancied that his smile was as forced as her laugh. She thought:

"Isn't he being a bit too casual about it, and a bit too attentive to me? Doesn't it prove that he's thoroughly shaken by the whole business?"

Yes, she was sure of it. The gay comradeship and intimacy of upstairs was all gone . . . spoiled, killed by Virginia's tragedy. She was alone with him, here, and he was her husband, and she his wife. But Virginia was with them; the shadowy third. Joan could almost feel her presence between them.

She had never felt less like separating from Barry than she did this evening. But she left him without betraying an atom of what she felt. That would have been a fatal thing to do, and she knew it. Whatever she did, she must not show what was in her mind now. As though the affair made no personal difference to them, she said:

"Well, so long, Barry darling. See you later. I'll be back soon after ten, I expect."

"Bye-bye," he said. "I'll put you in a taxi. I'll be back from the Club after a rubber or two. You'll tell Virginia how frightfully sorry I am, won't you?"

Very polite; formal; even stilted. Joan set her teeth and climbed into the taxi. She fancied she saw all the old hurt, all the old bitterness in his eyes, contradicting the indifference of his voice. The taxi rolled away and she lost sight of Barry. She sat back in a corner and stared blindly at the passing traffic.

CHAPTER VI

VIRGINIA'S boudoir, with a dim, religious light filtering through an exquisite Lalique glass lamp on a small table beside the sofa. Virginia lying on the sofa, her smooth dark head and pale face like a perfect cameo against great cushions of deep gold and blue and jade. Virginia in unrelieved black, accentuating the pallor of her throat and the slim pale hands clasped behind her head. No touch of colour except the bright vermilion of her lips; a cigarette between them;

long, lovely eyes veiled by heavy lashes which glittered with tears. An odd picture of grief and of devil-may-care. A true picture of the real Virginia, Joan thought when she entered that boudoir after a short conversation with Aunt Milly. Selfish, sensual, luxury-loving; with real emotion and tears hidden away for occasions.

Was she as shocked, as grieved by the sudden loss of her husband as she ought to be? Who could tell? The tears were there; gleaming on the heavy lashes. But the lipstick was there, too; the perfection of make-up on the beautiful face; the studied charm of the "cocktail suit" and mourning in one.

It was hot in Virginia's boudoir.

Joan took off her corded silk coat and sat down in a chair beside her cousin.

When she had left the hotel she had fancied she looked rather nice in one of the new dresses, bought in Paris, and her hair had been shampooed and "set" this morning in Dover Street. But as soon as she was with Virginia she felt the old sensation of inferiority so far as appearance went; of dowdiness. She could never be as perfect as Virginia. Somehow, tonight, she resented the feeling, bitterly.

"It's nice of you to come, Joan," said Virginia.

"I'm most terribly sorry about this, Gina."

"Yes, it's a ghastly thing to have happened."

"Tell me about it . . . if you want to."

Virginia took the cigarette from her lips and stubbed the end on an ash-tray beside her. Joan, studying her closely, saw that she looked tired and strained. No doubt the tragedy abroad and the subsequent events had been nerve-racking for her, poor girl. Joan's feelings softened.

"Would you rather not tell me about it, my dear? . . ."

"No. That's all right. There's so little to tell. I had no idea Ian had a bad heart. He kept it from me, but his physician over here tells me that he warned Ian months ago to go carefully. I feel so guilty. I wanted to climb up the mountains behind our hotel one afternoon. It was very hot. Ian didn't seem keen and I laughed at him. So he came, poor dear. And then it happened. He was lagging behind me. I heard him gasp. I turned round to rag him about 'old age'. He was bent with agony and he just collapsed and died—in my arms."

"Gina—how dreadful."

Virginia put a hand to her head for a moment.

"It was—I can't forgive myself—for making him come with me."

"You mustn't blame yourself. It wasn't your fault. You didn't know."

"No. Well—then I ran for help and he was taken back to the hotel, but of course he was beyond aid. It was angina pectoris. I sent for Mummy. She came out. Ian's solicitor, Mr. Appleton, came with her. Ian wished to be buried in England. So—we brought him home. It's only two weeks ago. It seems two years to me."

"Of course—poor old Gina!" Joan leaned forward, took her cousin's hand and pressed it.

Virginia drew a long sigh.

"Well—it's all over. Married—widowed within a month. I don't feel I've been married at all somehow. Poor old Ian must have known what a rocky condition he was in because he took care to make a will before our marriage. Mr. Appleton told me so. He has left me—everything."

"Yes, I suppose so," said Joan.

She thought:

"Virginia has always had everything. She didn't want to marry Ian really. She only wanted financial security, and now she has it—a title and her freedom. Everything!"

Everything except Barry. A fierce little feeling of exultation which she could not restrain gripped Joan as she thought of Barry. Barry was hers . . . yes, Virginia would never have him now.

"I've got about twenty thousand pounds a year, including my marriage settlement," continued Virginia. "And Claydown Manor down in Worth. Heavens—what shall I do with such a vast place? Sell it, I suppose?"

"Will you live with Aunt Milly now?"

"I think so. Perhaps we'll shut up this house and go to Worth for the rest of the summer. It all seems so queer —without Ian. I feel so—lost. He was awfully nice to me, Joan."

"He was a dear," said Joan.

"And now," said Virginia, "let's talk about you. Enough of me. How are things?"

She opened her eyes wide as though to take stock of her

cousin. Joan felt herself colouring for no reason at all. But her heart-beats quickened as she said:

"I'm very happy, Gina."

Virginia said:

"I can't get over your marrying Barry. It astounded me."

"Why?" said Joan defiantly.

"Well—you know why. Barry was supposed to be devoted to me——" Virginia averted her gaze now and took a cigarette from a shagreen box at her side. "And within a few weeks of coming back from the East—he married you."

"Not unnatural," said Joan, tight-lipped. "He couldn't be expected to go on adoring you when you'd married someone else—could he?"

"No." Virginia's pale face flushed and paled again. Her delicate nostrils dilated. "I suppose not. But he knew that I *had* to marry Ian—didn't he?"

"That was hardly excusable in his eyes."

"Did he say so?"

Joan also took a cigarette and lit it, but her hands trembled slightly. She hated this conversation. In a queer way it frightened her.

"No. He said you had a right to choose, but that he could not understand it. After all, he had adored you for four years. You let him down so suddenly. You ought to have played a bit fairer—that's all."

"I see," said Virginia. "So he turned to you for consolation."

Joan's chin went up.

"Barry and I were always pals."

"Were you in love with him?"

"Yes."

"I didn't know that."

"No—I don't suppose anybody did."

"Is he in love with you now?"

Joan's heart-beats hurt her. She looked at Virginia through a cloud of smoke and said, almost harshly:

"Don't let's dissect each other's feelings about this, Gina. It—isn't very pleasing to me."

"I'm sorry, my dear," Virginia shrugged her shoulders. "I was only asking you."

Joan swallowed hard. Only asking. Yes, wanting to find

out whether Barry was in love with her or had married her on the rebound. But she was not going to give Virginia the satisfaction of knowing that she still came first with Barry and that his wife occupied second place and always would.

"Barry and I are very happy," she said curtly.

"I'm glad. I'm sure you'd make a good wife to any man," said Virginia.

"Thanks," said Joan.

"Joan—why are you so horrid with me?"

Joan tried to stop trembling.

"I'm sorry, Gina. I—it doesn't seem decent somehow for us to discuss Barry like this. You used to be engaged to Barry. Well—he's married to me now. Can't we leave it at that?"

"Certainly," said Virginia coldly. "But why be so melodramatic about it all?"

Joan gritted her teeth. It was like Virginia to put her in the wrong, make her feel a fool. Perhaps she was being a fool. But it drove her crazy to discuss Barry with this woman whom she knew Barry had loved so much more than he loved her.

She said more calmly:

"Barry asked me to tell you how sorry he is about Ian's death."

"Tell him," said Virginia, "that I would like to see him."

Joan bit hard at her lip. She smoked in silence for an instant, then said:

"Do you think that's—wise?"

"Don't be a fool, Joan. Why can't we behave sensibly over this? Barry was a very old friend of mine, as well as a lover, and can still be a friend even if he is married to you, can't he? Or are you one of these jealous wives?"

Joan felt suddenly murderous. But she looked straight into her cousin's faintly mocking eyes and said:

"Not at all. I'll tell Barry you'd like to see him."

"I'll drop him a note," said Virginia. "There really isn't any reason why we shouldn't all be friends. And now Ian's dead I need a man friend. I've got so many responsibilities—I don't understand finance—but Barry does. He was always so good about investments and things."

It was on the tip of Joan's tongue to tell Virginia that

Ian's solicitors would be the best advisers so far as her investments were concerned, but she desisted. Gina obviously wanted to see Barry and renew their old friendship. Joan was jealous. She admitted it to herself. Horribly jealous. She could not bear the idea of Barry and Virginia meeting again. It made her feel wretched. But she was not going to prevent their meeting. That was the last thing she would do—if Barry wanted to see Gina. She would leave it to him.

All the same, she remembered that he had said it was best he should not see Gina. That had suggested to her at the time that he was afraid of seeing her again; that he knew his love for her was not dead.

The whole situation frightened Joan. But she told herself not to be a fool. She said:

"Barry and I won't be in Town much longer."

"Where will you be?"

"We're looking for a cottage near Horsham."

"That's only a short run from Worth. How nice."

Joan felt trapped. She did not want to stay here and talk to Virginia. Somehow she felt that she could never be friends with her cousin again; never revive the old, friendly feeling that had once existed between them. She wanted to walk out of this house, out of Virginia's life, and take Barry with her. But Virginia was coolly and calmly making plans to keep them both within the circle of her scheme of things. She got off the sofa and walked to her writing bureau and switched on another lamp.

"I'll write a line to Barry and perhaps you'll give it to him, Joan."

"Certainly."

Joan followed the tall, graceful figure with her gaze. She thought:

"What a beautiful figure Virginia has. Barry admires tall, slim women. No wonder he was madly in love with her. And he has a passion for nice hands. Virginia's hands are wonderful—so narrow—so tapering—oh, damn, *damn* . . . why did Gina have to come back?"

She stared at her own square, sensible hands. Much typewriting and office work had ruined her nails. They would never be filbert, delicate, beautiful like Gina's. And she was short; and she had freckles and she carried herself badly. Barry had laughed at her out in France and told her she was getting round shouldered. She would never have Gina's graceful, stately carriage.

Joan was ashamed of herself. But she did not want Barry to see Gina again and revive the past. It was beastly of her. She ought to trust him. But she had not married him under ordinary conditions. She had married him *knowing* that he was still in love with Gina. If only he would refuse to see Gina. Perhaps he would.

Virginia came back with a sealed letter.

" Give that to Barry—thanks awfully, Joan."

Joan folded it and put it in her bag.

" Right you are," she said.

Virginia paused beside her and picked up a fold of her dress.

" Nice stuff," she murmured. " Good shade of blue, too. Brings out the colour in your eyes. Get it in Town ? "

" No—in Paris. It's Balmain."

" I thought so. It's a good line, but your slip needs attention here——" she touched Joan's shoulder with one of her delicate fingers. " You want that tightened up."

Joan nodded. But she resented even that piece of advice. She knew Virginia was right about the straps. Somehow Virginia had a genius for dress and dressing. Joan always made a mistake. And Barry had such a quick eye for clothes ; for perfection in detail. Had he noticed the loose straps of the slip but been too nice to say so, just because he knew how she liked him to praise her ?

She rose and moved restlessly away from her cousin.

" I'm not going to stay, Gina, my dear. I've got to get back to Barry."

" How funny it seems—you as Barry's wife. I can't get over it."

" No—it seems a bit funny to me," said Joan dryly.

Virginia lit her third cigarette. Her nerves were bad and she was smoking too much. But she did not let Joan guess that she felt quite unreasonably irritated by the thought of any woman being married to Barry. She resented the fact that Joan was going back to him.

Barry had always seemed her possession. Virginia was essentially a possessive creature. She wanted to keep what was hers, even though she did not make any effort to keep it. Far from making an effort to keep Barry, she had deliberately shelved him for Ian. But now Ian was dead, and she was

free—and rich into the bargain. If only Barry had waited
... that thought ran riot in her brain tonight. What a
fool he had been to rush into matrimony with Joan. Joan was
a dear, but Barry could not be terribly in love; at least
not in the way he had been in love with *her*.

She knew, intuitively, that Barry had given something to
her that he would not give to another woman. She knew
him so well. He was built like that. She had been crazy
about him, in her selfish way. Tonight, face to face with
Barry's wife, she felt a more urgent desire to see him and
get in touch with him again than she had ever known in the
past. She had never cared for poor old Ian that way. Barry
had been first, so this was no disloyalty to Ian's memory.
The maddening thing was the fact that Barry had got married.
If it had not been for Joan, she felt that she could have
stretched out a hand and drawn Barry straight back ... on
the old footing. That would have been singularly pleasant.

"Well, thanks for coming round, Joan," she said, and
added, with one of her slow, attractive smiles: "Don't let
Barry be horrid to me, because I'd like us all to be friends,
now that Ian is gone."

Virginia's charm when she smiled like that, spoke like
that, was undeniable, and even Joan felt it. She had to
smile back.

"Blast my cousin Virginia," she thought. "She twists
everybody round her finger. Here she is, asking *me*, of all
people, to bring her and Barry together again. My God!"

But aloud she found herself saying:

"Barry will come and see you, I'm sure. Good night, Gina."

"Good night, my dear."

Joan took a taxi back to Brown's Hotel. It was half-past
ten. Barry was not yet back. Joan had a bath and went
to bed and started a book which Barry had bought from *The
Times* Book Club this morning. But she could not concentrate on the book. Her mind was such a confusion of
thought about Gina, Barry, herself. And Gina's letter to
Barry lay on the dressing-table, awaiting him. That letter,
summoning him back to her. Would he go? He had loved
her very much. If she wanted him, surely he would go.
Joan felt depressed and lonely. She wished Barry would
come back. She would like to feel his arms round her for a
few moments; to hold him close; to tell herself that he was

her husband and that a thousand Ginas could not take him from her.

He was late in coming back. He became thoroughly involved in bridge and could not get away. It was a quarter to twelve when Joan heard him open the door of his own room. She had abandoned her book and was lying in darkness, brooding over the thought of Virginia. She sat up when the light from Barry's bedroom slanted through the communicating door and pierced the gloom of her room.

"Barry!" she called out.

"Hello—you awake?" he answered.

She switched on her lamp. He came in, taking off his jacket; yawning. She felt absurdly pleased to see him. She wanted to stretch out her arms and draw him down to her breast. But somehow she could not do it tonight. If there was to be any love-making, it must come from him first of all.

Barry-like, he made no rush to kiss her. He strolled about her room, talking about the bridge and the Club and his good luck; he had won a fiver; and some man he had met there who had just lost a fortune on Wall Street. He seemed in no hurry to question her about her visit to Virginia, and he did not notice the forlorn and wistful look in her eyes as she watched him, her arms clasped about her hunched knees.

Then his gaze lighted on the envelope on Joan's dressing-table with the name "Barry" on it in a familiar hand. He put down the collar which he had just taken off and picked up the letter.

"This for me.

"Yes," said Joan.

"What's she want?" he asked abruptly. And added as he ripped open the flap: "How is she, by the way?"

"Very cut up, of course."

"A wealthy young widow," he said in a dry voice.

"Yes."

He read Virginia's note.

BARRY,—Will you please come and see me and let us wash out the past? I need a friend badly just now and you were always my greatest. Please come and see me tomorrow.

Yours always,
VIRGINIA

He read the note once, then crumpled it into his pocket.

Joan watched him with tearing anxiety in her heart and tried to speak casually:

"She wants to see you, doesn't she?"

"Yes," he said, yawned, and came up to the bed. "Good night, old thing. I'm frightfully tired—aren't you?"

Was that all? Wasn't he going to let her further into his thoughts, his feelings? Apparently not. Joan's heart sank. Her throat felt dry. He was so maddeningly reticent at times like these. How did she know what he felt about that note, or whether he meant to see Gina or not? And she was too proud to ask him. She felt that whatever happened she must not interfere with him. If she did she would lose him for certain; lose what she had of his affection.

She would have given a lot to pull him down to her and say: "Barry, Barry, don't see her . . . love me . . . only me!"

But she said nothing. He bent, kissed her hair lightly, and said:

"Good night, my dear. Sleep well."

"Good night," she whispered, and switched off the lamp so that he should not see that her eyes were filling with tears.

He shut the communicating door between them.

Joan turned her face to the pillow, and thought:

"Already . . . already she's between us . . . oh, why, why did Ian Kingleigh die and why has she come back?"

The man in the other room, on the other side of the door, lay in bed and read Virginia's note again. His eyes and lips were grim. He tore the letter in pieces and thought:

"Damn it, no—I won't see her. If she wants a friend, there are other men. I'm not going to see her. I've done with her. I'm married to Joan."

But there followed, at once, a host of memories of Virginia; of his old absorbing love and the happiness he had known with her. She wanted him; wanted his friendship. Wasn't he big enough to give it—to wipe out the past, as she asked?

It was a confession of weakness to refuse to see her. Damn it all, neither of them need refer to the past.

But could he see her and feel that the past was dead? That was the question.

He thought of the girl in the other room. His wife. His dear Joan, who was so frightfully decent to him, who so obviously worshipped him. He was very fond of her. But for the second time since he had heard of Kingleigh's death he wondered if he would have married Joan knowing that Virginia was free. It was not a very honourable thought.

He had married Joan and it was up to him to be faithful to her.

A man could be physically faithful, but he could not always control his thoughts. And Barry could not put Virginia and her freedom out of his thoughts.

The old lure was there, strong as ever, drawing him back, and he knew it. He told himself that he would go and see her. He must. He could not refuse. He hoped Joan would not mind. No—she was too sensible—and they had agreed not to question what the other did.

But for the first time since he had married Joan, the tie with her was irksome to him. He knew, definitely, that he had done wrong to marry her, feeling as he did about Virginia.

Like Joan he wished that Virginia's husband had not died and that she had not come back into his life.

CHAPTER VII

BARRY did not go at once to Virginia in answer to her request to see him. That much satisfaction had Joan. He waited quite a long time. He wrote to her. Joan did not know what, but he told her casually, that he had " dropped Virginia a line to tell her he would go and see her as soon as he could."

" We must get down to Horsham and hunt for the cottage," he said, the morning after Joan's visit to her cousin.

They stayed in a small hotel in Horsham; a pretty old place full of rambling passages, odd staircases, and oak-beamed bedrooms. They then scoured the countryside for a suitable cottage which they could rent. Barry was unwilling to purchase. He was, as usual, an entertaining companion and charming to Joan. But he showed no inclination to be her lover. He was in one of those moods which she had learnt to know and to dread—when he seemed out of touch with her in some queer way; living under the same roof with her as her husband; yet separated from her by a mysterious gulf which she could not begin to bridge.

It was only natural that she should attribute that gulf, at the moment, to the disastrous return of Virginia into their lives. Her widowhood and her demand that he should see and help her had inevitably affected him. She was in his thoughts constantly now. Joan knew that, intuitively. In the end he would go to her. She knew that, too. She tried not to make herself unhappy about it. It was not her custom to meet trouble half-way. But she loved Barry so entirely that it was impossible for this thing not to destroy her peace of mind.

In France, and when they had first come back to London, she had felt so confident of her success with him, and his love for her had seemed so much more passionate and voluntary. She had begun to feel secure—certain of him and their future happiness. Now it was all destroyed because Virginia was free and wanted Barry and he was face to face with those devastating facts. He had told Joan that he no longer loved Virginia and that he belonged to her, his wife. But Joan did not, could not, believe that. She told herself that she was, perhaps, mistaken in imagining that Barry was seriously affected by the fact that Virginia was once more accessible and had asked him to see her. Perhaps she was a fool to imagine that his present disinterest in her, in a passionate sense, was connected with Virginia. In any case she knew that it would be detrimental to her own position to question Barry on the subject or precipitate an argument from which she would only emerge the loser. So she said and did nothing. In her estimation the only way to deal with the position was to hold her peace and let things work out by themselves.

Joan had a particular love for the Downs. Up on the Dyke, that starry night two months ago, Barry had asked her to marry him and the great miracle had transformed the whole of her existence. She would like to have found a cottage with a view of those Downs, but Barry did not want to get too near the coast, so they toured the countryside further inland.

The week's search ended in disappointment. Only one place was offered them. A small cottage, genuinely old and with an attractive garden full of flowers, close to the Henfield Road. Joan fell in love with it at once. The oak-beamed rooms with lattice windows were adorable. The owners, a retired army officer and his wife, were willing to let furnished at a reasonable rent for two years.

For a day or two Joan was in a state of delightful anticipation. She talked to Barry of the little place, which was called " The Sparrow's Nest," in a proprietary fashion.

She effaced the thought of Virginia and made up her mind that once she was settled in " The Sparrow's Nest " with Barry, all would be well. They would lead a life of their own in which Lady Kingleigh would not play a part.

Then the whole thing crashed to the ground. Joan's castles in the air dissolved into nothingness. The army officer and his wife, who had been going to Canada to visit their son, altered their plans. The son wished them to settle out in Canada permanently. They decided to sell " The Sparrow's Nest " and refused, definitely, to rent it.

Joan was very disappointed when Barry came back to their hotel one afternoon from the estate agents' office and told her this news.

"Oh, darling, we *can't* let it go. We *must* have it, after all our plans ! " she exclaimed.

Barry was silent for a while. He sat on the edge of Joan's bed, smoking. She was sitting at her dressing-table, combing her hair. She had had a bad headache all day and had rested while Barry went to the estate agents with every intention of signing the agreement for " The Sparrow's Nest." Now she put down her comb and looked at him anxiously.

" We can't let it go," she repeated. " Won't you buy, Barry ? "

He did not look at her. His gaze was fixed on the carpet. He was frowning.

" No, I don't think so, my dear," at length he said. " To begin with, Colonel Anstey wants a fancy price for it. And the agents say he'll get it because the place is genuinely old and well restored and has electric light, etc. I don't want to chuck money away just because the cottage attracts us for the moment. We don't want to tie ourselves down to Henfield, do we ? "

Joan bit her lip. She would have liked to settle in the adorable cottage with Barry ; stayed there for ever. But he was so restless. She knew he could not bear to be tied down to any one spot for long. Wasn't restlessness nearly always a sign of unhappiness ? Only contented people liked to stay in one place. Yes, Barry was restless as the devil because he was not happy.

It was the thought of Virginia, worrying him. Joan reflected upon this with bitterness. But she said quietly:

"All right, darling. Then we must let the cottage go."

"Looks like it," he said.

"I'm frightfully disappointed."

"I'm sorry too. It's a charming place. But I'm not going to pay twice as much as it's worth."

"No," repeated Joan. She sighed. Alas for all her schemes for furnishing "The Sparrow's Nest" and making her home with Barry there.

"I've come to the conclusion we'd better find a small flat in Town for the moment," said Barry.

Joan's heart sank. London. How hateful! London... where Virginia lived; where it would be so easy to run into Virginia. Joan had yearned after that cottage in Sussex; hoped for isolation with Barry. Somehow she dreaded the thought of London.

Barry got up and walked across the room to her.

"Don't you want to go to Town, Joan?"

"Not much," she said, looking up at him with a faint smile. "But if you do——"

"Oh, I don't much care where we go," he broke in. "But it seems the best place to live in for the moment. I've got this estate to settle up and we may go abroad later."

That sounded more hopeful. Joan's eyes brightened.

"Well, let's take a flat in Town, then," she said cheerfully.

She looked with her fond and anxious gaze up at the thin, brown face of the man she adored. It seemed to her that the old strained, harassed look had come back into his eyes.

Wasn't he happy? Had he regretted marrying her and tying himself down? She felt a passionate wish to get close to him, mentally as well as physically close. He had not kissed her, except for a fleeting caress before he went to his own room at night, since they had left London.

She stretched up a hand to him, breaking her rule never to force demonstrations of affection from this queer and difficult husband of hers.

"Barry—darling——" she said.

He saw the hunger in her eyes. No man could have been blind to it. But he did not know how to meet it; how to comfort her. He felt so flat; so utterly unlike a lover should be. He was facing the grim fact that he had made a mistake when he had married her; from her point of view as well as his. She was much too nice, too sweet, to hurt. And he must, inevitably, hurt her. He had thought, in the beginning, that he would be happy with her. And in a way he was. He was never bored with her as a companion. But as a wife, a lover, he did not really want her. He did not deny to himself that his failure in this respect was due to Virginia's re-entry into the scheme of things. While she was totally lost to him as Kingleigh's wife, leading a life apart from him, he had been able to abstract his mind from her. He had turned to Joan's love and the intimacy of their marriage as a relief; an anodyne. He had hoped in time to annihilate the memory of that first unhappy love, and to make a good thing out of his life with Joan.

But Ian Kingleigh's death had been a calamitous affair. Virginia was free and Virginia wanted him to renew their old friendship. He could not get away from the fact that he wanted to renew it. Wanted, yet dreaded it; well aware that there could never be platonic friendship between him and the woman he had adored for four long years. If he went back to Virginia it would be with the knowledge that he still cared for her in the way that a man cares for the one woman in the world.

It was all hideously unfair to Joan. He ought to take Joan right away and refuse to see Virginia at all. That would be the strong thing to do. But he did not feel strong minded at the moment. He was nervy, restless, vacillating; playing about in his mind with the idea of answering Virginia's appeal, of seeing her again. He knew if he took Joan abroad and escaped from Virginia, physically, he could not escape from her mentally. He would merely become a mass of nerves and irritation which would react on Joan. Virginia had always been the one big thing in his life, and there was no destroying that knowledge. She had let him down. She had proved herself unworthy of his long devotion. But she was still the woman with whom he had been passionately in love from his boyhood, and if he had not rushed in that crazy fashion into marriage with Joan, he would have been at liberty to go to Virginia now. That was the thought which maddened him, and had kept him away from Joan during this week in the country.

He was desperately sorry for Joan. He was very genuinely

fond of her and he felt a cad, a swine, for bringing that look into her eyes and feeling himself incapable of assuaging her hunger. A mental, so much more than a physical, hunger. She wanted something from him which he could not give her. More than ever now Virginia was on the horizon again.

Wherever one is, one goes on loving, hating, regretting, desiring. And the one great thing which never left a man was hope. From that Barry did not wish to escape. Yet what was he hoping for? If he saw Virginia and revived the old affair with her, it could only wreck things utterly for Joan. That was the last thing he wished to do. He was, after all, responsible for her now. But unfortunately a man resents the object of his responsibility until in time he grows positively to dislike it. Barry knew enough about human nature to realise this and he did not want to feel that way towards Joan; to let a sense of duty become destructive to the affection he had for her.

He felt cornered, tormented with too much analysis of the affair, consequently he could not behave towards Joan as naturally as he had done on their honeymoon, nor extract the same pleasure from their union.

When she held up her hand to him this afternoon in her bedroom, he took it, but his clasp of her fingers was mechanical and she saw no answering spark in his eyes, and an indifferent cheerfulness in his smile. She withdrew her hand at once and turned to her dressing-table.

"He doesn't want me," she thought. "He hasn't wanted me for days."

He, feeling suddenly miserable because he had made her miserable, but unable to deal with the situation, walked into his own room, whistling.

"We'll go up to Town tomorrow, shall we?" he said.

"Yes, right you are," said Joan, and continued to comb her hair.

But when she knew he had gone along to his bath she put the comb down and covered her face with her hands, and for a moment her courage failed her. She thought:

"He doesn't want me at all. He wishes he had not married me now that Gina is free. When we get back to Town he'll see her. Oh, *God*, what can I do?"

The answer to that was—"Nothing." For the first time since she had married Barry she realised to the fullest extent what she had risked when she had married a man in whose affections she had only second place. And she was afraid . . . desperately afraid for her own happiness, as well as for his.

CHAPTER VIII

A MONTH later. The beginning of July. Grey skies and a chill, damp feeling in the air, and not at all the right sort of mid-summer weather, when Town folk usually desert their London houses for the green country or the blue sea.

Barry and Virginia met for the first time on one of these cold, grey days. Late afternoon; and in Virginia's luxurious boudoir, an electric fire and soft light filtering through the Lalique glass dispelling the gloom which had settled over Greyes Street, and Virginia, much more beautiful than even Barry remembered her, after the long years of remembering, of wanting her, while he was in Ceylon.

She was very pale; paler than usual, perhaps with excitement. Her hair was just as he remembered it; dark, with the lustre of a raven's wing; waving thickly back from her white forehead. Long, warm brown eyes with their fringe of heavy lashes; screwed up in the old familiar smile which had once so enchanted him. Low, attractive voice never forgotten, saying:

"Well, my dear——"

And a hand held out; ah, she had always had exquisite hands, and once he had covered every inch of them with kisses. He had never kissed any other woman's hands like that. Certainly not Joan's. But he did not want to think of Joan just now.

He took the hand Virginia held out. "Gina!" he said.

Nothing else. Only his voice was not the voice of the Barry whom Joan knew. It vibrated with feeling; was rough with it. His thin brown fingers gripped Virginia's white ones until she winced with pain. He saw her brows contract, dropped the hand, and said:

"Sorry——"

"That's all right, Barry," she said, and smiled again. And if her voice was cool she was inwardly the reverse. She was full of feverish excitement. Seeing this man again, she knew how crazy she had been to let him go out of her life for the sake of money; for her mother; for anything or anybody in the world.

And he, who had married another woman, hoping to forget her, watched Virginia walk across the room and sit down beside the fire and realised that he had never for a single instant ceased to want her. He must go on wanting her to the end of his days.

"Sit down," she said.

He sat down beside her. She held out the shagreen box of cigarettes. He took one with fingers that were not quite steady. He said:

"You still smoke the same old gaspers, Gina."

"Yes. The only cheap taste I've got, perhaps. I don't like expensive cigarettes."

"Neither do I."

"No. I know. You haven't altered, Barry," she said. "Except perhaps you look a bit older."

"You look exactly the same," he said.

"But I've changed a lot."

"Have you?"

He could not take his gaze from her; drinking in every detail of her loveliness. The old desire ran hot in his veins. Then he looked at her wedding-ring and his lips tightened. He sat back in his chair and drew a deep draught of his cigarette, exhaling it slowly through his nostrils. He said:

"Do you want me to say how sorry I am about—Kingleigh's death?"

Virginia looked him straight in the eyes.

"No, I don't. Whatever we do—whatever we have done —let's be frank with each other now."

"I quite agree."

"Very well. I've known you long enough, Barry, to tell you what I really feel. I was terribly shocked by Ian's death. It was terrible for him. But I can't frankly regret that I'm free again."

"Then why on earth did you marry him?"

"You know why."

"Because of finance?"

"Yes."

"That doesn't seem—worthy of you."

"I'm not very worthy, really," she said with a queer little smile. "Don't you know that by now?"

"I don't want to know it. All these years—all that long time out East I thought of you as a man thinks of—of a goddess, Gina . . . you were like a *religion* to me. Do you know that?"

Her face was soft and lovely in the rosy glow of the fire; tender, as Ian Kingleigh had never seen it. She said:

"Barry—my dear——"

"Well—you were—my religion," he cut in roughly. "And you smashed up everything—because of money. It hurt—like the devil, at the time. But now——"

"Now—it doesn't hurt?"

"Don't let's talk about it."

She drew in her breath. That meant it did hurt him still. And she had been so afraid that when he came he would tell her that he was in love with Joan. She said softly:

"Barry—I hurt myself, too. I *tortured* myself. I didn't want to give you up."

"But you did, and that's all over."

"Yes," she said in a low voice. "But it wasn't all over in my mind when I married Ian. If I cheated you, I cheated myself much more badly."

"Isn't it better for us not to talk about it?"

"I suppose so. But this is the first chance we've had of—understanding each other."

"I can't understand you chucking me in the way you did," he said bluntly. "So please, my dear, let's *not* talk about it."

Her head went back swiftly and her eyes flashed at him.

"Very well. But neither can I understand why you married Joan—so quickly."

He looked past her . . . at the shadowy end of the boudoir . . . a room pregnant with memories of his old passion for this woman. The thought of Joan cut like a knife through those memories and jarred on him. He said harshly:

"Well—I did—and she's damn good to me and I'm very fond of her. But the whole thing is a mess. You know it—I know it—*she* knows it. . . ."

"Poor Joan. . . ."

"Yes, poor Joan. She knew I was coming here today

and she smiled and sent you her love and inside she was *miserable*. She was afraid of my seeing you again...."

He broke off, drew another long breath of his cigarette, then pitched it savagely into the grate. His nerves were on edge. He felt suddenly raw with anger against this woman who sat looking at him with her lovely soft eyes; this girl who alone, out of all the women on earth, had power to make a weak, spineless fool of him. She had hurt him badly, and *he*—was he going to let her hurt him all over again? He got up.

"Virginia, I came to see you because you asked me to—you said you need my friendship. I didn't really want to come. And I'm not coming again."

She stood up—biting nervously at her lips.

"Barry—why?"

He looked her straight in the eyes. He was white under his tan.

"For a good many reasons, Virginia. Mainly because I'm married to Joan and I've got to give her a square deal."

"And can't you do that—and still see me?"

"No."

"But why?"

"Because, damn it, I'm still in love with you—that's why."

An instant's silence. Her face and throat flooded with colour. Barry turned on his heel and walked towards the door. Then he heard her crying and turned round quickly. Yes, she was crying, with her face in her hands. Through all the years of their old friendship and love affairs he had never seen Virginia cry. There was no room in his heart or his brain for Joan then. He walked straight back to Virginia. "Why are you crying—for heaven's sake—why?"

She took her hands away from her face. He saw that tears were pouring down her cheeks.

"Because," she said, "because I suppose I'm still in love with you."

Another short silence. Barry shook from head to foot. He said:

"What did you want to tell me that for?"

"Because it's true," she said. "I married Ian to save the situation, but I loved you and I still do."

"Do you realise what you're saying?"

"Yes."

"And do you realise that I'm tied up to Joan and that she cares for me?"

"Yes. But I don't care. You were my lover before you were hers."

"Damn you," said Barry. He caught her in his arms. "I've never really been *any* woman's lover but yours. . . ."

"Barry!"

Her long, slim body relaxed against his. He saw her face, white, reckless, passionate, lifted to his. He kissed her savagely on the lips and then pushed her away from him, and walked to the door.

"No, my dear. This ends it. We can't do this . . . to Joan . . . I'm sorry. Good-bye."

Virginia's knees trembled so that she could scarcely stand. She held on to the back of the sofa. She called him back.

"Barry—Barry—*please*—you can't leave me like this—you can't mean you won't see me any more."

He looked back at her. His eyes were bloodshot, but he smiled.

"I'm going to try not to see you any more." he said. "More than that I can't say. Good-bye, my dear."

He walked out of the room and shut the door. Virginia made no further attempt to detain him. She sat staring blindly before her.

"*I'm going to try not to see you any more* . . ." he had said.

But she knew, somehow, intuitively, that Joan or no Joan he would come back; that this could not possibly be the end.

Barry's thoughts were too confused for analysis as he walked away from Greyes Street and across St. James's.

The clouds had mysteriously lifted. At six o'clock the skies were clear blue and a bright sun was shining. Sudden warmth—a real atmosphere of summer—descended upon London. But Barry walked on with a set, stony face. He was thinking:

"Why the hell did I see Gina? Why the *hell*?"

That meeting with her; that revival of the old tempestuous passion that she had always managed to raise in him, had been disastrous. It had spoiled everything. He had found comparative peace and happiness with Joan before this. Now he knew he had lost any hope of peace or of happiness. The desire for Virginia was in his blood. When he had taken her in his arms and kissed her good-bye just now, he had felt himself come to life . . . he, who had been dead while she was lost to him. He had known how empty all the days with Joan had been. Poor Joan.

" How awful . . . for her . . . for everybody ! " he thought.

He was never going to see Virginia again. But that could not stamp out his desire for her.

Why did he want this one woman so passionately ? Why should she mean so much, rouse so much in him where others failed ? She was physically lovely and attractive, but no more so than a great many women. She was charming, but no more charming than his own wife ; not really half as amusing or such a first-rate companion. She was essentially selfish and spoiled. Joan was the most unselfish and unspoiled of women. Why, then, couldn't he love and want Joan ? There were no answers to these questions. No explanation. The whole of life—this question of love, of sex, was an enigma ; an insoluble problem.

He had married Joan. It was up to him to be faithful to her and to make her happy. But with Virginia free, Virginia *wanting* him, and her kiss, her embrace, just now, had told him that she wanted him ; it was going to be the very devil.

CHAPTER IX

JOAN was waiting for Barry to come back. She sat in front of the open window in her drawing-room, glad of the sudden sunshine and return to summer weather.

It was a very charming room, with low ceiling, like all the rooms, because they had found a penthouse, and two windows commanding a magnificent view right across the park. Barry had given Joan *carte blanche* with the decoration and furnishing and she had made her home just as she wanted it. This was a yellow room—primrose walls and ceiling ; pale gold curtains ; catching all the sunshine that there was. Only two pictures ; the Van Gogh—her old favourite—over the mantelpiece ; and an oil painting of a girl by an Italian master, in an old gold Florentine frame of exquisite design. This was Barry's possession ; the one and only picture of worth from his uncle's collection.

There were one or two low, comfortable chairs, two

beautiful rugs, a Queen Anne writing bureau, a radio-television set, and an old needlework stool. The sort of sitting-room Joan had craved for and never been able to afford until now.

She had been frightfully happy choosing these things with him and going off by herself to make other purchases of linen and small domestic things which were more in her zone than his. She had been amazingly happy from the day they took possession of their flat—their first home together. Too happy, perhaps, to notice that Barry was restless and subdued and not so ready as usual with his quip and jest.

The thought of Virginia had not worried Joan, so enthralled and busy had she been getting settled here. Barry had not seen Gina; nor seemed in a hurry to answer her summons. That was a good sign in Joan's estimation.

Then, today, at luncheon, Barry broke the news that he was going to call on Virginia this afternoon. Joan came down to earth with a sudden bump. So he had not forgotten that Gina wanted him. He was going to her. Joan wondered what the sequel to that visit would be, what effect the meeting with Gina would have upon Barry. She would not have been human and a woman in love if she had not trembled a little for her own happiness. But she had seen him off with a smile and said : " Give my love to Gina."

Now, waiting for him to come home, she tried not to worry about the thing at all. Barry and Gina had been friends for so many years. She could not expect them to avoid each other just because of their unfortunate love affair. Barry was her husband and there was nothing to be afraid of.

She amused herself while Barry was out by writing an article which Joe Halliday needed urgently for the *Hand Mirror*.

She wrote the article, posted it, and then sat at the open window, enjoying the sunshine after the grey day which had been so depressing.

She heard Barry's key in the lock and went to meet him with that light in her eyes which only he had power to kindle.

" Hello, darling," she said as he walked into the tiny hall. " Had any tea ? "

" Yes, thanks. What a marvellous evening, isn't it ? "

" Marvellous," she echoed.

She walked back into the room. She could never quite

stifle the absurd wish to throw an arm about him and kiss him when he came back to her, after a few hours' separation. But he was not given to spontaneous embraces of that kind and she was much too afraid of making herself and her affection a bore to show what she felt. So she just smiled and then strolled back to the drawing-room. Not before she had seen, with the quick, fatally discerning eyes of a woman in love, that something had upset him. She knew him well enough now to be quite sure that when Barry had that set, mask-like face, something was wrong. The meeting with Gina, of course.

Joan would have given a lot to ask him about that meeting, but nothing would have induced her to put a single question to him. And he, of course, did not volunteer to enlighten her. He followed her into the drawing-room and said:

"Look here, let's phone up and get some seats for a show. I feel I'd like to do something tonight."

"What about our economy plans?" she began, laughing.

Barry cut in, irritably:

"Oh, hang the economy."

Joan lit a cigarette and seated herself on the arm of a chair. She thought, with a sinking heart:

"Something *has* upset him. I wonder what Gina said. ... He wants to do a show and get away from his own thoughts. ..."

He began to walk restlessly up and down the room. She watched him covertly. Yes, that thin attractive face was hard as stone—quite grim. Heaven alone knew what was going on behind the mask.

"This," thought Joan, "is what I've got to put up with ... this *not knowing* about Virginia and what he's thinking."

But why should she put up with it? Why shouldn't she ask him, right out, about his meeting with Virginia? Well, she was quite at liberty to. But if she did, she might ruin all her chances with Barry. She had much better leave him alone and hope for the best. She had asked for this, when she had married a man, adoring him, and knowing that he belonged, in his heart, to another woman.

"Possibly nothing happened between them that matters," she told herself. "I don't know why I need work myself up into a stew ... but I do wish I *did* know."

She cast off depression bravely.

"Barry, I wrote an article for Joe this afternoon and I've

made three guineas. Aren't I clever? I can afford to treat *you* to a show tonight, my lamb."

He paused in front of her. His lips relaxed into a smile.

"Can you? That's nice of you, Infant."

Her heart warmed to the old pet-name.

"Will you let me?" she asked eagerly.

"Certainly not. I shall treat you. So you've started writing again."

"I must do something, and I hate having to ask you for every penny."

"That's rot."

"All the same, I'm independent—as you know."

He nodded. His eyes were softer as he looked at her. What a nice child she was. Thoroughly nice; and he liked that industrious and independent spirit of hers. He thought of Virginia; those lovely, delicate fingers of hers had never done a stroke of work; never would. Why couldn't he despise her for being lazy and spoiled? Why must he want her with every drop of blood in his body?

He felt remorseful about this wife of his. He put out a hand and pulled her hair gently.

"What show would you like to see?"

"Anything you'd like."

"I don't care."

"D'you remember when you first came back from Ceylon, taking me to see *Sonia*?"

"Yes, I do."

"You liked that. You always like a musical show. Let's go and see *Princess Prue*. The music's pretty. Margaret Mackay saw it with Joe the other night and loved it."

"All right. We'll go to *Princess Prue*."

His voice sounded flat, indifferent. But his casual fingers, touching her hair, had made her pulse-beats quicken. She wanted suddenly to be close to him and reassure her foolish heart that this afternoon with Gina had not really come between them. She stood up, put her arms round his waist, and pressed her cheek against his shoulder.

"Dear darling B . . ."

The man stood very still. He stared over the brown head. She looked so appealing with that starry light in those very blue eyes and the small, determined face with its golden sprinkling of freckles, flushed, inviting his kisses.

But the unhappy conviction settled on Barry that he could not love her in the way she wanted, and that body and brain clamoured still for that other woman; that woman who should have been his wife. If she had not failed him she would have belonged to him now. If he had not married in such reckless haste, she might still have belonged to him.

What sort of deal was he going to give Joan now? He did not want to be a brute to her. But he could not force himself to ape the lover. Not now, anyhow. He was no actor. He could not play a part. He hated himself for it, but he must be natural; she must allow him to be natural, or he would hate her, too. That would be a disaster and the last thing he wished to happen.

He did not kiss her. He patted her shoulder and moved away from her.

"I must have a bath, Infant. I walked across the park and I feel hot and sticky. It's suddenly grown hot, hasn't it?"

"Yes, frightfully," she said.

He went out of the room. She stood still, smoking, thinking. The warm colour had left her face. She felt chilled. Under normal conditions she would not have been so foolish as to feel hurt because he was undemonstrative. She was too used to Barry's moods for that. But this evening his reluctance to touch or kiss her seemed significant. Of what? She did not want to think. She could only take it for granted now that he had had a "scene" with Virginia and that the old fever, the old lure, had taken hold of him again.

She had known from the moment she had heard of Ian Kingleigh's death that this would happen. She did not quite see how to deal with the situation. But she went down to the depths of depression. She felt that she had lost Barry. As a husband, as a friend, he was still hers. But she had lost him as a lover. For how long? Perhaps only temporarily until he had had time to get over this business of Gina again. But there was just the chance that she had lost him, in that way for ever. Such a possibility to Joan—still in love with Barry, loving him with every fibre of her being—was intolerable—a thing too bitter to be endured.

She pitched her cigarette-end into the grate and put a

hand to her eyes for a moment. Her head ached with too much thought.

"I mustn't be an idiot. . . ." She whispered the words to herself. "I mustn't let him see that I'm hurt or worried. If I make a fuss I'll lose him altogether."

She might have felt resentment towards him for hurting her. But if she got hurt over this show, she had only herself to blame. She had married him *knowing* what she risked. True, she had not dreamed that Virginia would be widowed within so short a time and call Barry back. But she had known that Barry was not in love with her. He had said: "I don't want to hurt you . . ." that night up on the Dyke in his car, when she had cried in his arms and pride had gone to the winds. But she had been willing and eager to take the risk. Well, she must not squeal now if she got the worst of it. Joan faced facts squarely enough. But that made it no easier to bear the torment of jealousy which gripped every particle of her when she thought about Barry and Gina, her cousin. Supposing Gina won Barry back altogether; right away from her, his wife? That was a possibility. She knew nothing. But her imagination was vivid enough; and anything seemed possible.

"I couldn't bear it," she thought.

She felt a little distraught when she walked into her bedroom to change her dress. She wanted to call Barry; to throw herself into his arms, to say: "Tell me what happened today. Tell me what you're thinking. . . ."

But she did nothing of the sort. She put on a cocktail dress which she knew he liked. She took pains with her hair, with her whole appearance. She was cheerful and friendly with him when they met again in the sitting-room for a cocktail before going down to the restaurant. But she was torn with anxiety. How haggard he looked! He drank more than usual, too. It was only too obvious that his nerves were on edge and that he was repressing *something*.

He was grateful to her for not questioning him about Virginia. He appreciated her tact just as he admired her, always, for the pluck with which she faced a difficult situation. But he could not draw her into that intimate circle of thoughts . . . where she wanted to be. He knew that she was not happy and he could not make her any happier. He could answer her jests with his and echo her laughter and realise

that they remained a thousand miles apart. Virginia . . .
the memory of Virginia in his arms . . . had done that.

They neither of them enjoyed *Princess Prue*. It was a
good show; well acted, well produced; and the music was
charming. But they were both *distrait* and not really in the
mood for musical comedy. It was inevitable that Joan should
cast her mind back to that night when she had sat beside
Barry and they had laughed together over *Sonia*. It was
queer, but although she had not been married to him then
and had had no hopes of ever belonging to him, she had felt
closer to him that night than she did tonight at *Princess Prue*.
She had felt that he wanted her companionship and her
sympathy and she had given them with both hands. Tonight
she knew instinctively that he wanted nothing from her;
therefore her hands were tied. She told herself, when the
evening ended and they drove back to their flat, that her
marriage had been a failure. A heart-breaking thought to
foster. But she could not get away from it. She had failed
. . . through no fault of hers; no fault of his either. It was
just fate, just bad luck . . . because Virginia was free and
he still loved her.

"He must regret, terribly, that he married me," she told
herself. "He must want to be free. I wonder what I ought
to do."

She decided that she could do nothing yet. And after all,
"hope springs eternal . . ." and there was always the hope
that Barry would get over this phase and want her again
and put Virginia out of it.

When she was in bed Barry came in to say good night to
her, which was his custom.

She lay against the pillows, an open book in her hands.
The room was full of blue shadows; charming in the dim
light from the electric lamp beside her. Barry, seating himself
on the edge of the bed, thought how young she looked in her
creamy silk pyjamas with her ruffled brown hair. Young and
rather sad. He was making her unhappy. Yes, he knew it.
He knew how sensitive she was to his behaviour and how she
suffered when he was in these unlover-like moods. He
guessed that she was enduring the pangs of bitterest jealousy
about Virginia. And she did not show it. She did not
whine. He would like to have told her how much he admired
that and what a swine he felt for marrying her; for landing

her in this position. But he was tongue-tied. The worse he felt about things, the more reticent he became.

He looked at her in a worried way. She read what was in his mind. Starving for a little affection she put out a hand and took his.

"What's wrong, Barry?"

"Nothing," he said.

She went back into her own shell. He did not want to tell her. All right. But she knew; *she knew. Oh, damn Virginia.*

"What are you reading?" he asked.

"*Rebecca again.*"

"A good book."

"Yes. Daphne du Maurier understands human nature."

"Human nature . . ." he repeated the words, gave a little laugh and stood up, hands in his pyjama pockets. "Ye gods, it wants some understanding."

Joan shut the book. Her hands were cold, in spite of the warmth of the summer night. Her eyes looked up at him, very big and bright. He was in torment . . . she could see that. And so was she. Why couldn't they comfort each other? She broke her resolutions to say nothing to him. She felt that she must; that she could not let him leave her, go to his own room and let that blank wall between them grow higher and thicker. She wanted, desperately, to get nearer him.

"Darling, come here a moment," she said.

He sat on her bed again. He did not look at her, but he thought:

"I hope to heaven she doesn't mention Gina. . . ."

But Joan's defences were falling fast and furiously. She took both his hands in her small cold fingers.

"Darling—something's wrong. I can't bear you not to tell me."

"Don't let's have a personal discussion, please, old thing," he said.

"But something is wrong. We're friends—surely——"

"Much better to leave it alone," he broke in, and drew his fingers away from hers.

Suddenly, crazily, Joan lost her temper. The rarest thing in the world for her.

"Look here," she said, her face scarlet to the roots of her hair, "you can't expect me to be quite so angelic as all this, Barry. You went to see Gina this afternoon and since you've come back you've been . . . different to me . . . absolutely miles away from me. You haven't told me a thing and I can't stand it. I *must* know."

Silence. He sat still, neither moving nor looking at her. She was shaking from head to foot. She knew she had been foolish, but she could not draw back now. With tears in her eyes she added:

"I don't care a hell what you do—if only you'll tell me. I do deserve to be told at least!"

Then he looked at her. He shook his head slowly.

"I tried to avoid this," he said. "I wanted to avoid it. It can only hurt—both of us."

"I don't care," she said wildly. "Nothing can hurt more than not being in your confidence."

"What do you want me to tell you?" he asked abruptly.

"About—this afternoon. Barry, it isn't that I'm just a jealous wife . . ." her voice broke; tears of misery, of humiliation, poured down her cheeks. "It's all much more important than that . . . because of . . . what used to be between you two. Don't you understand . . . what it means to me . . . for you to see her again?"

"I do understand," he said quietly. "I understand the whole thing only too well. I thought it would be better if we didn't discuss Virginia. But since you want the truth—you'd better have it."

"Yes—please," she said, and looked at him with eyes full of dread.

He got up and walked to the open window. She saw the muscles of his cheeks working.

"When I saw Gina this afternoon I knew that I was still in love with her," he said.

Joan went down into that special little hell reserved for a woman in love with a man who cares for another woman. But the tears dried on her lashes. She said in a stiff voice:

"Yes . . . well?"

"I told her I was not going to see her again. That's all," he said.

"I see."

He remained at the window, staring out at the stars. She sat huddled up in the bed with her hands clasping her knees; her lips quivering. That was all. And he had told Gina

he would not see her any more. But he had found out
that he was still in love with Gina. He had never been in
love with her, his wife. Only too well she knew that. But
naturally, during their honeymoon, and at times here in
England, she had thought she was winning him; fancied
she had detected something more than ordinary passion in
his embrace. She had buoyed herself up with the thought:
" One day he may fall in love with me . . . because we're
friends and he likes me and he finds me attractive to make
love to. . . ."

She saw tonight the folly of such a hope; the tragic futility
of her yearning love for him. He had loved Virginia since
he was a boy and he loved her still. Even if he did not see
her again, Joan knew that he would go on wanting her. She
said:

" Tell me something—frankly—please, Barry. Are you
sorry you married me? Has Gina's being a widow made
you sorry? "

He swung round on her.

" What the hell's the good of asking such a question? "

" I want to know."

" You want to hurt yourself and make me feel a rotten
cad."

" No," she said, closing her eyes. " No . . . but I must
know, that's all."

" I won't answer that question."

" Then you *are* sorry."

" Joan, look here, you've been amazingly decent to me
—much nicer than I deserve and you've always left me
alone——"

He stopped. He wanted so much to get away from Joan's
eyes—they were so desperately hurt. He wanted to be alone.
He knew that if he stayed here he would only go on hurting her. She seemed to sense what was passing in his
mind. She lay back in bed and turned her face to the
pillows.

" Sorry," she said in a stifled voice. " I've been a complete fool . . . and I'm not playing fair, either. I knew when
you married me what you still felt for Gina. It's no good
my making a fuss now—is it? But it was frightfully hard
luck on me that Ian died. . . ."

She ended with a broken little laugh. Her shoulders were

shaking. And suddenly Barry forgot his own pain, his lacerated nerves. Immense pity and respect for Joan filled his heart. She was so very game and he had been brutally frank. He had not spared her.

He came to her bedside, leaned down, and kissed the top of her head.

"Poor Joan," he said huskily. "The whole thing's *bloody* —and especially for you."

She felt that light caress against her hair. She shivered. But she did not turn to him. She had humiliated herself sufficiently for one evening. She said in a stifled voice:

"Please go away. I'll be all right in the morning. Good night——"

"Good night, dear," he said miserably. "Try and forgive me and understand."

"You know I do. I ought to know what it is to be in love —hopelessly——" She laughed again.

Barry could not bear it. He walked quickly out of her room and shut the door between them.

For a long time she lay still, her face buried in the pillow. She reached out a hand and switched off the lamp. Then she turned on her back, sighed, and put her hands to her aching eyes.

"And now I know where I am," she thought. "Poor darling Barry. I suppose he's just about as hellishly unhappy about my precious cousin as I am about him. I pity him. What a mess! I oughtn't to have married him, of course. This was bound to happen. I did hope . . . but 'good-bye to all that,' as the well-known novel says."

Barry had promised not to see Gina again and he was going to try and wash out the whole affair. But that would not bring him any closer to her, Joan reflected bitterly. He must be chafing horribly against this matrimonial tie. If it were not for that he might step in and win Gina now and be quite happy.

Of course, if she were a real heroine, she would just run away from Barry, leave him free, give him a divorce, and let him marry Gina.

Perhaps that was what it would come to in the end. She would wait and see. But meanwhile she must suffer. During the brief period of her marriage, her deep and passionate love for him had thrived and increased. The idea of leaving him, of breaking up their home, of giving him to another woman, was worse to her than the thought of death.

But there was nothing to do but to wait and see and hope. But it seemed to Joan that she was going to die by inches.

CHAPTER X

DURING the weeks that followed Joan did not question Barry about Virginia and neither did she allow her mind to dwell on the affair.

She did not even know whether he saw Gina again. She did not ask. And Barry never mentioned Gina's name. The only intimation Joan had of what was going on under the surface with Barry was through his restlessness, his apparent disability to settle down anywhere or to anything. Although he was extremely nice to her in one way she felt that much of his attentiveness was studied; just as she was sure that his humour was forced. Loving him so well, Joan *knew* him. She knew that he was inwardly tormented, and that his torment was for Virginia. Bitter knowledge—made more bitter by the fact that she could do nothing to help him or herself.

Personally, Joan heard no news of Virginia. She avoided communication with Greyes Street and, since neither her aunt nor her cousin attempted to get into touch with her, there was little risk of meeting them. Joan did not even know whether they were still in Town. If Barry knew he said nothing about it.

During the last month or so, owing to his restless moods, they had scarcely stayed in the flat for more than three consecutive days. Everything in time appeared to bore him, fret his nerves. Joan was exquisitely patient, she did exactly what he wanted. They soon left France and came back to Town and here they were in their flat again. She wondered what the next move would be.

How long before he came back to her—*really* came back? How long before she would know whether he had really put Gina from his mind or not? And how long before her own endurance was broken?

Barry drained his glass and put it down.

"Well—to bed, I suppose, old thing. I liked your pal Halliday. He's a good fellow."

"Dear old Joe—yes, he is."

"Has a *penchant* for you, too, my child."

Joan interested herself in her cigarette-end.

"He used to have. I don't know about now. I rather think he and Margaret Mackay—Mac as we called her in the office—will fix things up one day. I hope so."

"Did you ever think of marrying Halliday?"

"No, never." She stood up and turned her back to him. Then she added lightly: "I was always a complete mutt about the man I married."

Barry looked after her in a worried way.

"I wish——" he began.

She swung round, her cheeks red.

"Don't say you wish I'd married Joe."

"My dear, I only wish you'd been happier than you are—with me. I'm not making you happy and I know it."

This was the first personal discussion they had had for long weeks, and Joan felt perilously on the edge of a breakdown, so she gave a wild little laugh and said:

"Well, you don't seem frantically happy yourself, darling, so I haven't done you much more good than you've done me. Sleep well, my lamb. Good night."

After she had gone Barry pitched his cigarette into the grate with a violent movement, then drew a letter from his coat pocket. He unfolded and read it. It was written in Virginia Kingleigh's untidy hand, headed "Claydown Manor, Worth," and dated the 29th of August. Two days ago. It said:

> When are you going to take me away? We can't go on like this. I can't stand it and surely you can't. When we saw each other down here last week-end we both realised that we can't keep away from each other. You say it isn't fair to Joan, but are we going to go on like this for the rest of our lives?
>
> For God's sake, come to me, Barry.
>
> GINA

He read the letter twice, then put it in the empty fireplace and burned it. His eyes were red-rimmed. His face bore the traces of mental and physical strain. He felt one of his bad headaches coming on. Every nerve was tortured. He stood a moment, his arm on the mantelpiece, and leaned his head against it.

When he had seen Gina down at Claydown Manor . . . what an afternoon . . . both of them strung to concert pitch . . . Gina at her loveliest, her most alluring . . . and he trying crazily to keep faith with Joan. It had not been pleasant. The whole thing had made a beast of him. He had turned on Gina and said:

"You chucked me when I was on my way home to marry you—why in the name of God do you want me now just because I'm tied up to Joan? Leave me alone."

She had only looked at him with dark, sorrowful eyes and said:

"Do you want never to see me again?"

And he had known he could not bear it if he did not see her again. He had broken his resolution to keep away from her six or seven times since he had made it that afternoon at Greyes Street.

Gina had said:

"*Are we going to go on like this for the rest of our lives?*"

Barry switched off the lights in the drawing-room and went to his room. While he stood at his chest of drawers taking off his collar and tie, he fancied he heard the muffled sound of weeping from the next room. His brows contracted. He hated and loathed the idea of Joan lying in bed, in there, crying. She was very unhappy. He knew it. What in God's name could he do?

When he had undressed, he went into her room. Joan heard him come. She said quickly:

"Don't turn on the light——"

She did not want him to see that she had been crying. She imagined he had come in to make his usual curt good night speech. When he sat down on her bed and put his arms around her, she was too astonished to speak, but her loving and hungry heart at once responded.

"Poor Infant," he said tenderly.

She cried then, terribly, with her bare arms clasping his neck, pulled his head down to hers, pressed her face against his shoulder.

"Oh, Barry," she whispered. "Barry. *Barry* . . ."

"I'm frightfully sorry, dear," he said. "And you've been such a brick to me."

"Stay with me," she said brokenly. "Stay with me for a little while tonight."

"I can't——" he began.

Her small, hot hands clung to him.

"Please, Barry."

In silence he acquiesced. For a few moments he held her close and she sobbed in his arms in the darkness. He felt sick with pity for her; sick and weary with his own long desire for Virginia's arms and lips.

"Why the hell does life do these things to us," he wondered. "If I'd let Joan alone, and never married her, she would not have been so miserable. She might have married Halliday."

Joan, extracting what comfort she could from his embrace —the first for so long—stopped crying. Her fingers touched his hair, his eyes. Her body trembled against his.

"Try and forget everything and love me a little," she whispered.

"It isn't fair on you, my dear."

"You mean because you're not in love with me. I know that. I don't care. Just forget everything."

He closed his eyes. Her heart leaped with the old fierce exultation when she felt his lips upon her mouth. But she thought, despairingly:

"Perhaps he'll imagine I'm the other woman. He doesn't want me, really . . ."

The brief moment of passion flared up between them; flickered out; left him with the taste of ashes in his mouth and a feeling of shame; of having wronged and cheapened his own life. And it left her with a more bitter sense of loneliness than she had known before. For what was physical union worth when their hearts, their minds, were so divided? In the morning things would be no better; perhaps worse.

After the ecstasy—reaction—an almost sullen resentment against life filling her heart and soul.

Barry left her with an apology and that made things ten times worse. There is such a fine line between passionate love and hatred, and she hung on the very precipice of disliking him when he muttered: "I'm sorry, Joan. . . ."

She sat up in bed, pushing her tumbled hair back from

her face. She could just see him in the faint light that filtered through from his bedroom into hers.

"Why should you be sorry? Oh, do you want to make me hate you?" she said in a choked voice.

"I wonder you don't," he said.

"Oh, get out and leave me alone," she said, and flung herself down on the pillows again.

He lit a cigarette with an unsteady hand.

"Joan, we can't go on like this."

"No, I agree," she said, pressing her closed fists against her eyeballs.

"Whatever I do, I'm damned if I'll go behind your back. I'll tell you straight—I've been seeing Virginia."

Joan shuddered.

Of course, she might have known that. She *had* known it, in her heart. But why must he tell her now, and destroy the comfort, the happiness she had drawn from that feverish moment of passion shared with him. He was utterly selfish and lacking in understanding of a woman's feelings. She didn't know why she loved him in this violent and persistent fashion and why she was such a fool to put up with the position.

She suddenly switched on her table lamp. He saw her, her face blotched, stained with tears; her eyes glaring at him. And he knew that her endurance was at an end. When she broke into bitter denunciation of him, he felt curiously soothed by it. It was more bearable than her kindness. He understood it better; and he did not blame her.

"You never think of me—of anybody but yourself. You hurt me and don't realise you're doing it—you're beastly—*beastly*—and it's absolute *hell* to live with you as you are now."

"I have been faithful to you," Barry said sullenly.

"Faithful—you mean you haven't actually *slept* with Gina!" Joan laughed wildly. "What does that matter? You've seen her—wanted her—you wanted her just now, when I was in your arms. Faithful! My God, do you imagine it's better for me just because you've been *physically* true to me? You aren't faithful in your mind at any hour of the day or night."

"Joan——"

"I won't be quiet!" she interrupted in an hysterical voice.

"Look here, Barry. I've finished. I've had months of this and I can't stand any more——"

"Joan——"

"I *will* speak. Listen, I say. I don't know whether you think it's been worth while for me lately—do you?"

"No—I'm sure it hasn't," he said quietly.

"Very well. You said you wouldn't see Gina any more. But you have seen her. And you want her. Now for God's sake go to her and take her. See if she can make you happy. I don't care. I'd ten thousand times rather you went to her and made up your mind whether you were going to be happy with her or not definitely, than stayed here in this flat, moping, brooding, *physically* faithful!"

He winced at the sneering tone in her voice. Joan was transformed from the sweet-tempered, charming girl he had known and married, into a bitter, sarcastic creature. And it was all his fault. He had done this to her.

"What a mess," he thought wearily.

"Go to her," repeated Joan. "Or if you don't go to her, I'll leave you."

Barry looked at her swiftly.

"Joan!"

"Well, I mean it. But whatever you do I'm not going to live with you as long as I know you're fretting after her, because I can't stand it."

He came nearer her. She switched out her lamp.

"Get out of my room, Barry, don't try and talk to me."

He turned at once and left her. She saw that even friendship between them was impossible now. She told herself that this was the end—really the end of her life with him. This was the price she must pay for allowing herself to be second best to any man. Much as she loved him, tonight it did not seem worth while.

CHAPTER XI

WHEN the "daily" awakened Joan with her tray of tea and toast that next morning, she brought also a note from Barry.

Her aching eyes read what he had written while Milly tidied up her clothes and retired, noiselessly, from the room.

"JOAN,—As we said last night, we can't go on like this, poppet. It only hurts you and I feel half crazy. I'm going away for a few days. I'll write to you and you might write me at the Club and tell me what you want to do about this damnable business. I'm more sorry than I can say for making you suffer because I owe you so much. You've been so good to me, dear. Try and forgive me. It's very queer, but I think my feelings for Virginia are stronger than I can cope with. When we see each other again we'll try and talk it all out sensibly. Meanwhile my affection and gratitude.

"BARRY."

Joan's eyes filled with tears when she looked up from this letter. So typical of Barry. Kind, apologetic, remorseful, and stabbing her with every word. But of course any mention of his feelings for Gina always hurt. His "affection and gratitude." Worth something—but not much—from the husband one loved with every drop of blood in one's miserable body ... and every thought in one's wretched brain.

It was a foregone conclusion that he would go to Gina. She had told him to, last night. But oh, heavens, how *damnably* the idea grated on her. She felt raw; broken to pieces over the whole business.

She no longer felt that she hated Barry or resented his conduct, as she had felt for a few moments last night. She could find it in her heart to pity him almost as much as she pitied herself. She knew that he had a conscience—quite a considerable one. And even if he did go to Virginia now, he would suffer. He would hate remembering about her, his wife.

Well—now what was she going to do? She would be alone in the flat for a day or two, anyhow, until Barry came back to "talk things out sensibly." Could she ever discuss such an affair as a separation or divorce sensibly ... with him? Could she ever bring herself to accept her dismissal and watch him walk out of her life, back to Virginia, for always?

Where was her pride? Dear God, she hadn't any. She loved him—just adored him—that was all. And she had been his wife for three months. Too short a time ... long enough to know indisputably that there was no one in this world who meant anything—but Barry. Nothing of any importance, except their life together.

But it was not a bit of good trying to keep Barry now. No use clutching at straws. She was drowning. And she must drown. She had lost him. She had never really had him. Their marriage meant nothing in the face of his unconquerable passion for the other woman.

When she was up and dressed, Joan wrote to Barry and sent the letter to his club.

> "I will wait at the flat till you come back and meanwhile I want you to know that you are free to do exactly what you like. If you want a divorce, tell me, and we will arrange it. Don't reproach yourself too bitterly. You warned me before I married you that you did not love me as you had loved *her*. And I *do* understand, darling, only I wish to God you had loved me instead. Don't be afraid that I shall be dramatic about things. I'll be quite reasonable and I want you to be happy.
>
> "JOAN."

She meant every word that she wrote. But that very human emotion of jealousy tore at her heart after she had posted the letter. Passionate jealousy of Virginia. She wanted Barry to be happy. And she would let him go. But oh, how she hated Gina! And she would go quite crazy if she allowed herself to dwell on the thought of Barry and Gina . . . going away together. Tonight, perhaps. Joan did not know. She might never know. But the idea of Gina in Barry's arms—Barry whole-heartedly her lover, giving her all that he had never been able to give the woman who came second in his affections—Joan could not bear and refused to harbour.

She decided at the end of a miserable morning that she could not endure being alone. She would phone up dear old Joe and ask him to dine with her.

It comforted her to hear Halliday's cheery voice. After all, it is comforting to know that somebody cares for you, and if only Barry had adored her . . . like Joe used to, but what in the world was the use of saying "if"?

"Hello, Joe," said Joan, forcing a bright note into her voice.

"Joan dear—how *are* you?"

"All right. And you and old Mac?"

"My dear, I was going to telephone to you to ask you and that nice husband of yours to dine with me tonight."

Joan winced.

"Barry's away just now," she said.

"What—you all alone?"

"Yes."

"Well, can you come tonight?"

"I'd like to very much."

"Splendid. Joan dear, shall I let you into a secret? . . ."

"What is it?"

"The dinner this evening is a celebration."

"Of what?"

"My engagement, my dear."

"*Engagement?*"

"Yes. Now, what will you say to me, Joan dear? Margaret and I fixed it up last night—bless her heart."

Joan laughed. It was just as well Joe could not see the cynicism in her eyes.

"Margaret—you mean—Mac?"

"Yes. We work together very well and we decided last night we might hit things off if we ran a little home together. What you say?"

"I think it's a lovely idea," said Joan. "I'm most awfully pleased."

"I knew you would be, dear child. Will you say a word to Maggie?"

"Here I am, Joan," came Miss Mackay's cheerful voice. "What do you think of it—Joe and I have been and gone and got ourselves engaged."

"Mac dear, I'm so glad . . ." Joan swallowed hard. "You're awfully bucked, aren't you?"

"Well, you know I've had a corner in my heart for the Boss for years."

"I do congratulate you. . . ."

"Are you going to dine with us?"

"I can't," said Joan wildly.

"But Joe said you were free. . . ."

"I thought I was—I find I've got an important engagement. . . ." she stammered the lie. "I'm so sorry, my dear. Some other evening. The best of luck—to you—both!"

She hung up the receiver. She put her elbows on the writing-bureau and buried her face in her hands. The tears were trickling down her cheeks. It was so weak, so stupid—but she could not control her emotions at all this morning. And she felt she just could not sit at a dinner with Joe and Mac and be gay and jolly and a witness to their new-found happiness.

She felt very much alone in her little flat; in that charming yellow room which she had decorated and arranged with such pleasure. It was no longer her's and Barry's home.

Was Barry with Virginia now?

Agonised, Joan walked into Barry's bedroom. She sat down on his bed. She was shaking; in tears. Through a mist she saw her photograph in a leather frame on top of the tallboy; an enlarged snapshot of her in her swimming-suit, standing on a rock, that had been taken out in France. She was laughing. Barry had said he liked that one of her laughing face; her eyes screwed up in the sunshine; her arms above her head; poised for a dive.

The sight of that photograph brought back a flood of memories of her honeymoon; those long, sunny days on the beach on the *Ile des Fleurs*; the sheer romance of golden days and moonlit nights shared with Barry.

He had seemed so much her lover then. And it was all over; all the hoping, the loving, the joy of living.

Joan threw herself down on Barry's pillows and cried as though her heart were broken.

When those tears, which seemed to be mingled with her heart's blood, had dried up and she could cry no more, something else seemed to dry within Joan. It was as though she withered and became dead. She went about the flat like a dead person with a white stony young face and a blank look in her eyes. What the future held she did not know, and the mood came upon her now that she did not care.

Let Barry go to Gina. Let him stay with her. Why should she pour her devotion like this upon a man who did not want it? He had hurt her enough. She would not be hurt any more. It was more her fault for marrying him than his for leaving her. But now she knew that she had been a fool. What she had suffered outweighed the little span of happiness.

She did not know what he meant to do nor what her next move would be, but she made up her mind never to love any other human being on this earth. She never would; no one on earth could love or suffer like this a second time. And even while that knowledge came to her, she found herself thinking, sadly, bitterly:

"How can I blame *him* . . . when he cared for Virginia in this way . . . how can I expect him to forget her and love me? If I had married Joe, who adored me once, I could not have forgotten Barry."

For three long days, for three nights that seemed even longer and terribly lonely, Joan merely existed from one moment to another.

She slept badly; ate practically nothing and felt ill in consequence. She went out; even went to a cinema, but emerged from it without knowing what she had seen.

No news came from him. She felt a sinking sensation now when she thought about him. It was as though an impenetrable curtain had fallen between them. She had not known it was possible for anybody to feel so unhappy as she felt that black and bitter week.

Then one morning she awoke to such a ghastly sensation of nausea that she thought she was going to be very ill. She felt suddenly afraid, she dragged herself from the bed, looked in her mirror and saw a livid little face and eyes with dark shadows like bruises under them.

When she was dressed she still felt deadly ill, and in a half-hearted fashion she telephoned for the doctor who had attended her at Victoria last year when she went down with the 'flu.

Later, after he had seen her and gone again, Joan faced a new and quite unexpected complication in this crisis.

She knew that she was going to have a child.

Such a possibility had never entered her head. And she was quite sure it had not entered Barry's. They had agreed that they did not wish to have such a domestic tie until they were more settled.

Her first emotion was one of exaltation. She was glad that she was going to have Barry's child. That was something he could not take from her. If he left her for Gina she would not have to face life quite alone. She would have her child. And because she had loved him so much she must inevitably love his child. Barry's son! . . . it must be a son . . . and like him . . . the thought overwhelmed Joan. She sat in her bedroom, after the doctor had gone, full of feverish excitement; her mind teeming with ideas.

But close upon the heels of ecstasy over her prospective motherhood came bitterness, fresh cause for depression. What effect would this news have upon Barry? She knew so well that he had very decided ideas and opinions about a thing of this sort. He was not the kind of man to desert a woman who was bearing his child. Hadn't he told her, many times before their marriage, that he particularly wanted a son? This might be a string which she could pull to bring him back. But did she want him back—under protest? Did she want him, knowing that he had come, reluctantly, believing it to be his duty? Forcing the hand of a man of his type was not going to improve his attitude towards her.

No—she must go away, alone—have her child and derive what consolation she could from motherhood. She sat down, wrote a letter to Barry, addressed it to his club, and posted it. And for the rest of that day a new and strange peace descended upon her. Fate had given her something to live for after all. She could not feel so solitary, so hopeless now, with Barry's child, like a secret flower, unfolding sweetly and mysteriously beneath her heart.

CHAPTER XII

THE library at Claydown Manor was the coolest room in the place on a warm September morning. There were big mullioned windows, wide open, showing a stretch of green, velvety lawn; the dark beauty of old clipped yew hedges, and the shadow of Worth Forest against a clear blue sky.

Barry and Virginia sat side by side on a low chesterfield which faced the big open fireplace. Above the magnificent oak beam which stretched across it hung the portrait of a handsome young man in the full-dress uniform of a Guards officer. The only picture in the library. All the walls were bound with books.

The portrait was of Ian Kingleigh in his twenty-fourth

year. Barry found himself regarding it gloomily. He bore Ian Kingleigh no grudge for having married Gina, and it was a grim thought that the once happy young man, endowed with so much of the world's goods, was now no more. He had loved Gina and won her ... and his happiness had lasted barely a month.

Virginia, too, was subdued and depressed. Barry had only just come down from Town, and she found him in a difficult mood. She wanted him, quite definitely, to break with Joan and, in time, marry her. But Barry, although he avowed himself madly in love, did not seem at all certain what he wanted to do about it.

When Barry turned his gaze from Kingleigh's portrait to the woman on the sofa beside him he was bound to admit to himself that she was lovely enough to make any man's pulses beat fast. The old thrill and desire for her stirred within him. She seemed to drop naturally into graceful poses. She sat back in her corner of the sofa, slim and youthful in a sleeveless dress of embroidered linen; pale yellow. He had always liked her in yellow. It suited her dark, sleek head and warm, black-lashed eyes, and the delicate colour in her cheeks. One bare beautiful arm was stretched along the back of the sofa close to him. He bent suddenly and kissed her hand.

She said nothing, but her eyes half closed and she drew in a quick breath. He gave an embarrassed laugh.

" Sorry," he said.

" What for ? "

" I oughtn't to have done that."

" Why not ? "

" Because I'm trying to keep my head and talk sensibly to you."

" Must we—talk sensibly ? "

" It's best, Gina. If I let myself go——"

" Well ? "

Barry stood up and moved restlessly round the library. A scent of roses and mignonette came through the open windows from the sunlit garden. The library was redolent of leather, and that particular faint perfume, so familiar to Barry, which Virginia always used.

He had come to her well aware that desire for her was a fever in his blood which he could not subdue. On the other hand, he found it quite impossible to eradicate the memory of Joan. She was his wife.

"Well?" came Virginia's low voice. "Supposing you do let yourself go, my darling?"

He turned to her, hands in his pockets. She thought how young and brown and attractive he looked in his grey flannels. She was imagining herself very deeply in love with him this morning.

"I don't often 'let go,' Gina," he said. "You know that. And I don't want to—until we've talked this all out and made up our minds what we're going to do. We're all in the devil of a tangle, my dear. Let's face it."

"I have faced it."

He stood in front of her, brows frowning.

"We must go into things deeper than that, my dear."

"Do you still love me, Barry?" She looked up at him with her long eyes screwed up in the smile which had never failed to pull at his heart-strings.

"You know I do and I suppose I always will. But I don't think you love me, Gina," he said.

"I've told you I do."

"Yes, but——"

"Barry, don't hold it against me that I married poor Ian. You know why—Mummy's position—my own——"

"We won't talk about that," he broke in. "Whatever mistakes there have been in the past don't count now. It's the future we've got to think of."

"You know what I want you to do."

"But you must not forget that I'm married to Joan."

"I'm not likely to forget it."

"Well—what about it?"

"That's for you to decide, Barry."

"I know," he said with some impatience. He took a cigarette from his case, lit it, and began to walk up and down the library again. "But it isn't as easy as all that, my dear."

"You told me you explained the situation when you married her."

"I told her I should never be able to care for her in the way I cared for you—yes."

"Well, then, she can't blame you for coming back to me."

"Oh, yes, she can. When I married her—I accepted a responsibility which I ought not to shirk. Look at the position! It's frightful. I've only been married three months."

Virginia bit her lip.

"Joan told you to come to me."

"Yes," he said dryly. "Because I behaved so rottenly. She got fed up with me, and no wonder."

"Does she know you are here now?"

"No. She may guess, but she doesn't actually know. I've been at my club since Monday. I had one letter from her."

"What to say, if I may ask?"

Barry stared out of the window.

"Oh, a typical sort of letter. She's damned sporting. She said she understood what I felt about you now that you were free and she offered to divorce me."

"Of course, Joan always was very decent," said Virginia half-heartedly. Praise to another woman, particularly when that woman was Barry's wife, did not please her at the moment.

"That's just it," said Barry. "If she were different, one wouldn't have so much compunction. You see—she does care for me. God knows why, but she does. I took certain vows when I married her, and here I am proposing to chuck the whole thing and leave her alone. It doesn't seem fair."

"Nothing's fair, if it comes to that," said Virginia. "And Joan took a risk when she married you."

"Not altogether, my dear. You were tied up then, remember."

Virginia's brooding eyes wandered to her husband's portrait.

"It seems to me it's a pity for all of us that my marriage to Ian came to such a sudden and untimely end," she said in a low voice. "I suppose if it hadn't—we'd have both just gone on leading our separate lives."

"Yes, I suppose so."

"But I wasn't really happy and nor were you. Were you?"

Barry paused beside her, bent suddenly and kissed her dark, rippling hair with passion.

"Oh, my God—it's all so difficult," he said. "I ought to hate you for what you did—in the beginning—and I can't. You know that you mean more to me than any other woman in my life. But *hell to it*, Gina . . . I must consider Joan.

I must, otherwise I'm going to be damned miserable and make you miserable, too."

She caught one of his hands between hers.

"Can't you forget Joan for a moment?"

"No—how can I?"

"Then what are we going to do?"

"I don't know," he said.

Virginia put an arm about his shoulders.

"Barry—my darling——"

He caught her in his arms and kissed her madly. For an instant she clung to him in a feverish embrace. When he let her go he was shaking and his eyes were bloodshot. He said:

"This is more than I can stand. Now, listen, Gina, if I shut my mind to duty and the rest of it and get a divorce from Joan—will you marry me?"

"Of course."

"Do you mind being cited?"

Virginia's face changed. She gave him a quick, anxious look.

"You wouldn't expect that?"

"I'm asking you. Would you mind?"

"Don't be silly, my dear. You can arrange a divorce without dragging me into it. After all—I've got Ian's name to consider."

Barry stood up. His nostrils dilated a little.

"You wouldn't go through a divorce scandal for my sake —presuming I was cad enough to drag you into one, eh?"

"Barry, don't be absurd. I—it's too much to expect."

"You and I have different ideas about loving," he said tersely. "I'd go through anything—for you."

"You're not a woman."

"I know women who would—women who do," he said. Instinctively he thought of Joan. If he had asked her to stand the trial of a divorce and a scandal in order to be with him, she would not have hesitated. He knew that.

He hated thinking about Joan at this stage of things with Gina. But the thought came and would not be denied. He wondered, in sudden bitter doubt, if Virginia knew how to love—or had ever known it. He felt seized with a devil of cruelty—the wish to probe her—hurt her—and find out once and for all what her passion for him was worth. After all, it had not been worth much in the past.

"Listen to me, Gina," he said harshly. "You and I have got to understand each other over this. You wouldn't go through a divorce with me. You'd want me to 'arrange it' with some wretched woman and come to you later. Is that the idea?"

Her heart beat fast. His attitude, the hard look in those queer light grey eyes of his, made her uneasy.

"Barry—I—I——"

"Well—*is* that the idea?"

"Y-yes," she said with some hesitation. "It's only fair."

"Then there's another thing," he broke in. "Kingleigh has left you a great deal of money. I'm not going to marry a woman with twenty thousand pounds a year and offer her one."

"Why one?"

"I've got two thousand and married Joan. I shall naturally support her."

Virginia's cheeks reddened.

"A wife in that case gets a third."

"My wife should have half."

"Rather quixotic, Barry."

He drew in a sharp breath.

"Don't you ever give two thoughts for Joan? She hasn't a soul on earth to care for her or support her but me."

"She used to earn her own living."

The crass selfishness of that remark astonished Barry. He looked at Virginia in sudden anger.

"You don't imagine I'm going off with you, calmly and cheerfully, leaving Joan to earn her own living again!"

Virginia sprang to her feet.

"I'm getting just a little tired of all this forethought for Joan. It's Joan—Joan—Joan!"

She stopped, a sob in her throat. Barry continued without relenting:

"Never mind—let's have this out once and for all. Another point—if you marry me, my dear, you'll have to give up Kingleigh's money and live with me on what I have."

She gasped. Her eyes, magnified by tears of sheer anger and passion, blazed at him.

"You're being absolutely unreasonable."

"Am I? Is that too much to ask? Do you love me

enough to come to me—on a thousand a year? You haven't got your mother to consider now. You can settle your fortune on her if it comes to that. But I won't take you plus the fortune. I couldn't stand a wife with all that money. Sorry, my dear, but I'm built like that."

"You're crazy!" she said. Her voice broke. "Barry—please——"

"I may be crazy, but those are my terms," he broke in. "I've loved you and wanted you for years, Gina, and you chucked me on account of money. Now—are you going to chuck me for the second time on the same account?"

"Barry—you aren't serious?"

"I am, my dear. Deadly serious. Don't you love me enough to give up everything?"

"I don't think any man has the right to ask a woman to give up everything," she said passionately.

Silence. He looked at her. And something that had been alive in his heart for so many years, for this girl, seemed to die there and then. The divine spark flickered out, and he knew that this time it was final. It would never be relit. He had cherished an ideal of Virginia which did not exist. He had loved a woman who was beautiful and attractive and utterly, hopelessly selfish. A man has no right to ask a woman to give up everything, she said. Perhaps she was right. But men do ask women to give up much and women who love give with both hands, uncomplaining. Like Joan had given.

He saw, suddenly, the beauty and sincerity of Joan's devotion. He had always seen it. But today, after the empty and egotistical passion which Gina offered him, it seemed to flame into a more radiant beauty.

He might not have insisted upon Gina sacrificing reputation and money. But he had wanted to know whether she was prepared to do so. He knew now that she was not.

He felt sick at heart and almost ashamed when he looked at her.

"Gina," he said, "I think this ends things, my dear."

She caught at the pearls which were wound about her throat. She was very pale.

"Barry, you've been extraordinarily unreasonable."

"Perhaps. But I know that you don't care for me."

She lost her temper.

"If you mean I am not ready to crawl to your feet and lick your boots like my dear cousin Joan, then you're quite right."

Another silence. Curiously enough, the insult to Joan hurt Barry more than the revelation of Virginia's lack of real feeling for himself. Then he gave a brief laugh.

"My dear, what melodrama! We aren't behaving at all like long-parted lovers anxious to fall into each other's arms and remain there. Well—now we know where we are. It's really the end of you and me this time. I'll get along back to Town if you don't mind."

Virginia's passion subsided. Her eyes, full of bitter disappointment, followed the tall figure in grey to the library door. She did not want to lose him. She had always felt him to be necessary to her. But she was so built that she could not abnegate self—even for the sake of her lover. All her life she had been spoiled. Barry was not prepared to spoil her, so she let him go.

"I'm sorry it's ended like this," she said more quietly. "But perhaps it's better you should go back to Joan."

"Good-bye, Virginia," he said, ignoring her remark.

He went from the room and shut the door. A blaze of hot sunshine poured down upon him as he let himself out of the big cool hall. He put on his hat and climbed into the Buick in which he had driven down to Worth. As he drove away from the Manor he heard a clock chiming one. He had meant to lunch with Virginia, of course. But now he would lunch at some pub on the road, on the way back to Town.

As he drove furiously he found himself shaking with grim laughter.

"What a jest. To eat your heart out for years for a woman who doesn't like you enough to drop a few thousand pounds for you. To leave your wife and go down to the other feeling that there isn't anybody in the world that means so much and then—find out what she is really like——"

Well, she didn't mean anything any more and never would again. She had killed him—stone dead today. She was not ready to "crawl to his feet," she had said, "like Joan."

Barry stared at the white sunlit road ahead of him and thought:

"Joan never crawled. That's where Gina was wrong. She never licked my boots. She just gave everything—magnificently. Next to Gina she *is*—magnificent!"

CHAPTER XIII

JOAN was on her knees in her bedroom before a raw hide trunk, packing. She was still in a curious condition of mind. The strange peace and calm which had come to her with the knowledge that she was to bear Barry's child, had not left her. But while she sorted her clothes and folded her dresses carefully in tissue-paper a feeling of intense sadness gripped her.

This was the trunk she had bought for her honeymoon. When she had packed her modest trousseau how terribly happy she had been, and hopeful that she would make a success of things with the man she had loved so long and so devotedly. It was a wretched thing to have to look back and admit failure and defeat. Today she was getting ready to go away for good and all. She had made up her mind to give Barry his freedom and make no effort to keep him from the woman he wanted.

Yesterday she had sent a letter to his club telling him about their child. But she had begged him to let it make no difference to his plans. She would be perfectly happy, she said, to divorce him and live her life with and for her child.

She expected to receive a reply to that letter tomorrow. Today she would pack all her personal possessions. Later this afternoon she would go to the house agents and ask them to let this flat furnished.

That was a hateful idea. Letting her penthouse full of the charming things which she and Barry had chosen. A home which they had occupied for so brief a period. What a fatal thing their marriage had been. He must have been unhappy, poor Barry. And she had fought a losing battle from the start.

She stood up, looked round her bedroom, and saw chaos. There was still much to pack. The bed, the chairs, the floor were littered with things. A depressing and untidy sight. Through the open communicating door she could see Barry's bedroom. All very neat and tidy. Nothing had been touched there. She did not know what he wished to do. But he would, of course, return to collect his things, and she felt sure she would be doing the right thing to let the flat.

She sat on the edge of the bed, lit a cigarette, and rested a few moments, staring at the confusion. Her feeling of melancholy increased. It was difficult to believe that never again would she lie in this bed and wait for Barry to come through that door to her. She had waited, always, her body and heart aching with love for him. His moods of tenderness, of passion, had meant everything. So much too much for her peace of mind. But now it was all over.

Joan sighed deeply. She caught sight of herself in the mirror opposite her bed. She looked rather like a schoolgirl in her light green tweed skirt, a white cotton shirt tucked into it. Her thick brown hair was untidy, one wave falling against a pink cheek. She was flushed with the exertion of packing. Only the dark shadows under the very blue eyes were evidence of strain and a fatigue that was mental rather than physical.

She felt so terribly tired. Tired of thinking and grieving and regretting. She had a passionate wish to get away from everything, everybody she had ever known; leave Town and find a haven somewhere in the country. She had made up her mind to go down to Sussex; to that inn at Horsham where she and Barry had stayed. She had liked that funny old place and been very happy there, and it was cheap.

When the question of finance arose in her mind she felt too weary to tackle it. Barry would, of course, support his child and she could do nothing but write a few articles until she was fit again. Then she would try and get a job. Perhaps the Chartwood Press would take her back. She must earn her own living. She could not depend entirely upon Barry. But, of course, there would be the baby to consider. Who would take care of it while she worked? She did not want anybody but herself to bring up her child.

She suddenly stubbed her cigarette on an ash-tray.

"I'm sure I oughtn't to smoke. It can't be good for my infant," she thought with a wry smile. And a small, bitter pain stabbed her. Infant! Barry had called her that. But she was not a child any more. She was going to be a mother and bring a human being into this world. Rather a hard, cruel world to be ushered into. Poor little brat, thought Joan. This business wasn't very fair on it. If it was a boy it would need a father and wouldn't have one. She hoped it would be a boy. She didn't want a girl who might grow into a foolish woman like herself and break her heart for a man who did not love her.

Joan walked to the dressing-table, combed her unruly hair and powdered her nose. It was half past three and she must go out and see these estate agents.

Then she put down the comb and swung round, facing the bedroom door, every nerve in her body tingling. She had heard a key scraping in the lock of the front door. Only one person other than herself had a latch-key. That was Barry. It *was* Barry. She recognised his footsteps now in the hall.

The colour faded from Joan's cheeks. She felt a sick, empty sensation. She did not know quite how she was going to face Barry. It was going to be a brutal business—saying good-bye to him for always—coolly and calmly arranging their separation.

"Pull yourself together," Joan whispered to herself. "Whatever you do, don't let him see that you *care*. You've let him see much too much of that sort of thing as it is!"

Barry walked into the room.

She saw vaguely that he was wearing grey flannels—he had had those made just before they last went abroad—and that he looked rather grim about the eyes and lips. Otherwise her vision was blurred, as though a film had come over her eyes. Her knees trembled, ridiculously. She put her hands behind her, clung to the dressing-table for support and wished she still had her cigarette.

"Hello, Joan," said Barry, cleared his throat as though he were embarrassed, and stared round the room. "What's happening? Why all this——?"

"Oh, I'm just packing up," she said, and was glad that she could speak coolly. She could see clearly now, too. His face and form were in focus. And she thought he looked very grim indeed and very weary.

"Packing up? You mean going away?"

"Yes."

"Where?"

"Oh—down to Horsham, I think. I haven't made any definite plans. But I expect you have."

He did not answer. He walked round the room in the old familiar, restless fashion. She followed him with her gaze, well aware that she still felt an unconquerable, crazy love for him in the depths of her heart. It was a maddening feeling—when she wanted to be quite indifferent and to let him see that she was. Hadn't he been to his club? Hadn't he had her letter? Surely he would say something about the baby in a moment.

Joan felt feeble; walked to the bed and sat on it. Barry turned his gaze to her. He thought she looked white and pinched and that there was a funny expression in her eyes. Yes, she had changed, in some strange way. Yet they had only been separated five days. It seemed to Barry, in this moment, that he had been away from Joan for five years. Well, if she had altered, so had he. He felt that he had come away from Virginia a different man. Certainly a sadder and wiser one. And he felt ashamed in the presence of his wife. That sensation of shame, coupled with a curious wish to humble himself before her, made him tongue-tied for a few moments. He could only look at her and think:

"I've been a swine and a fool and she's been amazingly decent to me. What the hell am I going to say?"

Joan spoke.

"Have you—been in Town this week?"

"The early part, yes."

"Did you get my letters?"

"One letter . . . in which you generously offered me my freedom," he said, and a slow red deepened the tan on his cheeks. Joan's brows lifted a little when she saw this. She had never known Barry to flush like that before. Was he feeling ashamed of himself? Poor Barry.

"I wrote to you twice," she said.

"I have only had that one letter. But I haven't called for any mail today. It may be waiting for me."

Joan drew a deep breath and clasped her hands over her knees.

"I see," she said.

So he did not know about the child . . . of course . . . that was why he made no comment. She bit nervously at her lip. It was strange how nervous she felt with him; it was as though they were strangers, or very distant acquaintances.

"I haven't been sleeping at the Club these last two nights," he added by way of explanation. "I went along to Brown's. I like it better than the Club. This morning I motored down to Sussex and I've only just got back."

"I see," repeated Joan.

She thought: "He's been at Worth with *her*. . . ."

Her heart was stabbed with pain again, but she tightened her lips and tilted her head in an almost arrogant way. She *would not* let him see that she suffered.

Barry said:

"I want to tell you right away that I saw Virginia for the first time since I quit the flat, this morning, down at Claydown Manor."

"It really doesn't matter to me," said Joan.

Barry thrust his hands in his pockets. He looked and felt more than ever uncomfortable.

Joan had never used that sort of tone to him before. On the night of their quarrel she had been stormy, passionate, even abusive—which he knew he had deserved. But today she was icily polite. He found her difficult to deal with—like this.

"Look here, my dear," he began, and paused.

Joan continued to hold her brown head high and her lips were a thin line. How often in the past he had begun a sentence with "Look here, my dear——" Well—now what was coming?

"Look here," repeated Barry, "I want you to understand straight away that Virginia and I have said good-bye to each other for good and all."

Joan's heart gave a peculiar throb and her eyes widened. This was a surprise, anyhow. She gave a set smile.

"Not on my account, I hope," she said. "I've quite made up my mind that we had better separate. I've put the flat into agent's hands and made my arrangements to go away."

"Joan——!" he exclaimed, and grew very red indeed.

"Oh, yes," she said calmly. "So if by any chance you've had a tearful farewell with my cousin because your conscience has pricked you—please go back to her. I'm perfectly happy."

"Are you?" said Barry grimly. "Well, I'm not."

"You're exceedingly hard to please, my dear Barry. You wanted Virginia. You can go to her. Why prolong the agony by saying good-bye to her and coming back to me, wishing you were dead?"

He ignored her sarcasm. He said quite gently:

"Wishing I were dead is more or less true. But not because I've left Virginia. Neither has there been any agony in saying good-bye to her."

Joan stared at him.

"My *dear* Barry——"

"Yes, it may seem difficult for you to understand, but, you see—everything is quite different. I mean—I just don't want Virginia any more, and if I wish I were dead it's because I feel such a swine and such a fool."

That held Joan speechless for a moment. Then she shook her head.

"You're crazy. You don't know what you do want."

"I didn't know—but I know now."

"Well—what do you want?"

"To admit my folly, settle down peacefully with you, and forget I ever knew Virginia."

Joan swallowed hard. Her cheeks flamed. She could not take her gaze from him. She had nerved herself to face the ordeal of a final separation from him. She had taken it for granted he would go to Virginia; that he had been with her all these days. And he was standing here, calmly telling her that he had never been with Virginia; that he no longer wanted her and that he wished to settle down with her, his wife. "*Peacefully,*" he said. Joan suddenly laughed, hysterically.

"Barry, you really are quite mad."

"No. I'm a bit saner than usual today," he said, his lips twisting into a smile.

"You honestly mean to tell me that you have come back because you don't want Virginia any more?"

"Yes."

"Why?"

"For a great many reasons. Mainly because I discovered this morning that she isn't worth all that I gave her, and certainly not worth breaking up my home for."

"Oh!" gasped Joan. "And why?"

"Must I go into details?"

It was the old, impatient Barry. But Joan had no mercy on him.

"Yes, I insist upon knowing."

"Very well. Gina didn't think it worth while to marry me on a thousand a year and I told her that is what she would have to do, as I intended to allow you a thousand, and refused to take her with Kingleigh's money. In addition, she was not prepared to face a divorce with me. *But* she wanted to marry me and loves me——" He laughed bitterly. "It wasn't my idea of loving, so I quit—for good and all. And I acknowledge myself a poor fool."

"Still loving her?"

"No. It's dead, I tell you—absolutely dead."

"I see." Joan was breathing quickly. And now she stood up and faced him, her shoulders squared, her hands clenched at her sides. "So—having been turned down once more you come back and wish to settle down with me—in fact you ask me to be second best all over again—do you?"

That hit him hard, but he took it smiling. He was white about the mouth.

"Of course, I deserved that," he said.

But she, as soon as she had hurled the insult, regretted it, broke down and cried.

"I won't," she said, gasping, tears streaming down her face. "I won't be second best again. I won't live with you and go through all that *torture* of loving you and knowing you don't care. If it's true that you don't care for Gina any more and that you've parted, it doesn't make any difference to me. If I lived with you, you'd tell me you were all dead inside, or something, and couldn't love me as you *used* to love her. No—I won't take it on—I *won't*!"

"Joan!" he said. "Oh, my dear——" Thoroughly shaken and distressed, he came nearer her and put a hand on her shoulder.

"Don't!" she said, moved away, put her face in her hands, and sobbed passionately.

"Joan," he said, "every word you say is justified. I was a cad to have married you and made you so unhappy, but I'm terribly sorry, my dear. Much sorrier than you can ever realise. I was crazy. When I realised how absolutely worthless Virginia's affection for me was, I asked myself why I ever spent so much time regretting her. Her love seemed so—so paltry—beside yours. I came away from her feeling how magnificent you were, my dear. I swear that. You must believe me."

Joan lifted her head. Her face was convulsed.

"But you can't just swing round in your affections from one woman to another—like that. You can't really want me now just because it's all over between you and Gina."

He made a hopeless gesture with his hand.

"Joan, my dear, these things don't bear too much dissection. One can't always explain what one feels or thinks nor can one account for the changes that take place in one's ideas. But it's like this. I *did* care very much for Gina, but it was an ideal Gina who did not exist. Today, somehow, the bubble broke . . . the whole damned thing bust up and I just feel dead about her. I've always been fond of you— more than fond. I have a tremendous respect and admiration for you. And you mean a hell of a lot. Even if I'd fixed things up with Gina I'd never have forgotten you and I'd have fretted about you all the time. If you can be generous enough to put up with me again and give me another chance——" He held out a hand and gave a sheepish schoolboy sort of smile that went to her very heart. "You never know what might happen," he ended. "In time. Will you chance it, my dear, or do you hate me now?"

She choked back a sob.

"No—I—don't hate you. I—I'm all sorts of a crazy fool myself, Barry, and I—can't stop—loving you."

He put both arms round her and held her very close. His throat smarted.

"My dear, you're much too nice to me and always have been. I'm damned sorry for hurting you so."

The warmth of his arms around her seemed the most satisfying thing that had happened to her for long, long days. Pride, resentment, all emotions went to the wind and there remained only the one white-hot, outstanding certainty of her incurable love for him.

"Barry," she said. "Darling, *darling* . . ."

Her hands held him very tightly indeed; her fingers threaded through his hair. Crying quietly, she drew his head down and pressed her wet cheek against his.

"Barry—I didn't want to lose you. God knows I didn't!"

"I don't deserve your love or your forgiveness, Joan."

"There isn't anything to forgive, but if you think there's

a chance that we can both be happy, let's start all over again."

" I'd be very, very thankful to, Joan."

" Then let's," she whispered.

" You're such a *dear*," he blurted out huskily.

She had to smile through her tears.

" Poor old boy. I'm sorry if——"

" Don't," he broke in. "Don't be sorry for me. I assure you I feel more at peace, more contented than I've felt for years—literally for years."

" I'm glad."

He held her closer and kissed her hair.

" You're so much nicer than any woman in the world and I've wasted five very good days away from you."

Joan felt suddenly rapturous. She did not know whether she was stupid to begin all over again with him or not. She did not know whether the future held success or failure. Barry wasn't easy to live with. He never would be. But he was the man she loved and the only man on earth she ever would love this way. Added to which, with Virginia really out of the running, she felt somehow that this time there were very good odds on their partnership being a success. And, of course, there was something else she had to tell him. She was glad now that he had wanted to begin again . . . before he knew. She need not feel he had come back merely from a sense of duty.

She felt ridiculously shy of him and of what she had to say. She reached up, kissed him passionately on the lips, and drew away from his arms. Her eyes were large and bright.

" By the way," she said in a casual voice. " That letter from me waiting for you at the Club may interest you."

" It won't if it was to make plans for our separation," he said, and lit a cigarette to calm his nerves. He felt uncommonly emotional and he could not possibly have said all the things to Joan that he wanted to say. He could only look at her and feel that she was a very wonderful person and much too good for him.

" It *was* about our separation," said Joan, her thick lashes hiding the light in her eyes. " But it was also about our—son and heir."

Barry stared. His face went scarlet. He put down the cigarette and walked quickly across the room to her.

"Joan—good God—do you—are you——"

"I'm going to have a baby, yes," she said, and gave a nervous little laugh. "I had to have the doctor yesterday and he told me. About March, I believe."

He did not touch her. He stood close to her, staring at her. She looked at him and saw something approaching awe in his eyes. Then he repeated in a choked voice:

"Good *God*!"

"It's true," she said.

"Joan, my dear, I feel *unspeakable*! And I was quitting you—at such a time."

"But you didn't know."

"I never for an instant imagined——"

"Supposing you had," she said curiously.

"Do you think I'd ever have left your side?" he said hotly. "I'm not as rotten as that. The mother of my child——"

Then she put her arms about his neck.

"Dear, darling Barry. So dutiful. Well, thank goodness you came back without knowing. I want to be loved for myself as well as for my son. I hope we do have a son—don't you? Can you bear being made a parent, darling?"

He could only say: "Joan!" And bury his face against her warm neck.

For a moment she was as happy as any human being can hope to be in this trying life. When Barry spoke again his voice was humble and his hand, smoothing the hair back from her forehead, full of new tenderness.

"Lord!" he said. "Little Joan with a son. Yes, I should like a boy—immensely. Dear, what a fool I've been —to think what I nearly missed——"

"I'm not the only infant now," she said.

"Two infants to look after," he said. "Sweetheart, what a responsibility."

"Are you taking it on in a cheerful spirit, my lamb?"

"I can't bear the idea of it—it's frightful!" he said.

But his arms and his lips told her otherwise.

THE END